D0041074

MIRAGE

MIRAGE

JENN REESE

CANDLEWICK PRESS

First edition 2013

Library of Congress Catalog Card Number 2012943643
ISBN 978-0-7636-5418-4

12 13 14 15 16 17 BVG 10 9 8 7 6 5 4 3 2 1

Printed in Berryville, VA, U.S.A.

This book was typeset in Plantin.

Candlewick Press
99 Dover Street
Somerville, Massachusetts 02144

visit us at www.candlewick.com

For every kid
who walks between worlds

And for Chris,
who bravely walks in mine

"THE WORLD NEEDS US, AND WE NEED EACH OTHER.
WE MUST NOT HIDE FOREVER."

> — *Ali'ikai of the Coral Kampii,*
> *born Sarah Jennings*

CHAPTER 1

ALUNA RAN TOWARD a patch of rocks and scrubby trees, trying to reach its shade before the next wave of pain struck. The sun's gaze followed her, searing the air and stifling the wind. The desert was no place for a Kampii, especially not a Kampii whose legs would soon begin fusing into a tail.

She stumbled and fell. Sand matted to the sweat on her face as she rolled on the ground, clutching her legs. The pain was her fault. She'd swallowed the Ocean Seed a month ago, when she was trying to rescue her sister from that evil monster Fathom. Now she was paying the price.

Underwater, a tail granted speed and agility. It shimmered and flowed. Growing a tail marked a Kampii's passage to adulthood and respect. But in the desert, weeks away from the ocean's embrace, a tail meant the opposite. It meant she'd no longer be able to walk or run or jump or fight. She'd be a fish on dry land. *Useless.*

When the pain ebbed, Aluna sat up and wiped the grit from her cheeks. She ran her hand over her ankles and calves, feeling for scales. Nothing. Only dark, tough Kampii skin. She tugged her cloth head wrap to better shade her eyes and tried to calm her breathing. She needed to tell Hoku about her legs. He was her best friend, and he deserved the truth.

But she'd been the one who insisted they come here, straight from their battle with Fathom. She'd wanted to warn the Equians about Karl Strand and his twisted clones. To stop Strand before he got a foothold in the desert. To help Dash protect his herd. They were all counting on her—not just Hoku and Dash and Calli, but all the Kampii back in the City of Shifting Tides. The Elders were smarter than her and Hoku, and the hunters, like her brothers, were stronger and faster. But none of them had legs. For better or for worse, the rest of the Kampii were trapped beneath the waves while she and Hoku tried to save them all.

Aluna needed to stay strong. Telling her friends about her weakness would make them worry. It would make them doubt her . . . as she was already doubting herself.

A familiar voice sounded in the distance. "Aluna?"

She turned as a tiny figure crested an outcropping of rock behind her. Hoku. She recognized his thin frame under the flowing desert tunic and pants that Dash insisted they all wear. She had no more time for self-pity. Aluna waved and stood slowly, testing her legs. Today they obeyed her. She dreaded the moment when they would stop.

She met Hoku halfway, excuses roiling in her mind like storm-tossed waves. But when she saw the wide-eyed expression on his freckled face, saw the tufts of reddish-brown hair escaping his hastily affixed head wrap, she knew she wouldn't need them.

"Mirage!" Hoku said. "Calli spotted it on the horizon. We can make it by high sun if we hurry." He grinned beneath a sunburned nose. "I've been dreaming about fresh water and real food for days."

She fell in beside him as they walked back toward camp. "Real food and maybe a place to sleep that isn't crawling with bugs," she said with a shudder. They'd had some rough nights in the last few weeks. Scorpions tasted good enough when cooked, but she didn't enjoy finding them in her bedroll.

"And the tech," Hoku said wistfully. "Surviving in the desert is so different from surviving underwater. I bet they've got stuff we've never even imagined."

Mirage. The greatest Equian city. Dash had been

filling their heads with stories about it since the day they left the HydroTek dome — the marketplace full of people, the brightly woven rugs, the smell of roasted delicacies filling the air, the word-weavers stomping their hooves and telling tales for the crowds, the artisans crafting the Equians' famed ever-sharp swords. Dash said they had so much water that it bubbled and flowed in a great fountain in the marketplace, and anyone who wanted could come up and drink their fill. Her heart beat faster every time Dash, his eyes bright as glowfish, spun another tale of Mirage's wonder.

It had been easy to get caught up in Dash's excitement. She'd laughed with the others and talked about grilled rabbit and all the new weapons she wanted to learn. It had been important to keep everyone's spirits up while they were hot and sweaty and living off bugs and berries. But the truth was, Dash would be in terrible danger the moment they set foot in Mirage. If someone from his old herd recognized him, they'd be fighting for Dash's life along with the fate of the desert.

Despite the danger, Dash still wouldn't tell them the details of his exile. In a small way, that made Aluna feel better about keeping her growing tail a secret. They'd been through so much, and yet . . . some words were still too hard to say.

When Aluna and Hoku got back to camp, Dash was

kicking out the remains of their campfire and gnawing on a tough piece of cactus. He wore his desert clothes with the ease of one born and raised in the unforgiving heat. His nose never burned; the light-brown skin of his hands tanned only slightly. Even though he didn't have a horse body like the other Equians, Dash belonged here in the desert, just as she and Hoku belonged under the waves.

And just as Calli belonged in the sky. Aluna looked up and saw Calli two dozen meters up, her tawny wings flapping lazily as she circled over the camp, her long brown hair trapped under a head wrap. The girl waved and Aluna smiled.

"Mirage!" Calli pointed to the west and her white teeth flashed in a grin, a stark contrast to her dirty face.

"So I heard," Aluna said. She bent down and helped Dash roll up the last of their bedding.

"Are you well?" Dash asked quietly. "You ran off so suddenly, I thought—"

"I'm fine," Aluna said. "I just needed some time by myself. I used to swim off all the time underwater. It's just more noticeable up here." Which wasn't a lie, not really. She'd always been darting off on her own or with Hoku, either avoiding her sister and brothers or escaping from her father.

Dash stared at her another moment while she finished the packing, then nodded once. Another person might have kept hounding her—Hoku certainly would have—but not Dash.

Aluna's nervousness about her legs disappeared as they trekked toward Mirage. She was tired of rationing her water, of always being thirsty. Once they got to the city, she planned to drink at that fountain for days. She wasn't alone in her good mood. Dash scrambled up each new hill, quick as a sand crab, and Hoku couldn't stop whistling. The wind had picked up, so Calli folded her wings against her back and walked with them, her mouth an endless stream of questions and facts and observations about the world.

"Do you think High Khan Onggur will welcome us?" Calli said. "My mother is very powerful. Maybe he'll treat us like visiting royalty."

Dash laughed, an easy sound Aluna didn't hear nearly enough. "Red Sky herd is renowned for its battle prowess, and High Khan Onggur is a man of great honor," he said. "He has taken the Gold Disc in the Thunder Trials for the last ten years in a row. I have no doubt that we will be treated with respect once he learns of our mission."

"Mirage belongs to Red Sky?" Aluna asked. She wanted to keep him talking, to keep the smile from fading from his face.

"Their ancestral home, yes," he said. "The largest of our cities, for the largest of our herds."

"And there definitely won't be any people from your herd here?" Hoku asked.

Dash's smile disappeared. "Shining Moon? No. They rarely travel this far east." Aluna wished he'd talk about his exile. Maybe she could help, or at least find a way to make him feel better.

Calli gasped. Aluna looked up and immediately saw why.

For weeks, they'd been traveling through a flat, parched expanse of cracked earth and sand, brittle shrubs, and jagged rocks that extended all the way to the distant mountains crouched at the horizon. Now a massive domed city flickered in and out of view a mere hundred meters in front of them. Aluna saw it one moment—a sprawl of squat buildings, banners of red and black, a haze of thick smoke—and in the next, only desert again.

Hoku whistled. "That's some tech."

"Projections and mirrors," Dash said proudly.

Mirage was hidden, Aluna thought, just like the Kampii's City of Shifting Tides, and just like the Aviars' mountaintop city of Skyfeather's Landing. The ancients had protected them all.

"Come," Dash said. "Let us speak with High Khan Onggur. And then I will find us rooms in the Market District—rooms with actual beds and basins of cool water and the best food you have ever eaten!"

Hoku and Calli cheered. Aluna laughed. It had been such a long trek, and they were so close to completing their mission. In just a few hours, they'd talk to the High Khan, warn him about Karl Strand and his clones, and form an alliance among the Kampii, the winged Aviars, and the Equian horse folk. Together, they'd stand a chance against Strand's army of Upgraders, slaves, and whomever else Strand had convinced to join him.

As they neared Mirage, Aluna's brain worked its way through the illusions. The city flickered less and less until finally it blinked into view and stayed, solid as stone. A layer of soot coated the inside of the dome, making it difficult to see details. Dark figures patrolled just beyond the entrance gate, their pikes and swords reflecting sunlight in sharp bursts.

She glanced at Dash and saw his eagerness fade, his jaw clench.

"What's wrong?" she asked.

He stared straight ahead at Mirage, his brown eyes searching. "I do not know," he said quietly. "Maybe nothing. But perhaps . . . everything."

CHAPTER 2

ALUNA HAD EXPECTED the gates of Mirage to be open and welcoming, had expected the sizzle of food and the laughter of Equians to greet them even before they set foot inside the city. Dash had promised them no less. Instead, Red Sky guards swarmed just inside the dome's walls like a school of giant, hungry fish.

Aluna stepped toward the entrance, a massive archway built into the dome's curved wall. A shimmering veil of energy filled the arch, separating the desert from the inside of the city. Dash had said that in times of danger, the gateway could be turned solid, sealing everyone inside an impenetrable barrier. Their enemies would be stranded outside in the desert, kilometers away from any other source of shade or water, slowly baking and dying of thirst in the sun.

A male guard noticed their approach. "Halt!" he called, drawing his sword. He had a curly brown beard and pale skin. A dirty bandage covered part of his sand-colored flank. Aluna could see blood seeping through it in dark lines. A fresh injury. "You will proceed through the checkpoint one at a time. Do not run. Do not reach for your weapons. Do not ask questions."

Aluna glanced at Dash and saw his jaw tense. "It's not supposed to work like this, is it?" she whispered.

He shook his head once.

"Maybe they're already at war with Scorch and Karl Strand," she said. "They're smart to be cautious. For all they know, we're enemy spies."

"My people assume that everyone is out to get them," Calli agreed. "It's a good survival tactic."

Hoku grunted. "I remember the Aviar prison cells with great fondness."

Dash relaxed slightly. "Let us not keep them waiting, then. We will win their trust when the High Khan hears our tale."

"I'll go first," Aluna said. She raised her hands and stepped forward, hoping her legs would stay strong with so many eyes on her. She spoke loudly. "Not touching my weapons. Not running. Not asking questions."

When she was directly under the archway, the guard with the curly beard motioned her to stop. She forced herself to stand there as tiny beams of light crisscrossed her skin. It reminded her of the shark she and Hoku had found at the forbidden Seahorse Alpha outpost, the one that had scanned her with its green net and sent pictures back to Fathom.

A mechanical voice spoke: "Race: Kampii. Age: twelve to fifteen cycles. Diseases: no known strains. Biotech: standard Kampii enhancements. Risk assessment: minimal."

Aluna swallowed thickly. Not only did the tech know she was a Kampii. It also knew how old she was. It knew if she was sick. It knew about her fast-healing skin and thick bones and dark sight. Could it see her tail forming, too? Would it tell the others?

"Wait there," Curly-Beard said, motioning to a spot beside him. Aluna jumped out of the scanner veil and took her place. Up close, she could see a dark bruise pillowed around the guard's left eye.

Curly-Beard motioned to a female guard with a dusty black flank and red hair. She clomped over and he whispered to her, "Did you hear? A Kampii. She will want to know right away. Maybe we should go now." His eyes darted to the bandage on his back.

"Shh," the female guard said quietly. "Let the rest come through. We will do what she wants—what the

High Khan wants, I mean. Do not worry. Your sister will be fine."

Curly-Beard nodded, but he didn't look happy.

Aluna pretended she hadn't heard a word of it, but the hairs pricked at the back of her neck. Her fingers curled up and touched the weapons strapped to her wrists, two tiny talon chains wound tightly in their canisters, just waiting to be unleashed. But not yet. Not until they'd seen the khan and found some way to win him to their cause.

Curly-Beard looked up through the archway and called, "Next!"

Calli walked into the archway, and the tech voice called, "Race: Aviar. Age: twelve to fifteen cycles. Diseases: no known strains. Biotech: standard Aviar enhancements. Risk assessment: minimal."

Hoku followed. A ring of red lights blinked as the voice said, "Diseases: dormant type 6-F. Recommend immediate inoculation."

Before Aluna could even move, a young Equian warrior cantered up to Hoku, grabbed his arm, and slapped a patch on the back of his hand. Hoku looked startled but unharmed.

"Disease 6-F? Is that bad?" Hoku said.

The lights around the entrance immediately turned green. "Dormant type 6-F neutralized. Diseases: no known strains. Biotech: standard Kampii enhancements. Risk assessment: minimal." Hoku joined the others in the waiting spot, still stunned.

"Was I going to die?" he asked Calli quietly.

"Disease 6-F," Calli said, pretending to think. "Boils. I'm almost certain your death would have been slow and involved oozing boils."

"Well, then, I'm glad I don't have it anymore," he said seriously, peeling the med-patch off his skin.

Dash came through last, his eyes down, his hands fisted. Aluna didn't understand why he was so agitated until the tech voice called, "Race: Equian, failed. Herd: Shining Moon. Age: twelve to fifteen cycles. Diseases: no known strains. Biotech: partial Equian enhancements; mechanical forearm, left, origin unknown. Risk assessment: minimal."

Equian, failed.

The guards snickered and some said, *"Aldagha."* The way they said the word made her want to punch each of them in the face. And then Dash was through. Aluna tried to catch his eye, but he continued to stare at the ground.

The female guard stepped forward. "Welcome to Mirage, glorious home of Red Sky herd, and seat of our most exalted High Khan Onggur, leader of the Equians."

Aluna heard Curly-Beard mumble, "Which should be enough."

The guard continued. "You are now prisoners of the High Khan—"

"Wait, what?" Dash interrupted. "Since when have visitors to Mirage been automatically taken prisoner? This is not our way!"

"Risk assessment minimal," Hoku added. "You heard it yourselves!"

"Times change," the female guard said to Dash. "And since when does an *aldagha* know what it means to be a real Equian?"

Aluna saw Dash's fists tighten. She had to act fast, before blades were drawn. She stepped between Dash and the woman. "We're here to see High Khan Onggur. If you're planning to take us to him, then that's fine. Call us whatever you want on the way."

She let her hand drift to Dash's forearm and squeezed. It was his mechanical arm, cool and unforgiving beneath her fingers, but she sensed him relax anyway.

The guard nodded to Curly-Beard. "Borte, take them to the High Khan. Do what you need to do." She called out four other names, and soon guards surrounded them, their swords out. Curly-Beard— Borte—took the lead. His tail swished behind him, but he held his weapon in a firm grip.

"Do not attempt escape," he said. "Do not give us a reason to hurt you." He glared at Calli. "If you try to fly away, we will give the High Khan a cape made from your feathers."

Calli crossed her arms and seemed to shrink. She tried to pull her wings tight to her back, but they were still wings—huge and conspicuous and impossible to ignore. Hoku stepped to her side, his eyes angry. He never carried a weapon, but he looked ready to attack Borte with the books in his satchel. Dash, on the other hand, seemed cool as stone, his face blank and without emotion.

"We won't cause any trouble," Aluna said, more to her friends than to Borte. At another time, Hoku, Calli, and Dash would have laughed that she was the one making that promise. Right now, nothing seemed funny.

"Wise Kampii," Borte said. He turned and led them into the city.

Her view of Mirage was blocked by the five massive Equian bodies surrounding them, but she could tell the city bore little resemblance to the Mirage of Dash's stories. Where were all the people? She'd expected vendors hawking their goods, stores brimming with jewelry and claywork, and musicians competing for tips. But the streets were empty. The only motion was the flutter of red-and-black banners in Mirage's artificial breeze and an occasional face at a window, always quick to disappear when she noticed.

"What happened to the city?" Dash asked.

"No questions," Borte answered, but Aluna saw the guard frown, saw his left foreleg stumble slightly.

The distant clanging of metal against metal got louder as they walked. Thick black smoke drifted through the streets like mist off the ocean. It stung Aluna's eyes and made Calli cough.

And suddenly the tightly packed buildings gave way to a vast, open area filled with blacksmiths and weapon forgers, with skinners and bow makers and fletchers whittling arrows. Smoke billowed from forges and stained the nearby buildings with soot. Some Equians wore chains around their hooves. Some wore bandages on their backs and faces and legs. Everyone, even young Equians no older than a few years, hauled supplies or hammered metal or molded leather. Guards with drawn swords patrolled the work areas and barked orders.

Dash's eyes widened, and his voice came out strangled. "This was once the Market of Ten Thousand Colors."

"It's the Market of Ten Thousand Blades now," Borte said brusquely. "When we have met our quotas and when the desert is secure, the old market will be back. It is for the good of the herd. It is for the good of all Equians." He spoke the last part as if he'd said it a million times before.

Dash pointed to a dusty stone structure sitting in the middle of the market. "The fountain. It has run dry."

"It is the underground river that ran dry," Borte said. "Almost two years ago. Water is now strictly rationed for all citizens."

"Does the High Khan know that some of his people are in chains?" Aluna asked.

"Only those who will not willingly serve the herd are punished. And yes, he knows. Everything done in Mirage is by order of the High Khan," Borte said. Then he added quietly, "Although he is not without his advisers."

"Who?" Dash blurted out. "Who advised him to do this?"

Dash's eagerness seemed to snap Borte out of his conspiratorial mood. His face returned to its hard lines. "It is for the good of the herd. It is for the good of all Equians."

At the southern edge of the market, they stopped at the bottom of a wide ramp leading up to a massive open-air palace that overlooked the rest of the city. Gold and gemstones covered the building's ornate pillars. At midday, it glinted like a second sun. Aluna couldn't look away.

"The seat of the High Khan," Borte announced with forced enthusiasm. The four other guards responded in perfect unison. "May the High Khan live and rule forever!"

"Tides' teeth, could they have crammed any more sparklies onto that thing?" Hoku mumbled.

Calli lowered her eyes. "I know! There's even gold inlay on the ground. Under our feet! Who needs to walk on gold?"

Dash frowned. "This building was not here before. Our people are practical. The desert demands it. High Khan Onggur is first and foremost one of his herd. I do not understand this . . . this *display*."

But deep down in her gut, Aluna was starting to see the big picture, and it terrified her. They'd come here to warn the desert Equians about Karl Strand and his clone Scorch.

Maybe they were too late.

CHAPTER 3

BORTE MADE THEM REMOVE their head wraps
before seeing the High Khan. Hoku didn't mind. He
had gotten used to the confining fabric, but missed
running his fingers through his hair when he got nervous. No one wore head wraps inside the city. Mirage's
dome blocked out the harmful parts of the sun's rays
and left only the light. "There is no need to hide from
her radiant glory," Borte said. "Those who continue
to wear head wraps are clearly hiding from something
else."

Hoku shoved his head wrap into his satchel, wishing for the millionth time that he hadn't left Zorro
back in the HydroTek dome. The Dome Meks had
convinced him that Zorro's mechanical raccoon body

hadn't been built for the desert, that the sand could damage his tech and break him forever. Hurting Zorro was not a risk Hoku was willing to take, despite how much he missed the furry little guy.

As they walked up the ramp toward the palace, Hoku noticed the horses. Horses painted on the stone beneath their feet, horses engraved on wide pillars holding up the palace's roof, horses embroidered on the black-and-red banners flying overhead. And the gold! Didn't the Equians understand how useful gold was as a conductor? That it resisted corrosion better than a lot of other metals? And here they were, slathering it on every depiction of the sun in their artwork instead of using it in their tech.

"Send a good bolt of electricity through this place, and the gold might electrocute all the Equians at once," Hoku muttered to Calli. She barely suppressed a giggle.

At the top of the platform, Mirage's artificial wind snapped the banners and blew Hoku's hair into his eyes. The High Khan stood at the center, surrounded by tables of food, piles of bright pillows, and a handful of advisers and servants all wearing Red Sky's colors. The contrast between the stinky, smoke-filled market below and the High Khan's breezy palace couldn't have been more stark.

To the High Khan's side, a handful of other

Equians stood in a clump. They each wore different styles of clothes—some in elaborate embroidered and beaded layers, others in simple desert tunics. A ring of Red Sky guards surrounded them, blocking Hoku's view. But if he'd had to guess, he'd say they had also arrived as guests and discovered that they were something else entirely.

High Khan Onggur's presence dominated the pavilion. He was easily the largest Equian Hoku had ever seen—not quite as big as Great White, but just as impressive. Onggur's muscled arms bulged. His black hair fell in one long braid at his side, a perfect match for the shiny black coat of his powerful horse body. Red and black had been worked into his tunic, wound into his tail, and enameled on his chest armor. He wore a large amulet of dull red around his neck, and the hilt of a massive sword jutted over his shoulder. Thin slivers of marred skin cut across his arms, his face, and his sleek horse flank. *Scars.* This man had already seen more fighting than Hoku ever wanted to.

"Who is that Human?" Dash asked quietly.

Borte's flank shivered. He replied coldly, "Our newest ally."

One of the servants moved, and Hoku saw her. A Human woman standing with the High Khan's Equian advisers. She had dark-brown hair cut close to her head and styled into a swoop over her forehead. Instead of muted desert clothes, she wore a tunic of bright-red silk cinched at the waist with a fluttery black sash. Her pants were black and sleek and disappeared into the tops of her knee-high black boots. Not a very practical desert outfit, but a stunning one.

He would have dismissed her as a visiting Human except for her eyes. The ancients had long ago discovered not only how to fix bad eyesight but also how to improve on it: to give the Deepfell and the Kampii the ability to see in dark water, to give the Aviars distance sight, to help the Equians keep their eyes from burning out from too much sun. Even the Upgraders knew how to replace their eyes with special tech, tech that could read heat shapes or estimate distance down to the millimeter.

And yet this woman wore glasses. Black-rimmed glasses that Hoku was sure he'd seen somewhere before. Somewhere important.

"That woman is Red Sky's new ally?" Aluna asked. "She's barely taller than me!"

"Do not let her size deceive you," Borte said. "She is a person of impressive cunning, and our High Khan listens to her council as if it comes from the sun herself."

They approached slowly, following Borte's lead. Hoku tried to watch the High Khan, but his eyes kept snapping to the woman, as if she were a magnet and he a bit of powerless iron. Her eyes found him and seemed to bore a hole through his head.

Borte stomped his foot. "Presenting to the High Khan, his allies, and his advisers a new batch of visit—prisoners. Two Kampii, one Aviar, and a failed Equian from Shining Moon."

Hoku cringed but didn't look at Dash. If the horseboy could ignore the insults, then Hoku could train himself to ignore them, too. Aluna didn't say anything, either. He glanced over and saw why. She seemed distracted, her gaze locked on the woman in red at Onggur's side, her brow creased in thought.

High Khan Onggur spoke, his voice almost as big as the rest of him: "What brings such an odd assortment of splinters to Mirage, home of Red Sky?"

"We bring important news from the oceans and skies," Aluna said, and Hoku felt a wave of pride at how strong her voice echoed in the stone pavilion. "A really old Human named Karl Strand—one of the ancients who's found some way to stay alive—is trying to conquer—"

"Stop," the Human woman said quickly. "The High Khan will hear no more of your lies."

Dash grunted in surprise. Hoku guessed that it was unusual for anyone, and a Human in particular, to presume to speak for High Khan Onggur. But instead of putting her in her place, Onggur said only, "Does our honored ally wish to speak first?" His voice sounded calm, but Hoku could hear an edge in it, as if the High Khan were balancing his words on the edge of a cliff.

"I do," the woman said.

Hoku saw several of the High Khan's advisers shuffle their hooves and swish their tails. They seemed uncomfortable but unwilling to speak out. Why? Then Hoku remembered Borte's fresh bandage and the bruises on his face. Maybe that's how the High Khan rewarded insolence. Then, on the edge of his vision, he saw the Human woman move.

No, she *blurred*. One moment she was standing beside the High Khan, and in the next flash she stood half a meter away, her hand around Calli's throat. Squeezing. Calli's eyes widened, and she clawed uselessly at the woman's arm.

"Stop!" Hoku yelled. "You're killing her!"

Aluna and Dash attacked. Aluna leaped behind the Human and pressed the blade of her knife to the woman's throat. Dash tried to peel the woman's fingers away from Calli's throat with his powerful mechanical hand. He could bend iron bars with that tech, but the Human's grip barely faltered.

"She is too strong," Dash said through gritted teeth.

"Not strong enough to resist a slice to the throat," Aluna said grimly. Hoku wondered if she could do it. If Aluna could actually cut someone's throat with a whole crowd of people watching. Then he saw the panic on Calli's face and knew the answer. He'd do it himself if he could. Aluna's blade cut deeper into the Human's neck, but the woman didn't budge. Didn't cry out. And not a single drop of blood slid down her throat.

"She's an Upgrader," Hoku said. "Her tech is on the inside!"

The woman's mouth twisted. "Allow me to introduce myself." She turned as if Aluna and Dash weren't attacking her and threw Calli to the ground in front the High Khan. Calli propped herself up on an elbow and gasped for air. Hoku was at her side in an instant, itching to hug her close. He settled for helping her to sit up. If the Human attacked Calli again, she'd have to go through him.

The Human swatted Dash and Aluna away as if they were guppies. Hoku watched Aluna stumble back, her expression shocked but her dark eyes still assessing.

The woman wasn't even breathing hard. "This winged harpy and her people killed my brother," she said. "I demand the girl's life in recompense."

Aluna crouched low and tucked her knife back in its sheath. "Ridiculous! Calli hasn't killed anybody." Hoku saw Aluna flick her wrists to ready her thin chain weapons.

"My brother's name was Tempest. Sky Master

Tempest," the woman said. "These flying rats killed him in cold blood at the SkyTek dome."

Suddenly, Hoku knew where he'd seen those glasses before. He'd seen them on an old photo of Sarah Jennings, the first Kampii, and her Above World family.

"Karl Strand," he croaked, even though he'd meant to only think it. "You're Scorch. You're one of Karl Strand's clones."

Scorch smiled. "I am his daughter, yes. And you, Kampii, are exactly the sort of specimen my brother Fathom has been looking for. Perhaps I will send him you and the girl Kampii, wrapped up with a bow. I don't agree with his experiments, but I do indulge them. We are family, after all."

Hoku clamped his mouth shut, afraid he might blurt out something that would get them killed. Scorch didn't know what had happened at HydroTek. She didn't know how they'd defeated her brother and taken back the dome. Fathom was in frozen sleep, not dead, but he doubted Scorch would see the distinction. It was only a matter of time before an Upgrader made it to Mirage and told her the news.

"I don't care who you are," Aluna said. "You're not killing Calli. You're not even touching her. We're here to see the High Khan, not you. And last time I checked, this city belonged to him."

"My father and I are allies of Red Sky," Scorch said. She turned to the High Khan. "I ask for the life of the bird-girl, as is my right, and for the two small Kampii to send as gifts of goodwill to my brother. Only three inconsequential lives."

Hoku had almost forgotten about High Khan Onggur and the other Equians. Why had they done nothing when Scorch attacked? He saw the High Khan's advisers stomping nervously and staring at their leader. A few fingered the hilts of their swords.

High Khan Onggur's face remained calm, but his words bit into the air. "No one is killed or attacked in my presence without my permission." Scorch's arrogant sneer faded slightly. Onggur held up his hand. "However, in light of the generosity your father has displayed to our people, we do not take offense. Soon you will better understand our customs, and such incidents will be merely a memory."

Scorch started to retort, then clamped her mouth shut and offered the High Khan a stiff bow. "Of course, Great Khan," she said. "I acted on impulse, and as you can see, the traitors are unharmed."

Traitors, Hoku thought. Nice how she worked that in there.

Onggur nodded briskly. "It is forgotten. Furthermore, I see no reason not to grant you the lives you have requested, to do with as you wish."

CHAPTER 4

Y OU CAN'T HAVE CALLI," Hoku said to Scorch. He felt Calli's wings brush his arm. He stood taller. "And you can't have us, either." He glanced at Aluna, hoping she'd back him up with more than just words. She nodded, her face grim.

"If you want to kill us, you'll get a fight," Aluna said.

Hoku heard a *snick* and saw Dash's retractable sword expand to its full, deadly size. Dash said nothing. He didn't need to. Calli struggled to her feet, her face still red from Scorch's attack. She didn't carry a weapon, but she glowered anyway.

"Wait," a new voice said. Everyone looked toward the group of Equians penned in at the khan's side. A young woman a few years older than Hoku clomped forward. She had skin almost as light as his and wore her long brown hair in two braids woven with dark-blue and white cords. Her horse flank was a deep reddish brown and turned to black at her hooves and tail. "I am Tayan, khan-daughter of Shining Moon, and I claim the lives of Dashiyn and his three companions."

Scorch started to interrupt, but the High Khan spoke over her. "By what right?"

Tayan spoke calmly. "The boy known as Dash is Shining Moon. He has broken his exile and must return to our homeland to face trial and punishment. I claim his companions as accomplices under herd law, until such time as their innocence can be determined."

There was a saying back in the ocean: *Escape a shark and find a Deepfell.* Just when you thought things were bad, they got a whole lot worse.

"Oh, we're definitely accomplices," Aluna said with a growl. "Whatever happens to Dash happens to us, too."

"This is ridiculous," Scorch said. "You're going to listen to these children?"

"I will listen to herd law," High Khan Onggur said. "Tradition must not be overlooked. It makes us strong." He turned to Tayan. "The *aldagha* and his companions are yours."

Tayan touched two fingers to her heart and bowed, but Scorch wasn't done. "Karl Strand will not be pleased to hear of this."

"Hold your threats," High Khan Onggur said impatiently. "I am not done."

Scorch raised an eyebrow and took a step back, giving the khan room. Onggur turned to the Equians penned in at his side, including Tayan. "Emissaries of the Equian herds, I give you this message to take back to your khans: the desert goes to war."

Hoku sucked in his breath and shared a look with Calli. He saw Aluna and Dash doing the same thing with each other. They'd come here to warn the Equians about Karl Strand, and they'd been too late. Way, way too late.

The High Khan waited until the Equians' shocked murmurs and hoof stomping subsided before continuing. "This year, the Thunder Trials will be more than contests of strength and skill. All herds will meet in peace, as we have done for hundreds of years. But when the games end and I once again earn the Sun Disc and am made High Khan, we will leave as an army."

"You will become the swift blade of Karl Strand," Scorch said, and Hoku could hear the pride in her voice. "You will become the agents of my father's justice throughout the land, from desert to ocean to mountaintop stronghold. Your High Khan will be king of all of that, and more. As payment for your loyalty, my father will give you our technology. If you want water brought to the desert, then we will turn the sands to rolling hills and fill the empty skies with clouds."

The Red Sky Equians cheered.

Hoku shook his head. Karl Strand was promising them water. How could their tiny band ever compete with such an offer?

"What about the herds that don't want war?" Aluna said.

"Karl Strand is not worthy of desert honor," Dash added. He touched fingers to his heart. "He is not worthy of *you*, High Khan."

"When the Thunder Trials are over, there will be only those who are loyal to me and those who are traitors," the High Khan said. "All traitors will be hunted down and killed. Their bloodlines will be crushed to dust so that their lines can never rise again. All memory of them will be extinguished, and even the sun herself will forget them."

Silence fell in the pavilion. Onggur's words hung in the air, dark as blood in water.

Tayan spoke next, her earlier bravado diminished. "Your message is clear, and I will deliver it to my father, High Khan. With your leave, I will take the four Shining Moon prisoners and go."

High Khan Onggur held up his hand, and Tayan waited, her black tail swishing. "The *aldagha* is yours by herd law, Tayan khan-daughter, but you will not harm the other three, even if they are found guilty for helping the exile. Bring them to the Thunder Trials. When the games are over, they will belong to Scorch."

Scorch grinned, looking like a hunter with a fat catch.

Tayan's back hooves shifted, but in the end, she bowed. "A fair compromise, High Khan."

"If you think we're going to give ourselves to her," Aluna said, glaring at Scorch, "then think again."

"If you do not arrive at the Thunder Trials, then Shining Moon will bear the punishment for your dishonor," the High Khan said.

"I will execute the Aviar in front of all the herds," Scorch said. "That will make up for this ludicrous"— she looked at the High Khan and paused—"this *understandable* delay. But if the winged girl is not there, then I'll make do with killing Shining Moon. One Equian for each of the girl's feathers seems fair. . . ."

"The prisoners will be there," Tayan said quickly. "You have my word."

The High Khan nodded. "Then go. Tell your father that by the Thunder Trials, Shining Moon should be ready for war. I am counting on his swords, his arrows, and his falcons."

"Oh, I will," Tayan said quietly, and bowed low before the High Khan. Hoku wondered if he was the only one who could hear the hint of dissent in her voice.

Their guard from earlier, Borte, motioned for Tayan to follow him. She paused to speak to Dash. "Dashiyn of the Shining Moon, you have knowingly broken your exile and returned to the desert. Do you acknowledge this?"

Dash looked up at her. "I do."

"And you will come willingly to face your judgment?"

He nodded. "I will."

Tayan stomped a foot. "Then I see no need for restraints. Bring your friends and follow me. We leave the city immediately." She walked past him, then past Borte and down the ramp.

Dash looked at Hoku, his dark eyes questioning.

"Yes, of course," Hoku said. "Calli, do you need help?"

She gave him a weak smile. "No, I'm fine. I'm looking forward to open air."

Hoku turned and found Aluna staring at Scorch from less than a meter away.

"This isn't the last you'll see of me," Aluna said to her.

Scorch chuckled. "I certainly hope not."

Hoku saw the talon weapons in Aluna's hands and whispered quickly, "Not here. Not now." He knew that the Kampii artifact in his throat would send the words directly to the device in her ears.

She didn't react at first. Her gaze stayed stuck on Scorch. But eventually she nodded and stepped away — though she wouldn't turn her back entirely, not with Strand's clone so close.

Hoku gave one last look at Scorch. Now he could see her resemblance to the Karl Strand from the ancient photo. Her brown hair was the same length as his, her chin the same shape. Strand's other clone, Fathom, had said the cloning process was imperfect, that all the clones came out a little different from Karl. Well, Scorch had come out female and smart. A lot smarter than Fathom. That made her a lot more dangerous, too.

Once Hoku made sure Aluna was really headed down the ramp and wasn't planning some sort of surprise attack, he followed. As they descended, the thick, choking smoke of the weapon forgers swallowed them up. Despite the smell, he was grateful for its protection. He wanted to be as far away from Scorch as possible. The entire desert might not be far enough.

At Mirage's gate, Borte handed them packs of dried cactus strips and water skins only a quarter filled. From what Hoku had seen of Mirage, it was a generous offer.

"May the sun guide you," Borte said as they affixed their headgear.

Tayan clapped him on the shoulder and said quietly, "Stay strong, Brother Red Sky. This isn't over."

Borte's back hoof stomped, but he said nothing.

And then they were through the dome scanner and back outside the city. The heat hit Hoku like a dolphin tail full in the face. He staggered and was tempted to head back inside, at least for another hour or two. But then Calli jumped into the air, unfurled her wings, and flew. A smile spread across her face, and although she didn't laugh, Hoku could tell she wanted to.

"Thank you for getting us out," Aluna said to Tayan. "I'm in your debt for that."

"You are welcome," Tayan said. "I would leave no person in the grasp of that woman, if I could help it. Nor with our High Khan while he listens to her counsel."

Aluna nodded. "We're heading back to HydroTek. We need to talk to the Aviars and our people, the Kampii, and figure out what to do next. We wanted to get here before Scorch, but we obviously failed. I'm not sure what our next move should be."

"You will come to the home of Shining Moon," Tayan said easily. It occurred to Hoku that with her horse body, she probably weighed more than the rest of them combined. "I gave my word that you would attend the Thunder Trials, and Dashiyn must stand trial. I thought I made myself clear."

Aluna stopped walking. "You said that to get us out."

"No," Tayan countered. "Everything I said was true." The Equian seemed untroubled by Aluna's growing agitation. Hoku felt his shoulders tense. After everything, he might still see blood today.

"We have no intention of being your prisoners," Aluna said gravely. "If you want us, you're going to have to take us."

There it was. The ultimatum. Hoku tried to signal Calli to fly back down. He wanted her by his side for whatever happened next. She waved and smiled. Clearly, his signaling skills needed work.

But it was Dash who spoke next, his voice as calm as ever. "Aluna, I have given my word to go with Tayan and abide by herd law, and Tayan has given her word that you will appear at the Thunder Trials. I am asking you, as a friend, to come with me. We will talk with Khan Arasen of Shining Moon and come up with a plan."

He touched Aluna's hand. "Please," he said. "Do not give up on the desert yet."

But Hoku heard the words he was really saying: *Do not give up on me.*

Aluna must have heard them, too. She stared at Dash, then sighed. "Okay. We'll go. We'll fight. We'll find some way to win."

CHAPTER 5

AS TAYAN LED THEM deeper into the desert, Aluna looked back and watched Mirage flicker briefly before it disappeared, hidden once again by its ancient tech. The city hadn't been the bastion of food and culture—and soft beds—that they'd been expecting. She frowned, remembering Dash's expression when he'd seen the marketplace transformed into a factory of war. How could High Khan Onggur force his people to work for a fight that wasn't even his own?

The High Khan said Karl Strand was giving them tech, had even promised to bring water to the desert. Maybe Onggur saw an alliance as the only way to help his people. Aluna needed to show him and the rest of the Equians that there were other options. Better options. Options that didn't involve letting Karl Strand and his clones run the world.

When they finally stopped for the night, Aluna and Hǫku started gathering twigs for the fire. They didn't need the flames for warmth, but Calli and Dash did. And besides, she'd grown accustomed to the crackle of dried wood, the smell of smoke, and the way the flames pulled everyone's faces out of the darkness.

Dash and Calli went looking for food. They'd proven a highly efficient team during the last few weeks, what with Calli's wings and keen eyesight and Dash's ability to know what bizarre desert plants and animals were actually edible. Dash could eat a much wider variety of things than the rest of them could, thanks to the SandTek ancients having given him a superstrong stomach, but he was good at finding things for all of them now.

Now that Dash was finally away from camp, Aluna saw her chance to get some answers. Tayan knelt on one knobby horse leg by the fire circle and began arranging the kindling with practiced ease. Aluna dropped a bunch of scrub brush by Tayan's side.

"So, you and your herd exiled Dash. Why? Just because he was born different? Because he doesn't have hooves?" She'd wanted to remain calm, but could hear the pitch of her voice rising anyway. "He risked everything to come back here and help you, and you're going to thank him by putting him on trial?"

Tayan stopped her work and stared. Her blue eyes reminded Aluna of an overcast sky. "Is that what you think? Is that what he told you?" Her tail swished. "Dash's exile had nothing to do with his status as *aldagha*. Shining Moon are not barbarians. We do not exile or kill our own people. Not without good reason." She shook her head as if she had a horse's mane instead of hair under a head wrap.

"If you've got a good reason, then I want to hear it," Aluna said. "If you want our help, then you need to win us over. Because right now, I may want Karl Strand dead, but I am *not* on your side."

"None of us are," Hoku said, dumping his small contribution of twigs near the smoldering fire.

Tayan looked across the darkening horizon in the direction Dash and Calli had gone. "Very well," she said. "I will tell you quickly, because despite what you may think, I do not wish to cause Dashiyn further dishonor." The Equian motioned to the fire, and Aluna sat, grateful for the chance to rest her legs. Hoku flopped down beside her with a grunt.

Tayan stoked the fire with a long stick. "Perhaps you know this already, but the Equians are not alone in the desert. The SandTek ancients created not one race but two—ours, and the half-Human, half-snake people called Serpenti."

"Snake people!" Hoku said. "We saw one at HydroTek. He was one of Fathom's prisoners."

Aluna remembered him from the cages, and later from the battle. He'd worn gold hoop earrings, and his long, dark hair had been half shorn to nothing by Fathom for one of his experiments. "That man fought bravely against Fathom's army. We had no idea where to send his body."

"I hope you sent it to the ever-dark," Tayan said coldly. "Oh, the Serpenti can fight. Their whole bodies are weapons, from the strength and reach of their tails to the poison hidden in their fangs. The SandTek ancients must have thought we could live together, share resources, perhaps even help one another. They were wrong."

Aluna gestured to the dusty flats surrounding them. "This place is huge, and you still fought over it?"

"The desert is vast, but water and food are scarce, and growing harder to find every year," Tayan said. "Why do you think the High Khan would even consider this alliance with Strand and his clones? Because the promise of water is too great a temptation. When your people begin to wither, you will do anything to save them.

"Performance in the Thunder Trials determines

how many foals each herd may birth in the following year. Win more honors, and your herd grows. In this way, our strongest bloodlines prosper and our weakest slowly diminish. Over the last few years, the High Khan has doubled the birthing rights granted to each herd, but our numbers do not increase. Fewer foals survive the birth chambers, and among those that do, there are more *aldagha*. More mistakes."

Aluna was already tired of hearing that word. It made her heart ache.

"Your tech is broken. Or breaking," Hoku said. "Maybe you just need to fix it."

"Which Karl Strand has offered to do," Tayan said solemnly. "Do you see now the position we are in?"

"Maybe if you didn't keep fighting with the Serpenti, you'd have more people," Aluna said bitterly. "Try making a few friends instead of going to war with everyone."

"Do you want to hear about Dashiyn or not?" Tayan asked coldly.

Aluna swallowed her anger. It felt like a fire in her gut, but she managed to control it. "Go on."

"As I have stated, war with the Serpenti was inevitable. When it came, it was bloody and terrible, and we were losing. We would have been utterly destroyed if our great heroes Altan and Chabi had not challenged the Serpenti to an honor duel in the Valley of the Dead. They defeated the Serpenti khans—whom the snake people called pharos—but were poisoned in the process. Both heroes died not long after."

"Just for once, I'd like to hear a story where the heroes *don't* die," Hoku grumbled.

"We crushed the Serpenti after that," Tayan said. "A few of them escaped into the desert, and we vowed to hunt them down, every last one, and put an end to the violence—and to the Venom War—forever." She paused and stared down at her front hooves for a moment before continuing. "We searched for the remaining Serpenti for years, and eventually Shining Moon managed to capture two of the beasts. One died during questioning, but we had high hopes of interrogating the second, of finally discovering the location of their hidden stronghold. We feared that they were planning another war, and we wanted to end it before it began."

"This is interesting, but I don't see what it has to do with Dash," Aluna said. She didn't like where this story was going. She didn't want Dash to have anything to do with the Serpenti or the Venom War.

"You will," Tayan said grimly. "The information we got from the prisoners would have brought great honor to Shining Moon. We would have been awarded greater birthing rights at the Thunder Trials. Our herd would have thrived. But when Khan Arasen, my father, went to interrogate the remaining prisoner, the Serpenti was gone—along with a crate of medical supplies needed by our own people."

Her accusation hung there, like smoke over the fire. Aluna thought she might choke on it.

"The Serpenti escaped," Aluna said finally. "That's the only explanation. All this time, you've been persecuting Dash for something he didn't even do. I bet it was easy to blame someone you were already calling a mistake."

"Which is exactly what I said to my father," Tayan said. "Only . . . Dashiyn admitted to the whole thing. He admitted to stealing the medicine, freeing the prisoner, and directly lending aid to our mortal enemies. We did not even have to ask him. He sought an audience with the khan and told us everything without prompting."

If Tayan was right, then Dash was a traitor. Aluna put her face in her hands. She wanted to scream at Tayan, to call her a liar and force her to retract what she'd said. But she knew Tayan wasn't a liar. Based on just the few hours since they'd met, Aluna would have staked her life on that.

The fire flickered in a sudden gust of wind. Aluna looked up and saw Calli swooping down for a landing, her tawny wings wide to slow her descent, her arms full of cactuses. Dash was still a way off, jogging back with two scrawny rabbits swinging from one hand.

She'd ask him about all of this. She'd listen to his side. The Dash she knew was honorable. He'd never betray his own people. Then again, it did explain why he'd been unwilling to talk about his exile before now. And why he sometimes seemed to be filled with equal parts regret and self-hate.

Maybe this time she didn't really want the truth at all.

CHAPTER 6

HOKU WAS STILL GNAWING on his last piece of grilled cactus when Tayan stood near the flames and cleared her throat. The sky covered them all in blackness. It wasn't the thick, cozy dark of the ocean at night, but it comforted him all the same. And he liked being able to see the stars.

"I think Tayan's going to tell a story," Aluna whispered. "I remember Dash telling us about this, about how the Equians tell stories all night long, trying to coax the sun back into the sky."

"All night?" Calli asked. "When do they sleep?"

"They take turns, but they don't have to sing all night if there are only a few of them," Aluna said. "I just hope we don't have to join in. After today's march, I could sleep like a whale."

Hoku looked across the fire at Dash. He hadn't spoken much since he'd been taken prisoner in Mirage. Hoku couldn't even imagine what dark thoughts were filling his head. If only Aluna would go sit next to him and ask him what was wrong. But no. Aluna respected him too much to pry. And Dash respected her too much to heap his problems on her. Hoku glanced over at Calli. She looked back at him and smiled, and his insides warmed.

Aluna and Dash were clearly doing it wrong. Although to be fair, he wasn't entirely sure what he and Calli were doing right. There was a lot of smiling and blushing and talking and occasionally some hand-holding. For now, that was all he needed.

Tayan started to speak. It was some sort of ritual calling to the missing sun. Hoku loved the way her voice got loud and high, then sank back lower and softer, pulling him in just like a wave. She stomped her hooves in the sand—sometimes just one or two, sometimes all four in quick succession—creating a rhythm that mesmerized him. When she began her first story, he forgot about their terrible day in Mirage. He forgot about all the sand and dirt caked to his skin. He even forgot about Scorch and High Khan Onggur and the long journey still ahead of them.

All he could do was listen.

Listen. Listen. To the sand, to the moon.
Listen. Listen.
Chabi was the last of her herd. Not the smartest.
Not the strongest. Not the sleekest. Not the
fastest. Chabi was the last Flame Heart.
She buried her kin. Buried her sire. Mourned
her dam. They were killed by Snakes in
the dark while fire blazed, killed while
the word-weavers called to the sun, killed
while the warriors slept. With knives and
with poison they were killed. Vile Snakes.
Venom-filled. Under the dark of no moon.
Chabi ran until her feet caught fire, until her
coat bled flames, until anger burned her
heart. Chabi was the last of her herd.
Listen. Listen.
Altan was the last of his herd. Not the smartest.
Not the strongest. Not the sleekest. Not the
fastest. Altan was the last Wind Seeker.
He buried his kin. Buried his dam. Mourned
his sire. They were killed by another herd
in bright of day, on the field of war, on
the clean white sand. Killed for their food.
Killed for their foals. Red Sky took them.

Claimed them. Grew stronger with their blood. Under the warm light, under the sun.

Altan ran until his feet froze, until his coat turned to ice, until his heart turned blue. Altan was the last of his herd.

Chabi and Altan ran. They ran for years. They ran for decades. They tried to outrun their pain. But no one runs faster than war.

Listen. Listen.

The Snakes came in numbers greater than the stars. Vile venom-vipers. Tail bashing, sword slashing. The sands turned red. The sands burned red. Khans fell. Herds died. No more Whispering Gait. Farewell, Golden Bow.

Brave were the warriors of the desert. Brave were our hoof-brothers, tail-sisters. But no one outruns war. No one outruns death. The sands turned red. The sands burned red.

The great desert herds gathered in the Valley of the Dead for one final battle, one last Snake slaughter. Outnumbered. Outmatched. Ten Snakes, fresh and fierce, for every horse blade. Ten for every sleek bow. We prepared to join the sun.

And then they came. Fire and cold ice. Anger and loss. Chabi and Altan, from the desert on hooves of flame and frost. They met

for the first time in the Valley of the Dead,
on the eve of our end. Red heat and silver
freeze. Where they first spoke, air sizzled.
Smoke twisted up to the sky.

Together they challenged the Snakes. Together
they fought the Snake kings, the Snake
pharos, in the Valley of the Dead. The
battle raged for eight days. Sword-slick,
blood-heavy.

Listen. Listen.

Altan and Chabi fought for us. The desert. Our
bloodlines. Our future. They were the last
of their herds, but not the last of their kind.

When Altan faltered, Chabi fought in his place.
When Chabi dropped her blade, Altan gave
her his own. Fire and ice. Ice and fire. The
Snake kings fell.

Singing. Dancing. Loving. Joy. The herds of the
desert outran war.

But as the herds sang and danced and loved
and laughed, Altan and Chabi fell. Green
venom in their veins. Green venom in their
blood. No one outruns death.

They died together. Fire and ice, anger and
sorrow. Altan and Chabi. And the place
where they fell sizzles still, smoke twining
into the air, hot and cold.

They were the last of their herds.

Listen. Listen. To the sand, to the moon.

Remember. Remember.

When Tayan finished her tale, she touched two fingers to her heart, lowered her head, and backed away from the fire. Dash stood up and began the next story almost immediately.

Hoku shook himself out of his stupor. He'd never seen the Valley of the Dead, but images of fire and ice, of swords and blood and sand, filled his mind. Even his heart thumped faster than normal. Maybe it was trying to outrun death.

It reminded him of the battle at the HydroTek dome, when Dash had held off the Upgraders while Hoku accessed the computer. If only the Equians could have seen Dash fight! Even with a wounded arm, he was brilliant and brave. A hero, just like Altan and Chabi. If Shining Moon had any sense, they wouldn't punish Dash; they'd write songs about him.

Fingertips touched his shoulder. He jumped, then relaxed when he saw Calli next to him.

"You off in the sky somewhere?" she whispered.

He smiled. "No, definitely still in the desert, on the ground. And still hungry."

Calli offered him a piece of cactus. He looked at it balefully. "I miss the sandwiches at Skyfeather's Landing."

"Be honest," Calli said, poking him in the arm. "You miss the mustard more than anything."

"You know me so well," he said.

Dash's story involved a legendary archer and his pet falcon, but Hoku missed most of it. His eyes slipped closed for longer and longer periods, until Calli nudged him and made him crawl over to the bedding pile.

Equians slept standing up to keep the desert's creepy-crawlies from getting into their ears and noses during the night. Hoku envied them. Dash's stories about brain parasites and bone-eating beetles had made sleeping impossible during the first few days of their journey to Mirage. But now he and Aluna and Calli had become experts at leaning against one another to keep their heads off the sand. It wasn't restful sleep. Calli's wings were soft but rustled too much and sometimes tickled his ears, and Aluna grunted in her dreams, as if she were perpetually fighting off Upgraders. Dash slept alone—if he slept at all.

But tonight Hoku didn't care about any of that. He made it to his blanket and collapsed, ear close to the sand. If the creepy-crawlies wanted him tonight, they could have him. Dash finished his story, and Tayan began the next. "Listen. Listen," she said, and that's all Hoku remembered.

Strangely, he wasn't the last one awake in the morning. Normally he opened his eyes and found Calli preening her feathers and Aluna already off stretching or practicing with her weapons. But this morning, he saw Calli circling high above their camp and Aluna's familiar shape curled nearby on her blanket.

"Hey, are you feeling okay?" he asked.

She groaned. "Go away. I'm sleeping."

"No, you're not," he said. "You never sleep later than me. Not even when you're sick. Something's wrong."

She rolled over. "I'm fine. Give me a minute, and I'll be fine."

He touched her shoulder. "Tides' teeth, if you're sick, I'll ask Tayan to carry you. It's stupid that Equians never let anyone ride on their backs. She could easily —"

"No," Aluna said harshly, pulling away from his touch. And then a word he rarely heard from her: "Please."

He let his hand drift back to his side but couldn't keep the frown off his face. A shadow blurred by. He shielded his eyes and looked up. Calli drifted and spun in the air. She couldn't fly most days because the blowing sand got in her eyes and feathers. Aviars were definitely not built for the desert.

He took one last look at Aluna, still scrunched up on her side, then went to help break camp. By the time they had everything loaded up and the fire stamped out, Aluna was up and ready to go.

Secrets, Hoku thought. When had they started collecting those?

CHAPTER 7

THEIR JOURNEY TO SHINING MOON blurred into a series of hot yellow days and cool ink-black nights. Even Aluna had trouble keeping up with the pace Tayan set. It was no secret why the SandTek ancients had given Equians four swift hooves instead of two legs. Tayan also seemed to need less water, could gnaw on cactus as she ran to keep her strength up, and, despite her light-colored skin, never burned.

Dash didn't have horse legs, but he ran as if he did. He never complained, never seemed to get tired. Aluna could only imagine what it must have been like for him, growing up in a place where everyone is faster and stronger and bigger than you.

At night, they barely had the energy to hunt for food, gather materials for the fire, and eat before collapsing. Sometimes Aluna managed to ask about the Thunder Trials, or they swapped stories from their homelands. Aluna never asked Dash why he helped the Serpenti. He'd tell her when he was ready, or she'd just have to assume that everything Tayan said was true.

One morning, when they'd stopped briefly to let Hoku pull some stones from his boots, Aluna heard Calli cry out from the sky.

"Tents!" she yelled, pointing northeast. "I see tents!"

Tayan galloped ahead to the next ridge and called back, "Shining Moon! We are home."

Aluna looked at Dash, expecting to see fear or apprehension on his face. Instead, it lit up as if he'd just seen the sun after years in darkness. He bolted for Tayan, and Aluna could only scramble to keep up.

Below them, hundreds of colorful tents sprouted out of the sandy, scrub-dusted landscape like a cluster of bright anemones. Hundreds of Equians walked and cantered through the settlement, far too many to count, and she guessed that there were a lot more inside the tents. Aluna could pick out a dozen training areas scattered around the perimeter, along with several large animal enclosures. One for horses, another for two huge rhinebras, and a third, covered in nets, that seemed to house birds. A huge meeting area at the western edge of the city contained a massive fire pit spitting a trickle of dark smoke into the sky.

"Tides' teeth," Hoku muttered. Aluna hadn't even noticed when he'd arrived.

An Equian down by the settlement spotted them and yelled.

Tayan grinned. "We made good time. Tonight is Darkest Night, when we celebrate the hidden moon. You will eat our best food, hear our best word-weavers. Then you will understand why we will defend this desert and our herd traditions with our lives."

Calli and Hoku whooped. Aluna knew that the trek had been hard on them—it was impossible not to see the exhaustion on Hoku's face each day—but she wasn't excited about reaching the herd. While they traveled, Dash was safe. A prisoner, but alive. Now that they'd arrived at Shining Moon, his fate was less certain.

A movement caught Aluna's eye. A lone gray-and-black horse cantered around the outskirts of the settlement. It reminded her of Conch, a dolphin that begged for food near her family nest in the City of Shifting Tides. Why wasn't the horse in the enclosure with the others? It didn't look injured or old, at least not from the way it danced out of range of passing Equians.

"Come," Tayan said. "We have much to tell my father and brother. Let us feel the wind in our faces."

Tayan burst into a gallop and headed toward the city. Hoku and Calli raced after her. Aluna was about to join them, *swift as a seal,* when Dash grabbed her elbow.

"Are you well?" he asked quietly. "You lie awake in the morning without moving. Three times now. Something is wrong."

Aluna's right foot stumbled in the sand, and she almost fell. He'd noticed? "Never mind that," she said. "We have more important problems to think about. Your trial—"

"So it *is* a problem," Dash said. "I knew it! You must let me help. We have many medics in the herd. Perhaps someone can—"

"No!" she snapped. She hadn't meant it to come out so harshly, but she'd found a new thick patch of skin near her knee that morning. A patch that looked suspiciously like scales. She'd been jumpy as a squid ever since. "No," she said again, much more calmly. "I don't want to talk about it, and I don't want help."

"Fine," he said, although the expression on his face told Aluna that he was anything *but* fine. He turned as if he were going to follow the others, but paused. "You are not alone, you know. You may prefer to be sometimes, but you are not."

He took off down the ridge before she could respond. Not that she knew what to say. The more she kept this secret to herself, the harder it was to even think about telling the others. It grew like a pearl inside her. The bigger it got, the tighter she wrapped her arms around it.

By the time she reached the edge of the Shining Moon settlement, Dash was gone. She joined Hoku and Calli near a cluster of Equians welcoming Tayan back to the herd.

"They took him away," Hoku whispered. "To prison. Or a prison tent. Or something like that. Tayan said they wouldn't hurt him."

"She gave us her word," Calli added.

Tayan broke out of the cluster and clomped over, still smiling. "Come, we will report to my father, Khan Arasen, and give the others time to prepare your tent." She looked at Aluna and had the good sense to drop the grin from her face. "Dash will not be harmed," she said. "Not until after his trial, and then only if he is found guilty."

"Which he will be," Aluna said. "You know he will be." *Lie to me,* she thought. *If you lie about this, then maybe you could have lied about Dash.*

Tayan stared at her. Her tail swished. Eventually, she said simply, "Follow me. My father is this way."

Equians stared as they followed Tayan through the settlement. Aluna had expected their horse bodies to be the same color, or at least similar, but they weren't. She saw blacks, browns, and light grays, reds like Tayan, and even sandy yellows. Some Equians wore solid colors that turned dark at their hooves and tails, while a few others had stripes. She didn't see any two alike.

Far too quickly, they reached the khan's tent. Inside, blue and silver light danced across the packed dirt floor. The fabric walls had appeared solid from the outside, but sunlight somehow streamed through. There were no windows, but the air felt cool and refreshing. A glorious change from the heat.

Khan Arasen wore his brown hair short and his beard neatly trimmed. His tunic seemed similar to Tayan's, with maybe a few more strands of blue and silver and white woven along the hems. A huge blood-red amulet hung from his neck, exactly like the one that she'd seen High Khan Onggur wearing. His horse flank glowed dark brown, even darker than his hair. He stood talking to another man, an older Equian in elaborate blue robes that complemented his spotted black flank.

"My father stands on the right," Tayan whispered. "The other man is Weaver Sokhor, a treasured adviser."

"What's that amulet around your father's neck?" Aluna asked. "High Khan Onggur wears one just like it."

"It is the Shining Moon bloodline," Tayan said.

Hoku grimaced. "There's actually blood inside it?"

Tayan shook her head. "No, not blood—something more precious. Biological codes. All the genetic information about our herd. When we are ready to birth new foals, our bloodline tells the tech how to make a new Shining Moon, not a new Red Sky or Arrow Fall or Cloud Hoof."

Hoku's grimace turned to wide-eyed wonder.

Aluna was about to ask how easy it would be to destroy the bloodline amulet when Khan Arasen turned, stepped over, and clapped Tayan on the shoulder. "It is good that the sun and sands have brought you back to us so swiftly, Daughter."

Tayan bowed. "Father, I bring urgent news from the High Khan about the coming war. But first I must speak of herd business."

"You would speak herd business in front of wetlanders?" Khan Arasen asked.

Wetlanders? Well, it made a certain kind of sense, Aluna thought. She looked over and saw Hoku mouthing the word to Calli.

Tayan flicked her tail. "I would, Father, for the business involves them . . . and Dashiyn."

"Dashiyn!" Weaver Sokhor said, clomping over to join them. His dark eyes seemed like pits under his graying eyebrows. "The boy has broken his exile?"

"He has," Tayan said solemnly. "He and his friends entered Mirage of their own free will. In their defense, they were trying—"

"No," Sokhor said. "We do not need to hear excuses. Herd law is herd law. The boy must be punished. Where is he? I will see to his death myself."

Aluna took a step forward, ready to bring out her talons, and found Tayan's hand on her shoulder, pushing her back.

"With all due respect, Weaver," Tayan said calmly, "I came here to tell my khan, not you."

Weaver Sokhor sputtered. He looked just like Elder Peleke back home, when Hoku figured out the answer to some tech problem before he did.

"You were quite right to mention this, Daughter," Khan Arasen said smoothly. "He came willingly?"

"He did."

Arasen nodded. "Yes, I would expect nothing less." Aluna noticed the darkness under the khan's eyes, the deep lines around his mouth. She hadn't realized how old he was until just now. "And why did you bring his friends?"

Much to Aluna's surprise, Tayan looked at her then, a question in her eyes. "Go ahead," Aluna said.

"He needs to know everything. The only weapon we have right now is that we know the enemy better than she — or Karl Strand — thinks."

That was all Tayan needed. She began with her arrival at Mirage, when she and the other emissaries had been taken prisoner. Aluna filled in the parts about Scorch and Karl Strand, and Hoku and Calli jumped in with details. Hoku remembered High Khan Onggur's exact words better than anyone. Calli mostly remembered Scorch hitting her.

Khan Arasen asked a few questions, and they went back further. Calli told them about Tempest and the Aviars' battle at the SkyTek dome. Aluna talked about Fathom. Hoku talked about how Dash had fought off the Upgraders long enough for Hoku to access the main computer system.

When they were done, no one spoke for a long time. The khan's brow was creased, and his hand stroked his beard.

"Well, the solution is clear," Weaver Sokhor said at last. "If Onggur wins the Sun Disc, then we will hand over the children and join Red Sky's alliance. Herd law and our honor demands it."

Tayan stomped both of her front hooves. "You did not see what has become of Mirage, Weaver Sokhor. If you had, you would not suggest that honor had anything to do with this alliance."

"You won't give us to her, " Aluna said. "Don't think for one flash of a tail that I'll let that happen."

"We're here because we want to work with you *against* Karl Strand," Hoku said. "Don't make us your enemies, too."

Calli rustled her wings. She lowered her chin, and her eyes fell into shadow. "You don't want see what happens when the Aviars call for revenge."

Aluna stared at the girl, a mix of horror and pride swelling in her chest.

"Enough," Khan Arasen said. "I must think."

Like magic, the flap of the tent opened, and they were ushered back out into the sun.

CHAPTER 8

W HEN THEY WERE OUTSIDE, Tayan held a finger to her lips. "Say nothing. Not here." She led them to a large round tent stitched from dyed fabrics in green, white, and blue. "I thought these colors might remind you of the ocean." She nodded to Calli. "Or possibly the sky." Tayan lifted the flap and motioned them inside.

The Equians had been busy. The khan's tent had been built for huge horse bodies that didn't need to lie down to sleep. But Shining Moon had filled this space with rugs and pillows and low tables piled with food. A tall curtain divided the room, and washbasins rested on short pedestals on both sides. Stacks of clean clothes were neatly piled by their sleeping rolls.

"For Hoku," Tayan said, pointing to the smaller side. "The girls can sleep here. My apologies that we cannot offer you all your own tents."

"This is perfect," Calli said. "Thank you."

Hoku went straight for the pitcher of water and filled three ceramic cups. Aluna took hers gratefully and downed it in one gulp.

"I must return to my father, but please," Tayan said, "do not lose faith yet. He listens to Weaver Sokhor because the Weaver is powerful in his own right, with many allies in the herd. But he listens to me, too, and to my brother, Dantai. We will help him see the honorable path." And she was gone.

Aluna didn't go after her. Her body ached. She wasn't sure her muscles would do what she wanted even if she begged. And besides, the Equian pillows felt smooth and soft as a sea slug on her fingertips.

Hoku flopped onto a rug and closed his eyes. "Wake me up when it's time for the Thunder Trials."

"If my mother knew I'd gone so many weeks without a bath, she'd disown me," Calli said. She tossed her pack by a table and headed to a washbasin. "I swear, we spend half our days cleaning our feathers and preening."

Aluna reluctantly let go of the pillow. After their trek through the desert and their frustrating meeting with the khan, there was only one thing she needed more than sleep: some time by herself. She grabbed two round pieces of food that she hoped were fruit, shoved them in a pouch tied to her belt, and headed for the exit. "I need to look around."

Calli looked up from the washbasin, her face caked in silvery soap. "You're going to look for Dash?"

Aluna sighed. "No, not yet. I think he'll be safe until his trial. I just need . . . space."

"Days in the open desert, and you're craving space." Hoku chuckled, his eyes closed. "Some things are as changeless as the tides." His eyes popped open. "Hey. Keep an eye out for cool tech, okay?"

"You know me," Aluna said, pushing open the tent flap. "That's all I ever think about."

She wandered slowly through the settlement, choosing paths randomly and trying to ignore the stares of Shining Moon's Equians. Some tried not to look interested in her and merely stole glances as they washed clothes in basins of sand or stood sewing fabrics in the shade of their tents. Others stopped and stared, making no secret of their distrust. No hands went to hilts or bows, but tails swished and hooves stomped. Even if she'd been born with a horse body herself, she was an outsider to these people. A person not of the desert. That set her apart more than her lack of hooves.

The layout of the settlement fascinated her. Shining Moon had to fit everything they needed across a flat plane, unlike the City of Shifting Tides, where nests could be dug out of the coral at different heights. It seemed so limiting, and yet the Above Worlders always made it work. Smaller tents seemed to be storage areas. Dwellings were larger. Big enough for at least five Equians, she guessed, and maybe even ten. The largest tents—the ones big enough to hold dozens of Equians at once—seemed to be work areas. She identified one for cloth makers, another for food preparers, and a blood-red tent housing the medics and the wounded. Foals and yearlings filled a cluster of tents and open areas apparently used for schooling and training. Aluna paused to watch the smallest ones stumble on knobby legs and try to mimic their elders.

On the edge of the settlement, she found the weapon makers. Tall anvils sat near forges spewing black smoke in the air. Bowyers and fletchers stood in groups, talking as they carved huge curved bows and pile after pile of arrows. Underwater, the Kampii could only reclaim metals from shipwrecks and ancient submerged cities or sharpen shells and animal bones for their spears. The Above World people had metal and wood, which they could shape into a much wider array of weapons and objects. Aluna was beginning to understand the truth about why the Kampii Elders had chosen isolation. In any war with the Above World, the Kampii would lose.

Her fingers itched to pick up a bow. The Aviars had used smaller ones occasionally, but preferred their spears, talons, and crossbows. During her imprisonment at Skyfeather's Landing, she'd never gotten a chance to learn how to shoot.

She headed to the animal enclosures next and stopped to marvel at the horses. Their shiny coats glistened in the sun and heat. She saw black, dark brown, reddish brown, gray—some speckled with white on their foreheads, some with dark patches around their feet, as if they'd stepped in mud. They came in the same variety as their Equian keepers. How strange it must be for the Equians to look at them and see a part of their past.

Every single horse wore white and dark blue in its tail and mane, woven in with colored beads, strips of cloth, or painted feathers. The way they pranced and played in their sandy field made them seem proud, as if they knew they were Shining Moon and would settle for being nothing less.

Reluctantly Aluna moved on to the rhinebra enclosures, which didn't interest her nearly as much. She hadn't been on one of the huge, horned pack animals since their escape from the SkyTek dome a few months ago, and she wanted to keep it that way. She didn't actually dislike the beasts, but it was hard to forget those long days of riding without a saddle.

She took a step toward the mysterious netted bird area, and her gut spasmed as if she'd been kicked. She collapsed on the ground, suddenly breathless. Her cheek slammed into the packed sand and her mouth filled with hot granules. She spat them out while invisible knives stabbed her legs. She barely controlled her screams. They came out as gasps and groans instead.

Only two Equians stood nearby, one in the horse enclosure and one shoveling feed with the rhinebras. Neither seemed to see her.

Normally an episode passed after a few seconds, but this one felt endless. Her legs burned as if flames had engulfed them. The invisible knives kept stabbing. With shaking arms, she pushed herself to her knees, just in time to retch up the fruit she'd eaten. Black circles swam before her eyes.

"Hoku," she whispered. "Hoku!"

Silence. She'd walked too far from their tent, out of range for their Kampii hearing devices. Her fault. She should have known. Her insides twisted, and she rolled back onto the sand, avoiding the mess she'd made.

"Hoku, where are you? . . ."

She squeezed her eyes shut and clutched at her

stomach. *One more second,* she told herself. *Breathe and make it through one more second.*

She tried to picture her sister, Daphine, calm and perfect, even with an Upgrader's scope instead of an eye. Daphine used to run her fingers through Aluna's short, tangled hair whenever she'd been sick. Daphine hummed, too. Some old song that their mother must have taught her before Aluna was born.

One more second. And just one more. And the agony started to fade, the wave of pain pulling itself back out to sea. She took a deep, shuddering breath. She felt hot tears on her face but couldn't remember crying.

Something soft brushed her cheek, and for a moment, she thought it was Daphine's hand, somehow made real from her memories. She squeezed her eyes shut harder and curled onto her side, wanting it to last.

The second time it brushed her cheek, she felt wetness. Then a puff of air and a snort, and the smell of cactus. Reluctantly she opened her eyes. A horse stared down at her.

Its head was long and tapered, dark gray except where it faded to black at its muzzle and around its wide-set eyes.

The horse nuzzled her face a third time, and Aluna laughed weakly. "Your nose feels just like an octopus. Did you know that?" She reached out her hand — slowly — and when the horse didn't jerk away, rested her fingertips between its big, open nostrils. "I didn't think you would be so soft."

She craned her neck to see the rest of the horse. Hundreds of tiny white specks dappled its dark-gray coat, like a field of stars at dusk. Knots and sand tangled in its inky-black mane and tail. Its four slender legs also ended in black from its knobby knees down. But its coat surprised her the most. Unlike all the other horses—the ones in the enclosure—its coat looked mangy. Battered. Completely unkempt.

"Don't care much about your appearance, do you, girl?" Aluna said. The horse reared its head with a quick snort, then lowered it back again, in range of Aluna's fingers. Aluna laughed, even though it made her stomach hurt. "I guess we have something in common."

The horse swung its head to Aluna's legs and nudged her knee with its nose.

"Oh, they still work," Aluna said, "but not for long. I'm growing my very own tail, which is perfect for life in the ocean. Where we aren't. Where I'm not sure I'll ever be again."

The horse swished its own tail, and Aluna chuckled again. "It's not exactly the same as yours, no. Imagine your back two legs fusing together into one long, scaly, flexible tail. . . ."

The horse's eyes widened and its nostrils flared. It twisted its neck to look back at its own legs. If Aluna hadn't known better, she would have sworn she saw the animal shudder.

Aluna froze. Did the horse understand what she was saying? Was it like Hoku's raccoon, Zorro, some mix of tech and animal? It certainly seemed friendly, but that was no excuse to let down her guard.

She rolled slowly onto her hands and knees and tried to push herself to her feet. When she got halfway up, the world started to spin—sand above, sky below—and she fell back to her knees.

"This is going to be harder than I thought."

The horse shuffled its feet, and suddenly it had one foreleg bent on the ground and the other out straight toward her. It was kneeling!

"Are you . . . trying to help me?"

The horse shoved its muzzle into her arm, almost knocking her off balance.

"Tides' teeth, I get the idea." She shifted her weight and lifted her hand to the top of the horse's head, just behind its pointy, black-tipped ears. She dug her hands into its mane and gripped as tightly as she could.

Slowly the horse lifted its head. Aluna hadn't intended to lean on the animal much, but when her legs quivered, she had no choice. She hefted her own body up and leaned it against the horse's neck. In a few moments, the black eels swimming in her vision dispersed, and the world seemed right-side up.

Aluna stood, keeping one hand on the horse, until she felt confident that her traitorous legs would support her. Only then did she let go.

The horse stood back up and whinnied. There was something so triumphant in the sound, as if they'd just killed a shark all by themselves.

Then again, maybe it *was* the same sort of victory.

Aluna touched two fingers to her heart, as she'd seen the Equians do, and bowed to her rescuer. "I am Aluna of the Coral Kampii, from the City of Shifting Tides, and I am in your debt."

The horse responded by lowering its nose to hers and snorting gently. Aluna breathed in the warm air it had just exhaled and laughed.

"Pleased to meet you, too."

CHAPTER 9

Hoku PULLED THE SCREEN separating his part of
the tent from the girls' and washed up. The Equians
had laid out a clean tunic and head wrap, but no
clean pants. Which made sense, since they didn't have
Human legs. He spent a moment trying to envision a
horse wearing pants and decided they'd made a wise
decision.

When he joined Calli, she was already halfway
through her plate of food. His stomach growled. "Hey,
save me some of the good stuff. If I have to eat
another piece of dried cactus, I'm going to . . . well, I
guess I'm going to eat another piece of dried cactus."
Calli laughed and handed him a skewer of grilled meat.

He took it without even asking what it was. Anything was a delicacy compared to cactus.

Hooves shuffled outside their tent, and a voice called, "It is Dantai khan-son, and I have come to visit the honored guests of Shining Moon. May I enter?"

Hoku looked at Calli. She shrugged, then wiped her mouth and tried to finish chewing. "Yes," he called. "Uh, please enter."

The flap opened, and a young Equian male clomped in. His horse coat was reddish brown, almost the exact color of the hair hanging in dozens of tiny beaded braids around his head. His desert tunic covered his Human torso, but Hoku imagined muscles. Lots of them. The Equian had the sort of confidence that almost *required* physical strength.

"I am Dantai khan-son," the visitor said again, doing that weird little bow Equians seemed so fond of.

"I'm Hoku," he said, bobbing his head. He pointed to Calli so he could introduce her, too, but she was already on her feet and making a clumsy yet adorable bow of her own.

"Calliope," she said. "Of Skyfeather's Landing."

If he didn't know better, he'd say that Calli was blushing. At Dantai. At a person who wasn't *him*.

"The Aviar!" Dantai said. "My sister tells me you are the daughter of the bird khan. Is this true?"

Oh, yes. Calli was definitely blushing now.

"My mother is the leader of our people," Calli said. "Not of all the Aviars, but of all the ones who live in Skyfeather's Landing."

"Where they don't allow boys to live," Hoku blurted out. It had sounded important in his head, but when he said it out loud . . .

"Truly? No men?" Dantai asked. "Fascinating! You must tell me more."

Not since Hoku had watched Aluna's older brother Pilipo seduce an entire pod of Kampii girls had he been both so impressed and appalled at the same time.

"Why don't we all sit and eat?" Calli said. "There's plenty of food."

Hoku frowned. If he tried to sit here and eat with the best-looking Equian ever, he'd probably blurt out one ridiculous thing after another. *Boys can't live there.* What was that? How was that relevant? Was "the ocean is wet" coming next? Or how about "the sun is so bright"?

Dantai said something, and Calli laughed. Hoku looked at her sharply. Was she just being polite, or was she flirting? Dantai was older than she was, but only by a few years. And they were both the children of leaders, while he was only the son of two workers, the sort of people who gathered mussels and deboned fish and lived in a tiny nest carved into the sand-side part of the coral reef.

This was his fault. He'd been so happy being with Calli that he'd never asked what they were. Was he her boyfriend? Then again, she grew up in a place with no boys. Did she even know what that meant?

"Are you going to sit with us?" Calli asked Hoku. Did she really want him to sit? Or was that her way of telling him that he should go? Her eyes offered no hints.

He chewed on his lip. He needed to spend more time understanding people and less time worrying about tech. But not now. Now he needed to flee before he said anything else that betrayed his dull-witted brain.

"Actually, no," he said carefully. "I'm going to look for Aluna."

"Good idea," Calli said quickly. Too quickly. Maybe she wanted him to leave after all. Calli added, "She's always more levelheaded when you're with her."

And then a compliment. Maybe. Was she implying that he had a thing for Aluna? Because that was ridiculous. They'd go together like Great White and an octopus. Somehow he managed to find his way out of the tent without saying any of the bizarre things swimming around in his head and started to walk. He headed up a large path first, trying to stay out of the way of the bustling Equians.

Shining Moon wasn't as big as Mirage, but Hoku

liked the humble settlement a whole lot more. The tents came in bright colors, most painted with horses and stylized Equians. For some reason he didn't mind them swooshed onto canvas in bold strokes. Smoke snaked into the sky from all over town, but it wasn't the choking, soot-black kind. It came from cooking fires and kilns. He smelled sizzling meat and vegetables, saw Equians laughing as they stirred huge pots of soup or chopped tubers outside their tents. Unlike Mirage, this settlement felt alive and joyful, full of people who had made the desert into a home.

He turned the corner onto a smaller path and spotted a figure digging through a sack in the shade of a tent wall. He thought at first it was a Human and was excited to introduce himself. Then the figure stood, and Hoku caught the glint of sunlight off metal. Metal that shouldn't have been anywhere near a normal face.

His heart thumped, and he stumbled backward. It wasn't a Human; it was an *Upgrader.*

He should have called for help. He should have alerted the Equians of the danger. But all Hoku could do was stare.

The Upgrader stood two meters tall. Short white hair spiked in a line over the top of its head, and the skin around its eyes and mouth was wrinkled with age. It wore a tight, sleeveless shirt revealing arms covered in tattoos, embedded with glowing lights and miscellaneous hardware. He couldn't even tell if it was male or female. Tools hung around the Upgrader's belt, a dozen or more devices that Hoku didn't recognize. Probably a dozen different weapons it used to kill its enemies.

One of the Upgrader's arms ended in a metal stump, to which the creature was attempting to attach the strange multibladed piece of tech it had pulled out of the sack.

Hoku gasped, and the creature looked up, startled. "What are you doing here?" Hoku said. "Are you spying for Scorch? I'll scream, and a thousand Equians will be on you in seconds."

The Upgrader stared at him. Its mouth hung open slightly, and Hoku could see metal inside. Did it have teeth, or something worse? He started to back away.

"Aluna will be here soon, too. She fought a dozen of your kind in the HydroTek dome and killed them all." Not technically true, but the Upgrader didn't need to know that.

The Upgrader closed its mouth, looked back down at its arm, and continued to screw the device onto its body.

"Name's Rollin," the Upgrader said. Its voice rumbled mechanically, and Hoku still couldn't tell if it was a man or a woman. Maybe such distinctions didn't matter when you were more metal than flesh.

He decided to go with female. "Scream your dunder-headed face off, if you want," Rollin said. "Give the four-feets a good laugh."

Hoku had expected gouts of flame, whirring blades of death, or a lightning-fast sword plunged at his own heart. He was unprepared for apathy.

"Are you here to kill everyone? Are you working for Karl Strand?"

The device on Rollin's hand clicked into place. The tiny blades started spinning. Hoku held his breath. Rollin pointed the arm at her own face and sighed.

It was a fan. Her implement of death turned out to be a fan.

"Hot one, yeah?" Rollin said. "Of course, they all are, out here. Gritty bit of business, living in a waste-land. But the four-feets seem to like it well enough. Figured I'd grow to love it, too."

"So . . . you're *not* working for Scorch and Karl Strand?" Hoku asked.

Rollin adjusted her fan-hand so the air was blowing straight up her nose. "I'm working for the Equians, as I think is obvious on account of me being here in this sun-blasted place," she said. "Even a *basic* like you should grasp the logic."

"I guess I thought you were all working for Karl Strand." Even as Hoku said the words, he could see how simplistic his assumption had been.

"So everyone who wants a little glint and hum, a little whir and fizz, is evil, then?" Rollin said. "I guess you'll tell me that all four-feets are good, and all basics like you are good, too? Add a little shimmy-pop, and we go from Human to bad?"

Hoku scratched his cheek where a line of sweat had started a slow trek down his face. "Okay, you have a point," he said. He thought back to the City of Shifting Tides. They'd certainly had their share of thieves and killers over the years. And some of the Elders weren't exactly "good" either. "I guess I just haven't met any Upgraders who weren't trying to kill me."

Rollin stared at him, then burst out laughing. Her mechanical voice fluttered up a full octave. "Well, you have now, Basic. You have now."

Hoku tried to laugh with her, to be polite, but only managed a strained chuckle. Then, the most wonderful thought in the world popped into his mind.

"Wait. You work for Shining Moon?" he asked, trying to keep the excitement out of his voice.

Rollin nodded. "I work for them now. Used to work other places, but they got too bloody for an old Gizmo like me. Nice place here, if you don't mind the smell of horse. Lots of tech to fix and fiddle with. Grub's no good, but everything has a price, yeah?"

Hoku blinked. An Upgrader—a *friendly* Upgrader. Right here, where they were going to be for two months until the Thunder Trials. He took a step closer, ignoring Rollin's surprise, and held out his hands.

"Teach me," he said. "I want to learn about tech. I want to learn everything. How that thing on your arm works, how to build a suntrap, how to fix artifacts. Everything you can teach me, I want to know!"

Rollin's jaw hung slack again. Hoku pressed on. "I want to learn how to talk to computers, how to mold metal into the shapes I want, how to build wings so I can fly with Calli. I'll work hard. I'll study. I'll do whatever you want, as long as it doesn't hurt anyone." He took another step closer, until he could almost feel the air from Rollin's fan.

"Take me on as your apprentice." He looked in her eyes and saw that one of them was fake, an artifact with tiny diagrams dancing across the lens. His heart raced. *"Please."*

Elder Peleke had always said no. Hoku wasn't smart enough, wasn't old enough, wasn't from the right kind of Kampii family. But Elder Peleke knew nothing about science and tech compared to the Above World people. This was Hoku's chance to finally learn. To finally do what his heart and mind had been driving him to do ever since he was a youngling.

Rollin closed her mouth and looked down at her fan. The air made the hairs in her shaggy white eyebrows dance as if they were alive.

Please-oh-please-oh-please . . .

Rollin shook her head, but when she lifted it back up to look at him, she was smiling. "Tell you what, Basic. You can start by finding me some grub. Real grub. I have special teeth for eating the grass the four-feets like, but I've got a craving for meat. You find me some of that, and I'll teach your little heart to pieces."

Hoku grinned so wide that he thought his face might split in two.

"You want mustard on that?"

CHAPTER 10

ALUNA MANAGED to get most of the debris out of the horse's mane and tail before it grew too restless to stand still. The whole while, she talked to it. Mostly about the City of Shifting Tides and her family. She hadn't intended to talk about her father—she was happiest when she never even thought about him—but the desert had apparently made her soft. Sometimes she almost missed the sad, faraway look in his eyes.

"There," Aluna said. "The worst is out. You need to stop rolling around in garbage."

The horse snorted and lifted its chin defiantly.

"Oh, I'm only being silly," she said quickly. "Roll around in whatever you want. There's not a lot to do out here in the middle of nowhere, unless killing scorpions counts. One of those little desert shrimps almost got me yesterday."

The horse lowered its head and huffed. Aluna was starting to get a sense of its moods. This one meant, "I'm still a little irked, but not really mad."

"I need to come back here with a brush," she said. The horse glowered. Aluna added, "If you want to be brushed, of course. I know what it's like to be groomed against your will."

The horse shoved her head against Aluna's arm and nibbled on her tunic, right near a huge stain acquired somewhere during their trek from Mirage. Aluna had somehow forgotten that she, too, was filthy. The sun had crept slowly across the sky and now hung centimeters above the distant mountains. She had very little time to get back to the tent and clean herself up before the Darkest Night celebration began.

"I've got to go." She dragged a hand along the horse's shaggy neck and marveled again at the feel of its coat beneath her hand. "Come with me? There's room in our tent. You can even sleep there if you want. Hoku and Calli won't mind."

The horse whinnied and stepped back nervously.

"I'm not going to force you," Aluna said. "I won't ever make you do something you don't want to do. Just think about it, okay?"

The horse's tail swished as it considered. Finally it shook its head. Still no.

Aluna considered skipping the evening's celebration to stay with the horse. She could find a brush, or maybe even convince the horse to take her for a ride. But it would be polite to participate in the Shining Moon's celebration—even the Kampii had special rituals for the one night a month when the moon disappeared from the sky.

Still, nothing could make her forget about Dash. The entire settlement would be enjoying the festivities tonight, and she wasn't sure if her spirit could pretend to be that light. Maybe she could make an appearance and then slip off to find Dash. He shouldn't be alone.

She turned to the horse. It seemed to know that Aluna was planning something; it slitted its eyes while it stared at her, much as Hoku sometimes did. The two of them would probably get along great.

"I'll find you again," she told the horse. "If you let me?"

The horse huffed and nodded and stamped a hoof in the sand.

Aluna bowed to it, turned, and headed back. She only turned around once, to see if the horse was following. It wasn't. In fact, it had completely disappeared.

Equians bustled through the settlement's streets as she made her way to the tent. She paused outside, surprised to hear laughter and a male voice that she didn't recognize coming from inside. She shoved the flap out of the way and strode in.

Calli and an Equian male sat on either side of a picked-over tray of food.

"Oh, Aluna," Calli said, scrambling to her feet. "Is Hoku with you? He said he was going to find you."

The girl's face flushed red as she babbled, but her companion remained unflustered. He stood slowly — probably the reason most Equians didn't sit very often — and offered a bow.

"Dantai khan-son," he said. "You must be Aluna. Calliope has spoken highly of you."

Aluna raised an eyebrow at Calli, but the girl quickly looked away.

"Swift currents, Dantai khan-son," Aluna said to the Equian, falling into a more formal Kampii greeting. She normally thought long hair and braids were impractical and unnecessary, but she had to admit that the Equian wore them well. "Am I interrupting . . . ?"

"No, of course not," Dantai replied smoothly. "Calliope and I were just discussing the intricacies of leadership."

"Fascinating," Aluna said. Her eyebrow tried to rise again, but she forced it back down into its normal position. "I didn't realize that . . . *Calliope* . . . cared so much about leadership."

Calli laughed nervously. "Well, truthfully, I haven't had much interest before. But I *am* the daughter of the president, and someday the burden will be mine, whether I want it or not."

"And so, better to embrace the unique challenges that come with leadership," Dantai said, folding his hand into a powerful fist. "A leader does not have the luxury of indifference nor the time for selfish indulgence."

Calli nodded. "It's true! And what have I been doing for so long? Ignoring my duties. Causing my mother no end of frustration. Skyfeather's Landing has other scientists, but I am my mother's only daughter. I must learn to live up to my legacy."

"Well spoken!" Dantai said, and Calli beamed.

Aluna wondered if they'd been nattering like this the entire time she was gone. She wasn't surprised to see that Hoku had bolted. Dantai reminded Aluna of her brothers—especially Pilipo—and Hoku could never tolerate being around him for more than a minute or two.

"I hate to change the subject," Aluna lied, "but I saw a strange horse a few minutes ago, gray and black with white spots? It wandered outside the horse enclosure."

"That would be Tal," Dantai said. "Her story is a sad one."

"Sad? How so?" Calli asked.

Dantai grew somber. "Because you know Dashiyn, you are already familiar with our concept of *aldagha,* a mistake. This is an Equian formed incorrectly during the birthing process."

Aluna ground her teeth together. "I'd rather not hear anyone use that word for Dash ever again."

"I agree," Dantai said smoothly. "The word is merely intended to be descriptive. Usually less than one percent of all our births result in . . . someone like Dashiyn," he finished carefully. "Dashiyn is an Equian, but born missing half of himself."

He's still worth more than you, Aluna thought. Calli stared at her, eyes wide, and Aluna took a long, slow breath to still the churning in her thoughts.

Dantai continued, oblivious to how much Aluna wanted to wrap a talon around his neck and pull. "Occasionally, another type of *aldagha* is born. It happens rarely, and I know of no others in the desert at this time," he said. "Tal is the first in our herd. The first Equian of our bloodline to be born without a Human side."

"Tides' teeth, she's an actual Equian?" Aluna said. No wonder the horse seemed to understand what she was saying! "Why doesn't she have her own tent? Why isn't she treated like . . . She refused to use the word *mistake.* "Why isn't she treated like Dash?"

The Equian shrugged. "The offer has always been open, but once Tal was capable of feeding herself, she has always chosen loneliness. She lets none of us near her, and yet she never strays far from the settlement."

"How old is she?" Aluna asked.

"She is not yet three," Dantai said, "but we do not know if her mind is aging as a horse or a Human. It is possible she is still a child, but we cannot know for sure."

"What does her name mean?" Calli asked.

Dantai spoke easily, as if the answer were the most appropriate and natural thing in the world. "She was born without her Humanity," he said. "*Tal* is our word for *half*."

Aluna's hands tightened into fists. She didn't even release her talons or reach for her knife. There wasn't time. She needed to punch every last bit of condescension off Dantai's face, and she needed to do it immediately. Words bubbled up in her throat. *Disgusting. Heartless. Cruel.* But she couldn't find the control to speak them.

Suddenly Calli stood between Aluna and Dantai, her wings half open and creating a barrier of feathers. The girl spoke quickly, but Aluna could barely hear her through the haze of her own anger.

"I'm sorry, but I'm feeling very tired," Calli said to

Dantai. "Would you mind giving me and Aluna some time alone to prepare for the celebration?"

"Certainly," Dantai said, "but I must state that—"

"Excellent," Calli interrupted. She grabbed his arm and propelled him toward the tent's exit. "We'll see you later. Please give our regards to your sister and father."

When his tail had disappeared out the tent flap, Calli turned but continued to block the door.

"He doesn't understand," Calli said quietly. "He doesn't know how it sounds."

"Oh, I think he knows exactly how it sounds," Aluna said. "I think they all do."

CHAPTER 11

BY THE TIME the sun had fallen into the mountains, half a dozen bonfires blazed, casting the whole settlement in a warm, flickering glow. Equians of all ages thronged to the flames. They passed food in baskets and on sticks, filled one another's cups with fruit-infused water, and wished each other "safety until the sun." Aluna watched a group of yearlings chase one another through the crowds, tossing a ball and laughing when they came close to hitting someone.

"Hoku, where are you?" she whispered. He and Calli had gone on ahead, hoping to find someplace for them to sit that was close to the festivities but safe from errant horse hooves.

She tugged at her new clothes. At least she hadn't spotted any new tough patches of skin on her legs. No new scales, either, although she was certain that the area by her knee was ready to bloom with them. She'd have to be careful in the tent with Calli so close. Her nightly examinations would have to wait until the bird-girl fell asleep. Thank the ancients for giving Kampii dark vision and keeping it from the Aviars.

"Finally done changing? Are you sure you don't need another hour?" Hoku whispered back, but then he let it go. "Head to the west side of the bonfire. Tayan saved us a spot."

"That's Tayan khan-daughter to you," Aluna said, and was gratified by his chuckle.

"We've got a surprise for you," Hoku whispered. "I think you'll like it."

"As long as it's not the company of Dantai khan-son, I'll be thrilled," she said.

He laughed again. She hadn't heard him so happy in a long, long time. What kind of day had he had?

It wasn't hard to find the khan's fire, not with the golden flames leaping half a dozen meters into the darkening sky. The official ceremony hadn't started yet, but the Equians had certainly gotten a head start on their celebrating.

She followed Hoku's directions, darting between dozens of huge Equians and heading toward the clearing around the fire. She didn't even bother to look for Tal, now that she understood more of her upbringing.

An Equian celebration was the last place an outcast would choose to be.

She spotted Hoku and Calli sitting together on a low pile of rugs and pillows. Calli's wings seemed to radiate light in the growing darkness, as if they were made of glowfish instead of feathers. And maybe that's why it took Aluna a moment to notice the dark figure sitting next to her.

"Dash," she whispered.

Hoku looked at her from across the clearing. "Surprise!" he whispered back. "They've given him the night off from prison."

Aluna could barely hear Hoku over the thudding of her heart. When Dash saw her approach, he moved over so Aluna could sit between him and Calli. She sat on the far side of him instead. She wanted him surrounded. Physically inside their tiny group. Protected.

"Hey," she croaked. Stupid voice.

"You look so clean," Dash said. "I had no idea your hair was that color."

She grinned. Firelight danced in his dark eyes. The effect made her brave. Or weak. She wasn't sure she could tell the difference tonight.

"Did you do it?" she asked. "Did you do what Tayan said?"

His lips pressed into a line. Just when she thought he wasn't going to answer, he did.

"The spies we captured," he said, "they were a mother and her son." He spoke so quietly that she could barely hear his voice amid the revelry surrounding them. "They had left the hidden Serpenti city in search of medicine. She had a young daughter, and the girl was ill. None of their own remedies had worked."

Dash looked up at the fire, his expression difficult to read.

"The woman died that night, before the khan could get any answers." He took a deep breath. "They had not realized how exhausted she was and how little food she had eaten. Her body could not survive even the smallest of tortures."

Aluna tore her eyes from his face and studied the Equians surrounding them. They spoke of honor. They fought like warriors. There was so much about them that she admired. And yet they treated Dash and Tal like mistakes, and they could torture a desperate woman to death. She could make no sense of them.

She felt a hand on her arm and looked down. Dash's warm fingers gripped her wrist. "Do not judge them too harshly. I can see it in your face. You do not understand the war. You do not know how many of us they killed."

Yes, yes. She understood, because she'd seen the war between her own people and the sharklike Deepfell.

She'd seen firsthand how death multiplied when things like honor and justice were used as war cries.

"So you helped the boy escape," Aluna said. "And you gave him medicine for his sister."

"Yes." Dash left his hand on her arm. Every second it stayed there, the heat intensified. "We were saving that medicine, and I chose to give it to him. I thought I was doing the right thing, that I was opening the way for peace between our people."

"You did do the right thing," Aluna said. Once upon a time, she'd given her breathing necklace to a dying Deepfell they'd found wounded on the shore. The Kampii needed every necklace they had. And yet if she hadn't done it, would Prince Eekikee have saved them later? Would they have become allies? Would Fathom have fallen? "It's harder to stand against your own than to stand against an enemy. You were brave."

"I was naive. When I told the khan what I had done, a part of me thought he would understand. That perhaps he would see how the Serpenti were no longer our enemy."

"It didn't go like that, did it?" she said.

Dash grunted. "No."

"You still honor him. The khan."

He nodded. "He did what he felt was right for our people. I may have done the same in his place. I accepted his judgment and thanked him for condemning me to exile instead of death."

"But this time . . . ?" She couldn't bring herself to finish the sentence.

Dash squeezed her arm gently, then released it. She could still feel his heat even after his fingers were gone.

"I broke exile," he said simply.

They sat quietly and listened to the crowd.

Eventually Dash spoke again. "My family came to see me today. Well, most of them did."

"Your family? You've never mentioned them before."

"Our families are . . . not like yours," he said. "Any number of Equians may make a family and live together. I was raised by eight parents—three of them elders—and have four brothers and sisters my age and younger. We all share the Shining Moon bloodline, but we are not siblings. Not like you are with Daphine and your brothers."

She thought about this. "No, you're siblings like me and Hoku. Siblings by choice."

He grinned. "Yes. We are a family by choice. That is a good way to phrase it."

"Will they talk to the khan about your situation?" she asked. She liked the idea of having so many new allies. But Dash shook his head.

"My family defended me at my first trial, but I will not let them do so again." He pulled on a tassel from one of the pillows with his mechanical hand and twirled the fabric between his fingers. "There is no defense for what I have done, and I wish to save them from further hardship. I have asked them to step away, and they have given me their promise." He turned to look in her eyes again. "Please. Do not try to involve them. It would hurt me if you did."

She nodded, wishing they were back home. Promises idly given under the waves were not so binding. Back there, a Kampii's word did not feel heavy as a whale, and it was easily washed away with the tide.

"I am worried for Erke and Gan, though," he said. "I am told that my fathers left the settlement to look for me shortly after I was exiled and have not returned. We were always so close. I would have liked for you to meet them."

"They'll be back," she said with feigned ease. "I'll meet them then."

"If they come to harm because of me . . ."

"They won't," she said quickly. "They raised you, so they must be good fighters. They can protect themselves."

He laughed then. A surprisingly light sound given their conversation.

"Oh, Gan can't even lift a sword," he said. "Erke

is decent, but unexceptional. My sword skills came from a need to defend myself at an early age, not from parental teaching. No, our family specializes in animals. Our falcons are renowned across all the desert."

"The birds in the enclosure," Aluna said. "I haven't gotten a chance to see them yet."

"Falcons are sleek and smart, quick and deadly. They are also far too stubborn for their own good. It is no wonder we took to each other early."

"You'll show me the falcons, then," Aluna said. "When this is all over, you can introduce me to every last one of them."

A drum sounded. The crowd fell silent immediately.

"It begins," Dash whispered. "Tayan and Dantai will speak first, and then our khan. The heads of each family will call the hidden moon. Some will offer gifts to coax him back into the sky. But then is the real wonder." His eyes glowed. His face lit with obvious joy. "Then the word-weavers will take over. You will hear stories that no Kampii has ever heard. There will be solos and duets, and if we are very, very lucky, even a quartet. Weaver Sokhor is a difficult man to like, but he trains his weavers well. Our herd is one of the only ones that still remembers the old ways."

He turned to her and took both her hands in his. She almost jerked them away in surprise but managed to stop herself.

"I want you to hear everything, Aluna. I want you to understand what is good about our people. No matter what happens to me, I want you to understand why I am proud to be an Equian. I want you to know that even if I die, I will die as one."

She nodded once and swallowed. Her voice had fled. Dash smiled briefly at her acknowledgment and turned back to the spectacle beginning in front of them. Eventually his hands slid from hers, although the memory of them lingered.

Together, they listened to the speeches, the songs, the stories, the pounding of hoofbeats on the sandy earth. One after another, each voice stronger or more practiced than the last.

Until finally, just before dawn, her eyes wet with tears, she understood.

CHAPTER 12

HOKU DRAGGED HIMSELF back to the tent just before dawn. He should have gone to bed hours ago, but he couldn't bear to miss any of the Equian songs. The rhythm created by hooves striking the ground made his heart beat faster and his ears strain to hear every syllable. He had no idea how to capture that power and energy in the song he was writing himself.

He wanted sleep, but he'd made a promise to Rollin. And to himself, too. Instead of curling up on the rug on his side of the tent, he quietly gathered his satchel and headed for Rollin's workshop.

The sun squinted over the top of the eastern mountains, layering the peaks in deep oranges and reds. It made him think of the solarphiles, the Kampii who swam to the surface every dawn and dusk to watch the sun. His mother had been one once, before she'd married his father. Hoku had gone with her a few times, when she'd had a craving for sunlight unfiltered by water. He'd complained every time . . . until they broke surface. Then all he could do was stare at the colors and grasp his mother's hand tighter and tighter. She'd be jealous now, if she knew how many sunrises and sunsets he'd seen. He made a note of this one, memorizing the particular colors and angles of the light. Maybe someday he'd get to describe it to her.

When he arrived at Rollin's tent, he announced himself outside the door. He heard a grunt from inside, which, he realized after another minute of standing there, must have been a command to enter. He pulled aside the flap and gasped.

Workbenches ringed the circular tent, every surface covered in bits of metal, jars of artifacts, pieces of plastic, saws, hammers, screwdrivers, and so many things he couldn't identify that he quickly lost count. Bigger artifacts and devices lay scattered on the ground and piled on carpets. He saw things that beeped. Things that whirred. Things that tried to limp across the ground of their own volition. Scraps of metal and spools of wire hung from hooks in the ceiling. Two huge devices, each big as a shark, chattered and hummed in the center of the tent. Rollin stood at one of them and dragged a rusty piece of metal through a beam of red light. Wherever the light touched the metal, it sizzled and broke in two.

Air inside the tent hung like a blanket of dank heat. And the smell—pungent metals and oil. Old food. Sweat.

Paradise.

"Close the flap. We already have enough bugs," Rollin said. She pushed more metal through her light cutter.

Hoku stepped inside and let the tent flap drop. The air grew even more dense and suffocating. Sweat pasted his hair to his head, his clothes to his back. He reached over and touched a thick iron tool, wondering at the notch on one end. A twister, but not like the smaller ones he'd had back home.

"Fingers off!" Rollin yelled. "No touching until you're trained on whatever it is you're touching. Rule number one." She held up her arm with the interchangeable tip. Today a claw was screwed on. "Too easy to lose a hand, even if you know what you're doing. Got me?"

Hoku gulped and pulled his hand back reluctantly. "I understand. But you can't show a Kampii the ocean and expect him not to swim."

"That so?" She chuckled. "You young ones are always so eager on the first day. The second day? Less eager. Day ten? Pretend to be sick. Oh, those four-feets are good at fake fevers! 'My skin is hot. I can't work. Poor me.'" She snorted so violently that the metal she was cutting jerked underneath the light cutter. Hoku was glad he didn't understand most of the words she uttered after that.

"I'm not like that," Hoku said. "I'll do whatever you say. I'll be here when I'm sick. I'll bring you food whenever you want."

She stopped her work and looked at him. He could hear the tiny buzzing of her mechanical eye as it focused. He sincerely hoped it couldn't shoot teeny-tiny harpoons or poisonous needles.

"Day one. Design a new attachment for this." She waved her clawed arm in the air. "Go."

Hoku's mouth went dry. Design a whole new artifact as his first assignment? Could this really be happening? He expected to be hauling metal scraps or washing Rollin's feet for the first few days, not actually building something. He reached for the notched tool on the nearby workbench.

"Stop!" Rollin said. "No touching. Did you forget rule one already?"

"But you said—"

Rollin shook her head. "The first step of designing, you use this." She touched her clawed hand to her head. "Not this." She wagged her hands at him. "Design starts in the brain."

"Oh, right," Hoku said. "Of course. I know that."

"Good. Now talk. I want to hear your brain," Rollin said. "Whatever you think, spew it out! Let's see how those gears are turning."

Hoku pulled his hand back from the tool he'd almost touched, took a deep breath, and tried again. "Well, first I have to figure out what I want the new attachment to do—"

"No!" Rollin yelled, and Hoku suddenly wished he'd stopped to eat breakfast before coming. He had a feeling his first lesson was going to be a long one.

"No?" he said. "But if we don't know what it's supposed to do, we can't begin to think about—"

"You have to find out what *I* want it to do," Rollin said. "It's my hand, yeah? My new bit of shiny you're designing. Who'll use it? Me! So you ask *me* what I want."

Hoku wanted to skip ahead to the thinking and building parts of the exercise, but he knew better than to argue. His Kampii teachers back home played the same sorts of games. The sooner he gave them what they wanted, the sooner he got what he needed. "Fine," he said. "What do you want the new attachment to do?"

Rollin grinned. Her specially modified teeth glinted silver. "I want . . . a weapon!"

He stared at her. "Really?"

"Yes! Something powerful and deadly. Instant death to my enemies, if you can manage it. That's what I want."

He could feel his face contorting with disappointment and made no attempt to stop it. "Weapons aren't exactly my thing," he said. "Aluna could invent a great weapon. In fact, she'd probably love the chance. But I like . . . *useful* things." He sighed. "Even your grass-chewing teeth are better than weapons. Can't I invent something like that? How about teeth good at chewing cactuses? Or a bigger fan for cooling the whole tent?"

Rollin shook her head and lowered her hand. "So weapons aren't tools? They aren't useful? That world you're living in—I want to live there, too. Everything so clean and fluffy and harmless."

"No, it's just that—"

"Your friends are your weapons," Rollin said. "I've heard about your friend, and I don't see any calluses on your hands. So other people will be your muscles and guts. Is that it?"

"No!" Then he thought about Aluna and cringed. "Yes. But they like it! They're good at it! I have other . . . skills."

Rollin plucked an apple-shaped artifact off the

workbench behind her. She tossed it in the air, caught it, then threw it at Hoku.

Hoku tried to twist out of the way, but she was too close and her aim was too good. The metal device slammed into his shoulder.

"Ow!" He rubbed his wounded arm with his good hand and backed toward the tent flap. "Why did you do that?"

"Where were your friends?" Rollin said. She didn't look sorry in the slightest. "Not here, that's where. If I were working for Scorch, I could kill you right now, before you even had time to scream."

He took another step back.

Rollin sighed and scratched her cheek with her claw. "Oh, settle down," she said. "I'm trying to make a point."

"You've certainly made a bruise," he said. He couldn't move his arm. It felt like a dead fish attached to his shoulder.

"Life isn't much fun if you don't survive long enough to live it," she said. "That's my point. Play all day with bits of metal, but don't think for one minute that we're not all trying to survive. Longer, better, easier. But survival is the key. No one in this world can get by being as helpless as a . . . Well, now, I don't even know any sort of animal that's as helpless as you."

"I hit someone in the head with a lantern once,"

Hoku said quietly. The Upgrader had been a little distracted fighting both Aluna and the Aviar Niobe at the time, but Rollin didn't need to know that.

"Did you? Good. You have a spine," she said, and nodded once. "That's not an easy thing to teach."

"The things I want to make will help people survive," Hoku said. "I understand that part. I want to make everyone's life better."

Rollin shuffled over and poked her claw into the center of his chest. Her spiked hair wobbled on top of her head. "Then start with yourself. There's not a person in this whole camp—four feet or two—who couldn't whip you in a fight. And if I'm going to spend my time teaching you what I know, you'd better survive long enough to make it worth my while."

That did seem like kind of a waste, Hoku thought. And he really wasn't in any hurry to die. And maybe, just maybe, it would be good to survive a fight. Not only for himself, but for Aluna and Calli, too.

"So, are you going to teach me how to fight?" he asked.

Rollin chuckled. "No. I'm old and you're scrawny. We need ways to defend ourselves that don't need brawn and bulk. That's where tech comes in, yeah? That's why I want you to build me a weapon."

Hoku frowned. He still didn't want to build a

weapon. Not even a little one, not even one that was mostly harmless.

"I won't build a weapon," he said. He didn't want to lose his apprenticeship, but he didn't want to lose himself, either. "But I will build armor. Or a way to deflect other weapons. Or something that helps you escape danger. All of that is survival, too."

He stared her in the eyes. Both of them, not just the neat one with the tiny display screen built into the iris. He wanted her to look at him. To see that it wasn't fear that was driving him, but something else. Something bigger.

Rollin held his gaze, then suddenly looked away. She turned her back and hobbled over to her light-cutting machine.

"All right, Basic. Tell me what you're going to build me that's going to help me survive a fight with a four-feet. You seen their swords? Nasty. Don't want to end up sliced up by one of those." She paused to wipe her nose on the back of her wrist. "Well, what are you waiting for? Let me hear your brain!"

Hoku started talking.

CHAPTER 13

WHEN TAYAN came to get them the next morning, Hoku was already gone. Aluna couldn't believe it. That little squid hadn't gotten up early one day in his life. Then again, he'd finally found someone willing to teach him about tech.

"We'll go without him," Aluna grumbled. A night without much sleep—no matter how magical—still left her prickly as an urchin.

Calli sighed. "I guess he doesn't understand the burden of leadership."

Aluna looked at her sharply. Calli taking her responsibility to the Aviars more seriously was one thing, but if she started spouting any more of Dantai khanson's wisdom, she and Calli were going to talk. Possibly with spears.

"Come," Tayan said, stomping her hoof. "My father wishes to speak with you about the Thunder Trials."

Dantai and Weaver Sokhor were waiting in the khan's tent when they arrived. Aluna suffered through the bowing and nodding as best she could. Fortunately Khan Arasen seemed as tired of it all as she was. Maybe the Equians didn't weather late nights as well as they seemed to.

"Enough formalities," Arasen said. "Here is where Shining Moon stands." He turned and paced in the tent. Dantai and Sokhor moved immediately to give him room. "If we go to the Thunder Trials, we must both turn you over to Scorch and pledge our loyalty to a war that will destroy everything we have built here in the desert—even if we win."

"We do not know that life under Karl Strand would be so terrible, my khan," Weaver Sokhor said, his voice raspy from the long night of stories. "He has promised us prosperity."

"Prosperity at what cost?" Tayan said. "You did not see Mirage. It is no longer the bright star it once was."

"Karl Strand's clone Fathom turned off our breathing necklaces to drive us to the surface," Aluna said. It still made her angry, even now. "He was willing to kill us all if we didn't agree to be his slaves."

Calli cleared her throat. Aluna turned to look

at her, surprised she wanted to speak with so many people in the room. "My people have been fighting Karl Strand longer than any of yours," she said quietly. "We would have chosen death before joining him."

"My khan," Weaver Sokhor said, "I am sure these children mean well, but what do they know of war? What do they know of the desert or our struggles?"

Khan Arasen stroked his small beard and continued to pace. "I do not need wetlanders to tell me what the issue is, Sokhor. It is a matter of honor. Which is better: to honorably follow our High Khan even though the path he takes us will lead to dishonor and the destruction of our very culture? Or to defend our ancient ways, break our oath to Onggur, and be slaughtered by Red Sky as traitors?"

"There's another option," Aluna said.

All eyes turned to her. The High Khan stopped pacing.

She shrugged. "If High Khan Onggur doesn't win the Sun Disc at the Thunder Trials, then he won't be the High Khan anymore. He won't be able to lead anyone but his own people, and he'll have to obey the new High Khan."

Weaver Sokhor scoffed. "Child, you have never seen Onggur fight. He is impossible to defeat."

Aluna ignored him and kept her eyes on Khan

Arasen. "We win the Thunder Trials. Then everything changes."

Dantai shook his head and made a sound like a whinny. "I could do it, Father. I've been training hard."

Arasen turned to Aluna. His eyes seemed a little brighter. "Tayan gave her word that you would be at the Thunder Trials. She did that to save you, and I would give my own life rather than see my daughter break her promise." Out of the corner of her eye, Aluna could see Tayan shifting on her feet. "However," the khan said slowly, "your lives were not hers to give away."

Aluna felt a dam break inside her chest; a pressure she didn't know had built up suddenly released.

Arasen touched two fingers to his heart. "Therefore, I must ask. Will you, Aluna of the Kampii, and you, Calliope of the Aviars, agree to accompany us to the Thunder Trials of your own will? Not only will you preserve my daughter's honor, but you will also undoubtedly save Shining Moon lives."

"I came here to stop Scorch, and the best place to do that is at the Thunder Trials," Aluna said. "I'll come."

Calli nodded. "May this mark the beginning of our future alliance."

Khan Arasen relaxed and leaned back. Aluna glanced at Sokhor and saw a small smile on his face.

Was he happy for his herd, or was there something more?

"Excellent," the khan said. "I will be sure to ask your companion Hoku as well. Now, please excuse me. We must begin our planning for the Trials immediately."

"I'd like to stay for that," Aluna said. "I'm a fighter, too. And Hoku and Calli are smart. We want to help Shining Moon win."

"Ridiculous," Weaver Sokhor scoffed. "You are not Equians. You are not even of the desert! And you most assuredly are not Shining Moon."

Tayan stomped a hoof. "But, Father—"

"No," Arasen said, holding up a hand. "On this, I must agree completely with Weaver Sokhor. It is clear that we must win the Thunder Trials in order to save our people, and so we will . . . as Shining Moon. The purity of our herd is without question, and it is that purity that will bring us victory."

The khan turned his back on them, his tail flicking so close that Aluna almost sneezed. Clearly the conversation was over. After everything they'd done, after everything they'd agreed to do . . . they still weren't good enough.

Aluna's breathing necklace pulsed rapidly at her throat. She needed to get away, far and fast, before she said or did something to ruin what little they'd accomplished today. She threw open the tent flap and stalked out. When Calli tried to join her, she waved the girl back.

She ran west, wishing for the speed and sense of freedom that swimming used to give her. Equians clopped their way through the settlement, either off to start their morning chores or stumbling back to their tents after the evening's revelry. Aluna stared straight ahead and refused to look at any of them. How far from town would she have to get before she could scream without being heard?

She reached the edge of the settlement and kept going. With each step, she told herself she'd stop soon. Just a little farther. Sand slid into her shoes, but she was used to it now. Eventually her legs slowed to a walk. She forced herself to breathe deep and slow, tried to coax a little calm into her anger-tossed insides.

Hooves clomped through the sand behind her. Aluna sighed and wondered which Equian had been sent to retrieve her. But when she opened her eyes, she saw the horse Tal standing a few meters away, watching.

Aluna smiled. Suddenly the khan and Weaver Sokhor didn't matter as much. Tal lowered her head and took a few steps closer.

"How come you never leave this place?" Aluna said. "Maybe you could find another herd or join up with a pack of wild horses, if there are any." She took a few steps closer.

Tal shook her head and stomped her right front hoof in the sand.

"Don't tell me," Aluna said, remembering her conversation with Dash the night before. "You're an Equian—a Shining Moon—and you always will be."

The horse bobbed her head yes, then reared onto her hind legs and whinnied.

Aluna sighed. "If loyalty were water, this place would be an ocean."

Tal dropped back to all four feet and trotted over to Aluna, all nervousness seemingly forgotten. Aluna ran her hand down Tal's sweat-slicked neck and cursed herself for not finding a brush.

But Tal didn't have grooming in mind. She knelt on one of her forelegs, used the other for balance, and huffed. The same position she'd used to help Aluna up when her legs were failing her.

Aluna's breath fluttered in her throat. "Do you want me to . . . ? Can I really . . . ? You wouldn't mind . . . ?"

Tal huffed again, then reached over and gently tugged on Aluna's tunic with her huge teeth.

"Ride," Aluna breathed. "You want me to ride."

She dragged her hand along Tal's coat, to the

lump where her neck met her back. Withers, Dash had called it.

"I'm going to jump," she said. "It's not going to be pretty."

Tal let go of her tunic and snickered.

"Oh, you're laughing now. Wait until I've broken my neck."

She put both her hands on Tal's back and leaped. She'd intended to swing one leg over so that she straddled Tal's back and could sit upright. Instead, she ended up landing on her stomach, bent over the horse's back like a sack of sand.

"Not what I wanted," Aluna muttered. Then again, when her legs were fused together into a tail, maybe this was how she'd have to do it. Find some way to ride with both her legs off to the side. But that was a problem for tomorrow. Today she had simpler goals. She struggled for a better grip so she could shift her leg into position. Tal chose that moment to stand up.

A second later, Aluna thudded to the ground. Miraculously she managed to land on her side instead of on her head. She spat sand out of her mouth and stared up at the horse.

"You're not making this easy," she said.

Tal reached down and tugged at her tunic again.

"Yeah, yeah," She hopped to her feet and shook the

sand from her hair. "Remember, this is a lot easier for you than it is for me."

Three falls later, Tal managed to stay still long enough for Aluna to swing her legs into position. Tal's bony back dug into her thighs, but she let out a whoop all the same.

"Tides' teeth, it's a whole new world up here!"

Tal took a step forward, and Aluna bobbed backward.

"Guess I'd better hold on." She grabbed Tal's mane just in time. The horse bolted into a canter. Aluna felt like she was floating on top of the waves, only with more fear of falling and a lot more pain on her backside. She clutched Tal's sides with her legs.

Tal cantered in slow circles as Aluna adjusted her grip. Her body was already sore from bouncing against Tal's back. She could feel the bruises forming through her light tunic and pants. But no amount of pain was going to stop her. Not today.

"Faster," Aluna said. "As fast as you can go."

One of Tal's ears swiveled back to listen, and she nodded. Aluna could feel the muscles in the horse's body bunching and extending. *So much power!* Tal gathered herself up and launched into a gallop.

Aluna tried to keep her grip, but was face-first in the sand within seconds. At least she'd managed to avoid the prickly cactus, which seemed to be watching with amusement half a meter away. She wiped the sand out of her mouth, shook the surprise from her head, and waited for Tal to circle back.

The next time she fell, she got sand up her nose. Ocean sand ended up everywhere, so she was used to the discomfort, but desert sand burned and stuck to anything wet. And since Aluna had been sweating all day, her face, hands, and neck were covered in the gritty yellow nuisance.

But Tal proved just as stubborn as Aluna and kept coming back for her after she fell. The horse didn't even need to kneel after a while—Aluna managed to vault onto her back and scramble into place without help. Two more falls and Aluna managed to keep her seat when Tal broke into her gallop.

Air rushed past Aluna's face, blowing the sticky sand away in sheets. She watched the golden landscape zooming by below Tal's hooves and felt the same exhilaration she got underwater, when she hit open ocean and could swim as fast as she wanted.

"We can go anywhere," Aluna said. "We can do anything!"

Tal whinnied and ran faster. Aluna laughed and tightened her grip. She loved the way the horse's hooves thundered against the sand in perfect rhythm. Her chest felt light. Her heart sang. She wanted the feeling to last forever.

CHAPTER 14

BY THE TIME Aluna returned to the settlement, the Equian word-weavers were already at their fires, telling stories to the sunken sun. Aluna limped slowly, each step causing an explosion of pain through her thighs, backside, and ribs. Tal had simply trotted off toward the food troughs when they were done, no worse for their day of exercise. Aluna felt mushy and weak, like a lobster without its shell.

She lifted the tent flap with a groan. Somehow she'd managed to bruise her arms today, too. Not since the day High Senator Electra had taught her the basics of the Aviar spear had she so wished for a bottle of stinging jellyfish goo to ease the pain in her muscles.

"Aluna! Where have you been?" Calli said. "You look terrible. Is that cactus in your hair?"

"Food," Aluna said, stumbling inside. "Wash."

"I'd suggest grabbing some food first," said Calli. "Hoku's been taking all the best morsels for his teacher."

"Food," Aluna agreed.

"Have you met Rollin yet?" Calli asked. "I was nervous at first. I've never met a nice Upgrader. Er . . . and maybe I still haven't. But Hoku likes her."

Rollin. Aluna wasn't ready to trust any Human willing to disfigure herself with tech, but she trusted Hoku. That was enough.

Aluna devoured two chunks of smoky meat, then stumbled to the washbasin and stared mournfully at the water. The idea of pulling off her clothes sounded excruciating. After a moment's indecision, she picked up the cloth, wetted it, and covered her face with its cool bliss. But it wasn't enough. She wanted to dump the whole thing over her head, let the water race down her face in rivulets, trip over her lips, soak into her shirt.

But she couldn't. Not here. Shining Moon had given them a whole basin of water, more than most Equians would see in a month. It was one of the greatest gifts they could bestow. If she wasted it, the Equians would think she was just another rude, ignorant wetlander.

As she did her best to wipe the grime from her face

and hands, her thoughts began to clear. "What did you do today?" she asked Calli.

Calli appeared next to her as if she'd been waiting for a chance to spring. "I learned about the Thunder Trials. I have so much to tell you and Hoku."

"No fair starting without me," came Hoku's voice from the front of the tent. "Well, at least you left me some food. I'm starving."

"Save some for Aluna," Calli yelled back, and scurried off to greet him.

Aluna smiled. Calli wasn't the best warrior, but more and more, Aluna was grateful for her friendship.

"Is there a single centimeter of you that's not dirty?" Calli asked.

"I think the inside of my elbow is okay," Hoku replied. "Nope. Guess that's pretty gross, too."

"The Thunder Trials," Aluna said loudly. "You were going to tell us about the Thunder Trials?" She joined the others in the main room and sat carefully, arranging the pillows and trying several positions until she found one that didn't make her squeal from the pain. If she could sleep at all tonight, it would be on her stomach.

Then again, this was good pain. The kind she understood. The kind she had *earned*. Her brother Anadar used to say, "Pain scares your weakness away."

She'd pushed her body hard and would be stronger for it tomorrow. This feeling was nothing like what she felt from her growing tail. That pain came out of nowhere, confused her, left her feeling fragile instead of fierce. It didn't scare the weakness away; it scared *her.*

Hoku, his sunburned face covered in dark smears, grinned and handed her a hunk of rabbit. "You're moving a little slow tonight," he said.

She glared at him halfheartedly and took the food. "Funny comment coming from a walking oil slick."

He opened his mouth to reply, then filled it with rabbit instead.

Calli picked up a piece of fruit but didn't eat it. "Well, you already know that the Thunder Trials are contests, and that the winners earn more birthing rights for their herds."

Aluna nodded. "The faster, tougher herds grow larger, and the weaker herds die off. They're just accelerating what happens in nature anyway."

"Spoken like one of the faster, tougher people," Hoku grumbled.

"Except the Thunder Trials aren't only for warriors," Calli said, popping the fruit into her mouth. It bulged in her cheek. "They've got competitions for tech, too! And for working with animals, cooking, and even word-weaving. There are three paths — Sun,

Moon, and Sand. Sun is for one-on-one fighting, Moon is for artisan skills, and Sand is for other skills, like shooting and falconry."

"Fiddling with tech makes me an artisan?" Hoku asked.

Aluna snorted. She grabbed a small bundle of cactus flowers from the food tray and bit off a petal.

"Shining Moon has traditionally done well at the Trials," Calli continued. "Khan Arasen himself won the coveted Sun Disc in his youth, the one for fighting. He was High Khan for three years. But Onggur and the Red Sky always win that now. Shining Moon is known for their falcons and horses. They've won every year for decades, only . . ."

Calli scrunched up her face, gnawed on her lip, then started again. "Only their best falconers are gone. Erke and Gan. Two of Dash's parents. Dantai didn't want to say more, but I convinced him to tell me everything. He said that after Erke and Gan, Dash was the best falconer in the herd. Dantai isn't sure they can win this year, not when they're missing all three of them."

"But why wouldn't they have Dash?" Hoku said. "He's right . . . *Oh.*"

Blood pounded in Aluna's ears. Dantai wasn't counting on Dash because he expected Dash to be dead. They all expected Dash to be dead.

"Maybe prisoners aren't allowed to compete," Hoku said.

Calli shook her head. "They're going to judge him soon. As soon as everyone recovers from the celebration," she said. "But the situation is more complicated that we thought. Not all the Equians here are happy that Arasen wants to defy the High Khan. Weaver Sokhor seems to have a lot of power, and . . . he hates Dash. I don't know why, but he does. I don't know what the khan will do, but I heard Tayan arguing with him."

"I bet she wants Dash dead," Aluna said. "Why else would she have brought him back here?"

"No, it's not like that," Calli said. "Tayan believes in herd law, maybe too much, but I don't think she wants Dash to be hurt. She asked the khan to be lenient, to ignore Sokhor's demand for his life. She didn't want me to overhear, so I kept walking. But I heard enough."

Aluna stared down at the green plant in her hands, her appetite suddenly gone. "She doesn't want him to die, but she won't go against her father."

"No, I don't think she will," Calli said. "Honor and tradition are powerful here."

"Not everyone is as strong as you, Aluna," Hoku said softly.

She didn't feel strong right now. Not even a little. Riding all day had fed her spirit but destroyed her body.

All she wanted to do was swim into her sticky bed back in her nest in the City of Shifting Tides. She wanted to forget she'd ever heard of Karl Strand or Scorch. She almost wanted to forget Dash.

No. She didn't mean that.

Later that night, when Hoku's snores drifted over from the other side of the tent and echoed in Aluna's ears, Calli's voice emerged from the darkness.

"We'll save him, you know," she whispered. "After everything we've been through, I feel like you and Hoku and Dash are the only people in the whole world I can really count on. I can count on my mom, too, and Electra . . . but they're so far away. Sometimes I wonder if I'll ever see them again, you know? I miss the sky. Not the desert sky, all full of grit all the time, but the clear sharpness of the mountain air. The blueness. The white clouds. I feel like I came all this distance but part of me stayed behind. Is still back there soaring."

Aluna stayed perfectly still. She barely breathed. She didn't want to hear Calli's confessions. They scared her. The darkness was a shield, a protective bubble. It made you feel safe to say things you'd never say in the bright of the sun. If she and Calli started talking, Aluna couldn't trust herself to keep the secret about her growing tail. Telling someone—telling Calli— would make everything harder. Even so, she wanted to do it. She wanted someone to have her back, to cover for her, to *understand*.

No, the darkness was too dangerous.

"I guess you're asleep," Calli said with a sigh. "Good night, then. Sleep well. We'll figure out how to save Dash. I promise."

After Calli's breathing had slowed, Aluna sat up and began inspecting her legs. She found two more patches of thick skin and a strange softness by her ankle. She wrapped her feet in bandages made from her old tunic and hid them under pillows.

CHAPTER 15

A FEW DAYS LATER, Tayan burst into their tent just as Hoku was heading to Rollin's for a day of lessons, arguments, and unexpected injuries. Aluna and Calli were on their feet in a flash.

"The trial is today," Tayan said, her voice tight. "Dash has been taken to the khan. I am about to join them."

"Tides' teeth," Hoku said. "So soon?"

"We're coming with you," Aluna said. Hoku could see waves crashing behind her eyes. "Dash asked me not to involve his family, but he didn't make me promise not to go myself."

Thankfully Tayan merely nodded.

"Wait. We need a plan," Hoku said. "Some way to get through to Khan Arasen and Weaver Sokhor." He hadn't shown the story-song he'd been writing about Dash to the others yet. It wasn't done, and it wasn't very good. He'd thought he'd have more time.

"Hoku's right," Calli said. "We need to stay allies with Shining Moon. We can't jeopardize our relationship with them. It's not what Dash would want."

"Wise words," Tayan said. "Perhaps my father will be swayed by your restraint—"

"I'm done with restraint," Aluna said. "This is Dash we're talking about. *Dash.* I'm not going to bow and curtsy and play dutiful little visitor when his life is in their hands."

She stalked toward the door. Hoku considered stopping her, but her eyes held an emotion he rarely saw on her face. They held *fear*. He touched her arm. "Come on," he said softly. "We do this together. We do everything together."

Aluna looked as if she might rip his arm off. Instead, she sighed. Hoku fell into place at her side, and the four of them headed to the khan's tent. Two Equian guards with extremely sharp-looking spears blocked their entrance.

"Welcome, Tayan khan-daughter. You may, of course, enter," the female warrior said. She frowned at the rest of them. "The khan warned me that the three of you might also seek an audience. You are to keep your words brief."

Inside the tent, Shining Moon's most powerful Equians stood in a great semicircle around the tent's rim, looking as terrible and imposing as the Kampii Elders. Aluna's father would have fit in perfectly. Hoku recognized Weaver Sokhor by his curling gray hair and sour expression. The man looked like he'd swallowed a stinkfish.

Dash stood in the center of the tent. His cheeks seemed sharper than Hoku remembered, his eyes brighter.

Strangely, Aluna ignored Dash. She stomped to the center of the tent and stood right next to Dash but never looked at him. Instead, she addressed the khan—and only the khan. Weaver Sokhor glowered even more.

"Khan Arasen," Aluna said, "this is all my fault. I want to take full responsibility for Dashiyn's breaking of his exile. There must be some herd law that lets me do that." The Equians in the tent clomped their feet, shifted their weight, flicked their tails. Dash turned to Aluna, shocked, but she still wouldn't look at him. She kept her gaze locked on the khan. "I convinced Dash to enter the desert because of my crusade against Scorch. He didn't want to. He wanted to honor the terms of his exile." She shrugged and gave a wry smile. "So you see? If anyone should be blamed for this, it's me."

"Preposterous!" Weaver Sokhor blurted out. He turned to the khan. "She should not even be allowed in this tent during judgment, let alone be permitted to speak such obvious fabrications."

"Silence, Sokhor," the khan said. "You made your argument already, and I have granted the wetlanders permission to speak."

Sokhor clearly had more to say, but he swished his tail and settled for glaring at Aluna.

"May I speak, my khan?" Dash asked. It was the first time Hoku had heard his voice since the night of the celebration.

"You may not," the khan replied.

Hoku watched Dash struggle with this answer. It was probably killing him that Aluna was trying to take punishment in his stead. But instead of arguing, Dash simply bowed his head and said nothing.

"Aluna of the Kampii, you would suffer the consequences of Dashiyn's crime in his place?" There was something calculating behind the khan's eyes, and it made Hoku nervous.

"Yes," Aluna said clearly. "Dashiyn has done nothing but honor Shining Moon. He risked everything to come back here and warn your people about Scorch and Karl Strand."

"And you?" the khan said to Calli. "What has Calliope of the Aviar, daughter of the bird khan, to say about this criminal?"

"Please, my khan," Sokhor urged him, "end this nonsense now. These outsiders can have nothing to add to this matter of honor."

Instead of yelling at the word-weaver again, Khan Arasen nodded. "Only one minute more, Sokhor."

Sokhor nodded and backed off, clearly pleased. Hoku gripped the worn piece of paper in his pocket and wondered if he'd have the guts to read it when his turn came.

"Dashiyn has been nothing but brave and loyal," Calli said. "He has gone out into the world and represented you well. Everyone who meets Dash soon learns to honor Shining Moon as well."

Hoku gulped. Dash hadn't actually told any of them about his herd until they were already a few days into the desert. But the khan didn't need to know that.

"He's more than brave," Hoku blurted. If he waited for his turn, he might lose his nerve. "He's a hero. I . . . I wrote a story-song about him. And me. And the battle at the HydroTek dome." He could feel Aluna's and Calli's eyes on him, their shock and apprehension. He pulled the paper out of his pocket and unfolded it. "It's not very good," he added. "I don't know all the rules for Equian songs, and I only have two legs instead of four hooves, and I don't have a very good singing voice, not even for a Kampii. But . . . it's about Dash, and I'd like to share it, if that's okay."

Weaver Sokhor crossed his arms in front of his chest. The twisted smile on his face was anything but kind. "Oh, yes, my khan. Please, let us hear this boy's attempt. Our own word-weavers study and train their whole lives before attempting to add to our legends. And yet this boy thinks he can live in the desert for a handful of days and understand our ways. I beg you, my khan—let us hear this offering."

And suddenly Hoku's plan seemed a lot more dangerous than he'd intended. He hadn't realized that just the act of writing a story-song would insult the very Equians he was trying to reach.

"I'm sorry," he mumbled. "I didn't intend disrespect." He crumpled his page of lyrics and started to shove it back in his pocket.

"Stop," Khan Arasen said. "I would hear your song."

Hoku blinked up at him, frozen.

Aluna nudged him in the arm. "I hope you're as good with words as you are with tech," she whispered.

I'm not, he thought. *I'm not!* But it was too late. He swallowed thickly, cleared his throat, and began.

Listen. Listen. To the waves, to the whales. Listen. Listen.

The dome was full of Upgraders. Too many arms, too many eyes. Way too many weapons. Fathom's fiends.

Dash was already wounded, his wrist broken. But his sword was still whole. Silver steel. His heart was still strong. The heart of a horse.

Listen. Listen.

I needed time to access the computer, to stop Fathom, to save my people, to figure our futures.

But the Upgraders kept coming, bringing blood. Bringing fire. Bringing pointy green-tipped needles.

Dash fought them all, kept them at the door. His bright blade flashing, one-armed, honor-bound.

He never cried out or begged or gave up.

Dozens came. One after the next. Bent on death, bent on our death.

Dash fought them all, kept them at the door, his bright blade flashing. He gave me time.

And with time, I solved the puzzle. Words

trailed across the screen. Letters made of light. The dome was ours. Fathom defeated.

Dash lost his arm. A small sacrifice in the grand scheme, but more than I made. He'd been willing to lose his life.

Listen. Listen.

Dash is the one who saved me. Who almost died to save us all.

Dash brings honor to his herd. He brings honor to us all.

We need him.

Listen. Listen. To the waves, to the whales.

And please understand.

———

His hands shook by the end. His voice quavered, but he didn't stop or apologize or ask to start over. And when he finished speaking the last line, the khan's tent fell silent.

Until Weaver Sokhor snorted.

Hoku's face burned. He stared at the faded rug beneath his feet.

"His rhythms were completely off," Sokhor said. "No sense of power. Multiple language mistakes. I found the use of Dashiyn's nickname an insult to our heritage. And—"

"Enough," Khan Arasen said. He looked angry

enough to strangle a shark. Hoku pitied that shark. "I have heard all I need to hear," the khan said. He directed his remark not to Hoku but to Weaver Sokhor. "I am ready to decide the fate of Dashiyn."

Hoku looked at Aluna, but her face was blank. Almost empty. She stared at the khan, waiting, her hands thankfully devoid of weapons. He felt a tug on his arm and breathed deeply as Calli edged closer to him. He was grateful for her touch. She always seemed to know when he needed it most.

Khan Arasen stepped forward into the circle. "Almost two years ago, our beloved blood-brother Dashiyn betrayed us. Not only did he release a prisoner against our wishes and give him valuable medical supplies needed by the herd, but he also cost us birthing rights. If Shining Moon had found the Serpenti stronghold, we would now be in a position of far greater strength. Strength that we need to combat Red Sky and Scorch, and to take the Thunder Trials."

Barnacles. This did not seem like a promising start.

The khan continued. "Because Dashiyn and his family have, in the past, brought honor to Shining Moon, the normal penalty of death was waived. In an act of mercy, Dashiyn was exiled and forbidden to return to the desert."

Hoku glanced over at Weaver Sokhor and saw a self-satisfied smile. He had no idea why Sokhor seemed to hate Dash so much, but there was clearly no mercy left in that man's heart.

"The arguments in favor of Dashiyn are strong," Khan Arasen said, and Hoku's heart fluttered with hope. "We are particularly moved by our Kampii visitors. Aluna, you do your own herd honor by claiming responsibility for the failure of one of our own."

Aluna's hands bunched into fists for a moment, then opened again.

"Hoku," the khan said, "while you are clearly no word-weaver, your willingness to respect our ways also honors your herd. If your subject were not a symbol of shame to us, no doubt your story would find a home around our fires."

Hoku nodded, his face once again hot from the attention. He hadn't embarrassed them or made things worse. That wasn't much of a victory, but was more than he'd been expecting.

The khan paused, as if he were collecting his thoughts. His face remained unreadable, smooth as sand at low tide. "Unfortunately, we have already stayed our hand once, and we cannot afford to stay it again."

Time seemed to slow. Hoku could hear his heart in his ears, along with Aluna's now-ragged breathing.

Khan Arasen turned to Dash. "Dashiyn, once beloved son of Shining Moon, you are hereby condemned to sundeath."

CHAPTER 16

THE ROOM ERUPTED. All the Equians started talking at once, and Hoku heard Calli's voice behind him, "No, no, no." But he knew his job. He reached for Aluna's arm just as she was releasing her talons.

"Aluna, we'll die," he said. "Do this now, and we'll *all* die."

She shrugged him off and took a step forward. She would have kept going, straight at the khan, if Dash himself hadn't barred her way. The horse-boy put both his hands on Aluna's shoulders and looked her straight in the face.

"Stop," he said. Dash never raised his voice, not even now. "If you care for me at all, Aluna, please stop. This is not what I want. You are not helping me."

Hoku expected Aluna to brush his arms out of the way, scream her defiance, and launch herself at Khan Arasen. A few months ago, she'd done almost exactly that when they'd met Calli's mother, the president of the Aviars.

But instead, Aluna stopped. Her arms fell to her sides, and the anger in her face drained away. Just like that.

Dash smiled. "Thank you."

Two Equians grabbed Dash's arms and pulled them roughly behind his back. The smile stayed on his face as they marched him out of the tent and toward his terrible fate.

Hoku reached for Aluna. She stood there numbly as he pulled her into a hug. Calli stood at his side, murmuring. "It's not over. There's still time. Maybe I can fly him away—"

Tayan left the khan's side and joined them.

"You get your wish," Aluna hissed. "You wanted him dead all along."

"Go," Tayan said, ignoring Aluna and speaking directly to Hoku. "I have a plan. I'll find you later."

"What plan—?" he started to ask, but she had already clomped away to whisper in her father's ear. The khan nodded once. Tayan touched her fingers to her heart, then disappeared out of the tent.

"Let's go," Hoku said. "There's nothing more

for us here." He turned, pulling Aluna with him. She wore a deep scowl on her face, the one she always got when she was trying to be angry instead of sad. "Calli's right," he said. "This isn't over yet."

Back in their tent, Hoku paced, trying to make time go faster with his mind. Aluna sat by a tray of food and water, but didn't touch any of it. "Does anyone know what sundeath is?" he asked. He didn't really want to know the answer, but he knew it could be important.

"I do," Calli said. "It's . . . not good. They take the Equian out into the desert. Sometimes days out. And then they leave him without food or water or a head wrap. It's part death penalty, part sacrifice to the sun." She shook her head. "It's a miserable way to die, but they think it's honorable."

He'd expected Aluna to say something, but she only stared at her hands. Hoku tried to imagine wandering over the hot sands without water or protection from the sun. He licked his lips and fingered the canteen hooked to his belt. If that's how the Equians honored their own, he never wanted to see what they did to their enemies. Did Rollin have any devices that might help Dash survive? And if she did, how could he possibly get them to Dash without his captors seeing?

The tent flap swished open, and Tayan slipped inside.

"Good. All of you are here. I do not have much

time." She paused, listening to noise outside the tent, then relaxed slightly. "We are not taking Dashiyn to the desert until tonight. That is part of the ritual. He must be out in the desert when the sun rises. The longer he lasts, the greater the honor he pays to the sun."

Aluna spat. "Sounds like a convenient excuse to keep him from seeing landmarks when you drag him out there. It'll be too dark for him to tell which way you're taking him. He won't even have the sun to gauge which direction you've headed."

"The situation here is more tenuous than it seems," Tayan said. "Weaver Sokhor has many allies. If my father had not condemned Dashiyn to death, Sokhor would have used that as a sign of weakness and usurped him as khan. And believe me, that is not something any reasonable person would want."

"I don't care which one of you is in charge," Aluna growled. "Using Dash's life as if it were part of some game — that's just wrong."

Tayan nodded. "I agree, Aluna. I actually agree with you on a large number of things, if you would only deign to listen."

"Tell us how we're going to save Dash, and I'll listen to whatever you want," Aluna said.

Tayan sighed. She motioned them closer and then spoke quietly: "My father knew he had to sentence Dashiyn to death, at least publicly. But he chose sundeath so Dashiyn would not be killed immediately. I will ride with the party that escorts him to the desert. I will see the direction we ride and find some way to tell you. You will follow and rescue Dashiyn when we leave."

"How will you tell us?" Calli asked.

Tayan's tail swished. "I have not determined that part yet."

"And how are we supposed to follow?" Calli asked. "I can't fly that far into the desert, especially at night, and Aluna and Hoku can only walk. We'll never get to Dash in time."

"You must steal four of our horses," Tayan said quietly. "I will choose them for you, and Dantai will see that you have access to the gate. We will give you provisions, but you will never be able to come back."

"No," Aluna said. "We need to defeat Karl Strand, and for that we need to stay allies. Besides, if we don't show up at the Thunder Trials, Scorch will kill one of your people for every one of Calli's feathers. You heard her say it, and we both know she'd follow through on the threat." She shook her head. "No, there's a better way. I can follow without stealing a horse. I can ride Tal."

"Tal!" Tayan snorted. "She will never let you near her."

"Who's Tal?" Hoku asked. But even as the words

were forming in his mouth, he knew. "That outcast horse. Is that where you've been the last few days?"

"She's not an outcast, at least not on purpose," Aluna said. She lifted her chin, daring anyone to argue with her. "She's my friend, and we can go after Dash. She'll be able to carry me, plus Dash when I find him."

Tayan shook her head. "Tal is unpredictable, possibly damaged mentally. You have been here a week, and you think you can ride her? No. You will never make it."

"Yes, I will," Aluna said. "I'm not a good rider, but Tal is smart. She'll make up for me. I trust her."

"I could fly with you," Calli said. "I might be able to spot Dash from a distance."

"No," Hoku said. "Aluna wants to leave us behind. Again."

Aluna winced. "It's not like that. Not this time. I'm not the same foolish youngling I was back before the HydroTek battle. I know what you're capable of. But my plan is better. While I get Dash and take him some-place safe, you and Calli work on stopping Scorch. Find some way to help Shining Moon win the Thunder Trials, even if they don't want you to. I'll meet you there."

"But—"

"And besides"—she stepped forward and put her hand on Hoku's shoulder, something she hadn't done in weeks; he could feel the calluses on her palms through the light desert fabric—"if I don't make it, you'll need to keep going. You and Calli. You're the only ones who know how dangerous Karl Strand is and what he's trying to do. Our own people won't be safe until he's been destroyed."

He looked at her and saw determination instead of anger in her familiar brown eyes. They'd come so far, Aluna and him. He tried believe that this wasn't the end of their journey together. "We'll need supplies for Aluna and Tal."

"I'll get them," Calli said.

"Extra clothes for Dashiyn, and medicine," Tayan said. "Dantai will know what to bring. Be discreet. Weaver Sokhor and his allies must not see you."

"They won't."

Hoku mentally scanned the contents of Rollin's tent, trying to think of something that might help Aluna track Tayan through the desert. "Iron!" he said. He lowered his voice. "Tayan, can you carry a filled sack on your back without making the other Equians suspicious?"

She furrowed her brow as her hand drifted to her sword hilt. Her thinking look, alarmingly similar to Aluna's. "Yes, we will have some supplies with us in case something goes wrong. You can never be too cautious on open sand. One more pack will be easy to hide."

"Good," Hoku said. "You'll need to ride on the side of the group. There will be a small hole in the sack so the iron can trickle out while you run."

"What's the iron for?" Aluna asked.

He knew he was talking too fast, but when the ideas surged inside his brain, all he could do was open his mouth and hope that something sensible came out. "Tech hunting," he said. "The Upgraders build these amazing artifacts that can locate metal—all kinds of metal—even when it's underground. They use the scanners to find old tech and spare parts and even entire citywrecks that have been buried over the years. Rollin has two: one calibrated for iron and one specializing in lighter metals. The iron one is more sensitive."

Aluna rolled her eyes and motioned for him to continue. Could she really not see where he was going with this? He crouched down and rolled back a section of carpet, exposing the sandy earth. He drew a line with his fingertip.

"Tayan goes with Dash and leaves a trail of iron behind her. It'll be too small for anyone else to see. But there's not much metal in the desert." He drew a circle at one end of the line. "You know where she's starting from, so you can use Rollin's device to see the iron. It should be as obvious as a school of glowfish all swimming in a line."

Tayan clomped over and looked at his simplistic diagram. "We will be running for hours. I will not be able to carry enough iron to mark the whole way."

"Vectors," Hoku said. He leaned down and, with some small additions, turned the line indicating Tayan's path into an arrow. "If you start the trail and stay on the same trajectory—keep going exactly the same direction in a line—then Aluna can use her compass to stay on that line even after the iron has run out." He extended the line in the sand all the way to the edge of the next carpet. "Just don't alter your direction after the iron runs out. If you suddenly veer south, Aluna will lose you."

Aluna looked at Tayan and raised an eyebrow. Slowly, Tayan nodded.

"This will work."

Hoku hopped to his feet. "Meet me at Rollin's tent with your supply bag so I can get the compasses and we can test the iron dispersal."

Tayan turned to Aluna. "Is he always like this?"

"Only when he's awake," Aluna said.

CHAPTER 17

ALUNA STOOD WITH HOKU in the darkness, a small, battered compass gripped tightly in her palm. She'd sent Calli into the sky, hoping the girl might see the dust clouds from Tayan's group when they left Shining Moon. If she knew her prey's starting point and direction, then Hoku's tricks would do the rest.

Tal stood nearby, her back laden with supplies, and huffed. She wouldn't let Hoku touch her, but she'd allowed him to attach the metal scanner to her packs. Aluna made sure he explained how it worked within earshot of Tal. She had a sneaking suspicion that the horse might be smarter than she was.

Now they stood in the darkness, waiting for the signal and listening to the word-weavers call to the sun around Shining Moon's fires. Aluna's stomach grumbled and whined. She struggled to still her muscles and her mind. Her entire body felt coiled, ready to spring. Did all warriors feel like this right before battle?

"Where will you go after you rescue him?" Hoku asked. He kept his voice low, so only she could hear him.

"I don't know," she said. "It's too big a question. I need to stay focused on the first part—on the impossible task of finding a single boy in the middle of an endless desert."

"Your family would be proud of you, you know," he said. "Probably even your father. You've done so many brave things."

She shook her head and looked down at the compass in her hand. "And so many foolish things, too. I should have found a way to save Dash before now. I should never have let him get captured in the first place."

"He's got his own mind, Aluna," Hoku said. "You can't control him any more than he can control you." He nudged her shoulder with his own. "Besides, that hardheadedness is one of the reasons you like him."

She opened her mouth to protest, but clamped it shut when she saw the huge grin on Hoku's face. He was baiting her, the little squid. After years of it, she ought to have developed some sort of defense.

Hoku turned back to the stars. Calli was up there, but even with her Kampii dark vision, Aluna couldn't see her in the night sky.

"You'll find him," Hoku said. "I've never seen you fail, not at something you attack with all your heart."

Aluna wrapped her fingers around the compass and squeezed. "Hoku . . ." She'd imagined telling Hoku about her tail in the middle of a fight. *Clash, clatter.* "*Guess what!*" He'd have no time to ask questions, to yell at her for not telling him sooner, or worse, to offer pity.

But the Ocean Seed inside her assaulted her body unpredictably. If it happened while she was stranded out in the middle of the desert, there'd be no medics, no water to wet her blooming scales, no hope of comfort from a friend. And if the Ocean Seed she swallowed had gone bad—a possibility since she'd carried it around for so long—then who even knew what it was doing to her?

"Hoku, I'm growing my tail," she said quietly.

He continued to stare at the sky. "You mean, eventually? Are you sure? Legs are stupid underwater, but they're kind of fantastic up here."

"No, I mean I'm already growing it. Back in

HydroTek, I wanted to rescue my sister from Fathom. So . . . I made a trade. I swallowed the Ocean Seed and told Fathom he could observe the process."

Hoku turned his pale face to hers. She could count the freckles on his nose and cheeks.

"You stole the Ocean Seed during the ceremony?" he asked.

She nodded.

"And you kept it the entire time we were traveling? At Skyfeather's Landing and the Deepfell cave? All the way to HydroTek?"

She nodded again.

"And you never told me? Not even after you swallowed it?"

She cringed but said nothing.

Hoku ran his hand through his hair and sighed. "Well, you probably know how I feel about all that. Not good. I told you when I had my first crush on Elder Maylea. I told you when I gave her that seashell and she patted me on the head. I won't dwell. I know it's not the right time. But seriously? I tell you everything. You know what I eat for lunch, all my favorite foods, and even the first meal I'm going to share with Calli once I figure out a way to get her beneath the waves. And yet something like this—something that changes everything—and you don't tell me even when you have months to say something?"

His anger pulsed like a wave, rising up and crashing, then pulling back and rising up again. She let him go. She deserved it.

"Aluna, don't you see? The time for secrets has passed. We're not children, and this isn't a game. You know that better than anyone. You were the one who found Makina's body in the kelp, who found the Deepfell slaughtered on the beach, who barely survived a fight with Fathom." He kept his voice hushed, but she could see his frustration building. He threw up his hands. "You're about to go out into the desert in the middle of the night, on a freak horse, without knowing how to ride, to rescue a boy condemned to death. The time for secrets is over."

He grabbed her shoulders and shook her. He wasn't strong, but it still surprised her. "If you'd told me sooner, maybe I could have helped. I could be researching genetic resequencing instead of playing Rollin's games. I could have been helping you this whole time! Don't you see?"

She could see him straining to keep his voice under control when he clearly wanted to yell and scream. His pain cut through her like a spear.

"Now you're leaving," he said. "You're leaving and I can't help you. And if something goes wrong, I won't be there. I won't even know. You could be lying out there somewhere, in the sand, dying, and I won't ever even know where you are. Do you see? Do you understand?"

She grabbed him. He shoved her, tried to push her away, but she was stronger. She pulled him in and wrapped her arms around him. "I'm sorry," she whispered. "Everything you've said, it's all true. I'm sorry. You're my best friend. I'm sorry I hurt you."

And just like that, all the fight dropped out of him. He stood in her arms and let himself be hugged. After a minute, she felt his arms start to hug her back.

"You're my best friend, too," Hoku whispered.

She snorted. "I don't deserve to be."

"I know," he said. "Don't let it go to your head."

Tal clomped her hooves. A moment later, Aluna felt the horse lipping her hair. Tal grunted and lifted her head to the sky. Aluna followed her gaze and saw Calli plummeting toward the ground. She released Hoku.

"Calli's seen something," he said. "It's time."

Aluna tucked her compass into a pocket and leaped onto Tal's back from the ground. The packs made it more difficult, but she'd been practicing all week and managed to do it with minimal embarrassment.

"Barnacles," she said as her bruised backside hit Tal's bony withers.

"That explains all the groaning you've been doing this week," Hoku said.

"Remember how bad we were after the rhinebra?"

"I'll never forget," Hoku groaned.

"Well, this is worse." She patted the pocket with the compass. Still there. Hoku helped her adjust the metal scanner so it wouldn't clank against her leg as Tal ran.

Calli landed with a whoosh of air and a great cloud of dust.

"Northeast," she said quietly. "They started near the foundry, where they make weapons. I think they were holding Dash somewhere near there."

Aluna nodded. "I'll give them a few minutes and then head out. I can stay closer at night, since my vision in darkness is better than theirs." She clicked on the scanner. "I hope this thing works."

"Rollin's been using it for years," Hoku said. "Then again, she hasn't found very much."

"I am filled with confidence," she said.

"Be careful," Calli said. The girl's cheeks were red from her flying. From Aluna's position astride Tal's back, Calli seemed small despite her wings.

"You too," Aluna said. "The politics here are more dangerous than in our colonies. If you become one of Sokhor's enemies, it may not be safe for you. Especially because of your friendship with Dantai."

"While the khan lives, I'm sure we'll be fine," Calli said. "If he dies or is killed, Hoku and I will run." She reached out and pressed one of Aluna's hands between both of her own. "Don't worry about us. We can take care of ourselves."

"So I've heard," Aluna said, looking at Hoku.

She stared at him, wanting to remember every detail. She'd need something to hold on to in the coming days.

"It's time," Hoku said. "Swift currents, Aluna."

"Swift currents," she replied. She turned to Tal and patted her on the neck. "Let's swim."

Tal took a few steps forward, then vaulted into a gallop. Aluna never looked back.

CHAPTER 18

ALUNA AND TAL raced over the sand. The cold desert air felt almost like water as it washed over Aluna. Lit only by the stars, the desert became a beautiful shadowy landscape not unlike the ocean floor. Cactus were almost like kelp, but more straight-backed and stubborn. Tiny animals darted out of their path, just like goldenboys and shiny-blues, little fish too quick to be caught. Aluna imagined that they were racing along at the bottom of the sea, sand puffing up behind them in the water.

She hated stopping, but she couldn't risk losing Tayan's trail. Tal didn't want to stop, either. She whinnied her objection but slowed to a trot, then a walk.

The metal scanner beeped weakly. They zigzagged across the sand until the signal strengthened. Once they'd found it, Aluna pulled out the compass and checked their direction. The needle always pointed north, which meant they were heading a little north of east.

"Got it." She pointed and Tal bounded off again.

For days, they'd been practicing their riding in the desert. Stopping and starting, galloping and trotting, turning quick like a shark. Aluna did not ride well, but Tal's occasional nips at her feet or snorts of irritation helped her improve quickly. If she'd been sitting atop a regular horse instead of an Equian, she'd still be at a walk.

The next time they slowed, Aluna couldn't find the trail of iron with the scanner. Either she'd read the compass wrong or Tayan had. Or maybe the two other guards had altered the group's direction.

Tal weaved north and south along the path they'd been following, trying to pick up the iron trail. The scanner offered a weak beep every few minutes, but nothing Aluna could follow. The minutes passed painfully. Each one meant that Dash was that much farther away, the trail that much colder. If the wind picked up, it might blow the light iron dust into the air and scatter it kilometers away.

Even in the cold of darkness, beads of clammy

sweat formed on her scalp and dripped slowly down her forehead. "Beep, you stupid artifact. Beep!"

The scanner ignored her. She checked the settings, hoping nothing had been broken or dislodged during their run. Hoku had told her not to touch any of the knobs, but what if they'd moved while she and Tal were galloping? She'd never figure out how to reset them.

And then a miraculous beep. And another. And a whole stuttering cluster of them.

"Tides' teeth," Aluna muttered. She and Tal navigated back to the trail. "They're headed due east now," Aluna said. "We'd better stop more often." Tal whinnied in disgust but didn't argue. She vaulted into a gallop, and Aluna barely had time to grab hold of her mane.

They rode for hours. Aluna sipped sparingly from her canteen, wanting to save as many of her supplies as possible. Dash would need food and water badly when she found him, and who knows how many days they'd be traveling after that. She offered water to Tal, but the horse shook her head and ran faster.

Aluna smiled. Tal was more similar to her than her own siblings were.

Eventually the sky began to lighten and Tayan's trail ended. The signal had grown weaker and weaker on the scanner until, finally, they couldn't find any trace of iron at all. Now everything depended on the compass, and on Tayan's ability to keep the group headed in the same direction.

The sun peaked over the gray mountains, and the air started to warm. Tayan and the other guards would have abandoned Dash by now and might even be headed back this way. Even so, she stayed on course. She'd rather run into the guards than risk missing Dash.

A dark smudge appeared in the distance, a black lump lying on the blinding gold ground. Tal slowed as they neared, and Aluna's pulse quickened.

An Equian. Dead. One of Dash's guards.

She dismounted and toppled into the sand, her legs refusing to hold her weight. She landed on her hands and knees beside the body. Her nose wrinkled at the smell. A deep-red stain soaked the cloth of the man's tunic near his Human stomach. A gut wound, the most painful kind. He'd lived long enough to run from whatever he'd fought but hadn't made it far.

Another wave of stench assaulted her nose. She turned and retched into the sand, painfully aware of how much water she was wasting with such foolishness.

Tal stomped a hoof and whinnied.

"I don't like death, either," Aluna said. "No one does."

She pushed herself to her feet. Her legs obeyed this

time, and she was relieved that their earlier betrayal had more to do with riding for hours than with her growing tail. She stumbled back to the dead Equian and unhooked his canteen from his packs. Water was too precious out here to waste just because she didn't want to touch a dead body.

A stain in the sand a few feet away from the Equian caught her eye. The guard had been bleeding as he ran.

"Come on," Aluna said to Tal. "We have a new trail to follow."

Tal trotted over. Aluna hefted herself onto the horse's back with a groan. Her legs ached, but she found her seat.

"There," she said, pointing. Tal burst into a trot. The trail proved easy to follow, far easier than the iron had been. Even the guard's hoofprints were still visible in the sand. "Whatever happened was recent."

Who had killed the Equian? Had the group been attacked by bandits? A rival herd? The Serpenti? Scorch? If the others were alive, why hadn't they followed the dead guard and tried to save him? Tal seemed to sense Aluna's growing unrest and ran faster. She had no trouble following the trail without Aluna's help.

And then, in the distance, she saw the rest of them. The rest of the bodies.

Her heart thudded painfully inside her chest, her

rib cage suddenly too small. Tal slowed instinctively. Aluna's eyes struggled to resolve what her mind didn't want her to see.

Tayan and the other guard, down on the sand. Down, though Equians never *chose* to lie down, not even when they slept.

A flash of silver. The third figure looked up at them, his eyes bright and alive, a long, bloody sword clutched in his hand.

CHAPTER 19

DASH!" Aluna cried. Tal galloped forward. Aluna swung her legs over and dropped to the ground before the horse finished slowing to a stop.

"Aluna," he said. He had no head wrap. His straight dark hair streamed behind him like a black sash.

She stumbled toward him. No wounds. She didn't see any wounds. The blood must be from the others. "Are you okay?"

He nodded. "It's Tayan. She's hurt."

Aluna pulled her eyes away from him and looked down. Tayan lay beside him. He'd been shading her face with his shadow.

"The others attacked," Dash said. "They belong to Weaver Sokhor. They tried to murder us. They were going to tell the khan that I killed Tayan. That I killed his daughter."

She knelt by Tayan and dropped her ear to the Equian's mouth. "She's still alive."

"They got the first blow. The dishonorable one," Dash said. "We got the rest."

Aluna searched Tayan for the wound and found it. A deep puncture dangerously close to her heart.

"Berrin got away," Dash said. "He will spread lies about us as soon as he gets to the settlement. Sokhor wants to hurt the khan. He wants to weaken him with grief."

"Berrin will never get there," she said. "He's dead. You got him, too."

"Good," Dash said, and sat back on his heels. Aluna glanced at him and saw clouds in his eyes. He'd killed before—some of the Upgraders in the HydroTek dome had died. Was this the first time he had killed one of his own?

She said nothing but began to rummage through the packs tied to Tayan's back. "Help me remove these. We need to lighten her burden. Maybe she has medical supplies in here somewhere."

Dash snapped out of his reverie. "Yes, of course. She always has supplies. She is ridiculous that way. I do not know why I failed to think of that."

I know, Aluna thought, looking at the sword still gripped tightly in his hand.

They found bottles and ointments and bandages, and Dash set to work applying them. Aluna had never been much for tending wounds, not even her own. She headed over to the other Equian and began sifting through his supplies. More food, more water. Two knives. A compass. Special tools for making fire without wood. She took it all but left the bedding and extra clothes. Tal couldn't carry much more.

"Traitors!" Tayan breathed.

Aluna looked up and saw Tayan struggling to lift her head.

"Slow," Dash said. "They are dead. The traitors are dead."

The panic washed out of her eyes, and she sighed. She groaned and touched her wound. "I should have known," she hissed. "I should have insisted on bringing only warriors loyal to my father."

Dash finished taping a bandage around her shoulder. She'd have to keep the whole arm immobile to stop the gash from reopening. "Can you stand?"

She nodded. "With help."

Aluna called to Tal. The horse had been keeping her distance, but now she stepped carefully into place beside Tayan.

"Thank you," Aluna whispered to her. Tal didn't like the Equians of Shining Moon. Or at least she didn't trust them. But Tal understood life and death, and she knew what she had to do.

Tayan gripped Tal's mane with her good arm, while Dash supported her on the other side. From what Aluna had seen, horses never looked graceful when they tried to stand. Wounded Equians were so much worse. Tal grunted as Tayan cursed and pulled herself up.

"Careful," Dash said. "Try not to reopen the wound."

"Of course I am trying not to aggravate the wound," Tayan said bitterly, then added, "My apologies. My anger is not with you."

"Be as angry as you need to be—just get to your feet," Aluna said. "We're shark meat if we can't get you walking."

Another few curses and Tayan got all four hooves underneath her. Aluna and Dash lifted, Tayan pulled on Tal, and the Equian managed to stand.

"Keep hold of Tal," Aluna said. "You're likely to be dizzy."

As she finished speaking the words, Tayan stumbled forward and almost toppled over again.

"The desert spins," she said.

"Here, water. Drink as much as you can." Aluna

handed her the canteen. Tayan sipped carefully at first, then lifted her head and gulped.

"The sun climbs," Dash said. "We should start moving."

"No," Tayan said, handing the water canteen back to Aluna. "We must bury the dead. These men were Shining Moon."

"Shining Moon who tried to kill you," Aluna said. "We're not wasting our energy, our water, or our time on them. Not when we need every minute we have to find shelter."

"I agree," Dash said. "We have no idea how long it will take us to cross the desert."

"We know exactly how long," Tayan said. "It took us six hours to ride here. It will take us slightly longer to get back. We have more than enough supplies."

Aluna looked at Dash. He shrugged and gave her a small grin. She felt her face break into a smile in return. "Tayan, we're not going back to Shining Moon," Aluna said firmly. "Dash will be killed, and you're too weak to make the journey on your own. We must go forward."

"Never!" Tayan said. "I must warn my father. I will go back by myself if I must." She let go of Tal and clomped forward. Her legs wobbled, and she fell to her forelegs in the sand. "Uhhh . . ."

"Easy," Dash said. He put a hand to her head.

"Fever. And I have already given her all of our painkillers."

Aluna stood near Tayan as the Equian struggled to stand again. "Listen," she said. "I understand what it's like to think you're in charge and then find out that you aren't, but it's happening to you now."

"I must—"

"No. No arguments," Aluna said. "Dash and I are making the decisions. We'll find someplace safe to get you fixed up, and we'll find some way to get word back to Shining Moon. Our friends are back there, too. We won't forget. But now, and until we say otherwise, you'll listen to us."

Tayan wanted to fight. Aluna could see it all over her pale, bloodless face. But the woman was also feverish and dizzy and suffering and seemed to realize that she'd lost.

"Good," Aluna said. "Now, you hang on to Tal. Dash and I will walk alongside." She turned to Dash. "We're east of Shining Moon. What direction do we walk?"

He looked up and studied the sun. "Southeast," he said. "I may have some allies in that direction. They won't care that Shining Moon has condemned me to death."

Tayan snorted. "Then they cannot be honorable allies, to ignore desert law without care."

"Equian law is not desert law," Dash said easily. He could have said more—Aluna saw it in his eyes— and yet he didn't. His restraint seemed to vex Tayan all the more.

She wanted to ask about these allies, too, but not in front of Tayan. It would be so much easier if they could just let her go back to Shining Moon. She and Dash could make good time riding Tal without a wounded Equian to care for.

But letting Tayan have her way would kill her, and Aluna didn't want her to die. Tayan had told them how to save Dash and had risked everything to carry out her part of the plan. Aluna could do no less for Tayan now.

"Dash, there are extra clothes for you in Tal's pack," Aluna said. "And I'm sure you need food and water, too."

"I can wait on the food and water, but not the clothes," he said. He walked around Tayan but stopped when he stood in front of Tal. "Thank you for your assistance, friend," he said to her. Then he touched his fingers to his heart and bowed as low as she'd ever seen him bow. Tal responded by huffing air into his face. Dash smiled. "It's good to see you again, too."

When Dash had once again tied his hair into its accustomed tail and donned his head wrap, they set off. Slower than Aluna wanted, but probably faster than was good for Tayan.

Tayan walked between Tal and Dash, protected on both sides. Aluna floated around, first walking next to Tal, then finding her way to the other side of Dash. His mood seemed lighter now; his eyes held more spark. She guessed that surviving a death sentence might make you playful as a porpoise, even under bad circumstances.

"Thank you," he said when she fell in beside him. "For rescuing me."

"It wasn't just me. Hoku was brilliant, and so was Calli," she said. "Besides, I haven't rescued you yet. Not entirely."

"Yes," he said. "You have."

They kept walking, and despite everything, Aluna felt light as a bubble rising in the waves.

CHAPTER 20

Fingers!" Rollin yelled for the third time.

Hoku pulled his hand off the sheet of metal just as the slicing light cut through it.

"You're too far away to use the slicer. Too far away up here," Rollin said, tapping her temple. "Do something else. Something not involving sharp, pointed, hot, or otherwise dangerous tools. Unless maybe you want to design new fingers next?"

He sighed and shut off the slicer. It was almost dusk, but Tayan and the other Equians hadn't returned. They should have been back hours ago. A net of anxiety had fallen on the whole settlement. Everyone was talking about what might have happened.

Well, everyone except Rollin. She'd assigned Hoku a series of mindless tasks: cut strips of metal, coil wire, uncoil wire, solder strips of metal back together. She didn't seem to care about Tayan or Dash or much of anything besides the tech in her tent. But he had to admit, he'd have gone wild with worry if she hadn't kept him so busy.

Rollin stood hunched at the desk dedicated to "fiddly bits and micro-making"—the place where she worked on tiny tech. Once she started a new project, she could focus on it for days. He made sure to bring her food and water when she got like that. And to sneak as many looks over her shoulder as he could.

Now, released from his senseless slicing duties, he surveyed the room, looking for something harmless to occupy his time. He spotted a squat machine covered in loose wires hunkered at the back of a table. It had the same configuration of knobs that Calli's radio had, plus a keyboard, a viewscreen, and a few more knobs of various shapes and sizes. Was it some sort of communication device?

He made a path to the table by moving three sacks of miscellaneous parts, a humming machine with no apparent purpose, and a stack of old, crumbly suntraps. The wires strewn across the machine were buried in sand and dust and seemed impossibly knotted.

He lifted the whole mess of them off the artifact and dropped them to the floor.

"Commbox," Rollin said without looking up from her work. "Most of the settlements got 'em. Smaller units than those in the big cities. Not that useful when you only have one. Talking to yourself gets old, yeah?" She laughed at her own joke. Apparently that part of talking to yourself *never* got old.

"So it works?" He reached over and twisted a knob. The commbox whirred to life, sputtered, and choked back to silence.

"Nope," Rollin said.

He rolled his eyes. She loved to answer his questions when he already knew the answer. He was probably supposed to learn to stop asking dumb questions that way, but so far, it hadn't worked.

A quick examination of the commbox led him to a series of tiny screws keeping the faceplate in place. He headed back into the chaos to look for a screwdriver small enough to fit.

A shadow fell across the tent's entrance flap. "It's Calli. May I come in?"

Hoku smiled. Hearing Calli's voice still did that to him.

Rollin huffed. "Why not? The basic's no good to me or himself today. Not without a brain."

Calli lifted the flap and entered. "Oh, it's very . . . full . . . in here." She tried to snug her wings to her back, but it was no use. If she moved around too much, she'd be knocking gizmos off their ceiling hooks and toppling them off their precarious stacks.

"Hey," Hoku said. He tried to make it no big deal. That's what Aluna's brothers always did—they pretended they didn't care one way or another if the girl they liked paid attention to them.

"I'm sorry to interrupt," Calli said. "The khan has sent out a search party. I . . . thought you should know that I told them what direction to look."

"Good," he said. "I'm glad they're doing something. I feel so useless."

Rollin snorted.

"What are you working on?" Calli asked, pointing at the newly visible artifact. "Looks like a commbox. We have one of those at Skyfeather's Landing."

"You do? Do you know how it works? Can you help me fix it?" *Barnacles.* He'd channeled Aluna's brothers for approximately thirty seconds before lapsing back into himself.

"Ours hasn't needed fixing since I've been alive," Calli said. "We only turned it on a few times a year, to talk to the Aviar colony in Talon's Peak. But it can't be much different from my radio, and I got that working by myself."

"Don't you have to get back to Dantai?" Hoku asked. He hadn't meant the question to sound so . . . well, the way it sounded—equal parts jealous and afraid.

Calli tilted her head, clearly uncertain about what his question really meant. "Dantai and most of the others are preparing for the Thunder Trials. Even the khan is on the practice field—although I wouldn't want to be his sparring partner. Not until Tayan returns."

Rollin turned. "The khan fights? At his age? Ridiculous! What fresh foolishness is this?"

"Dantai and Tayan were supposed to champion Shining Moon in the Thunder Trials, at least in the warrior arts. But Weaver Sokhor convinced the council that it would better display their strength, and bring more honor to the herd, if the khan himself took up his sword."

"Weaver Sokhor wants the khan dead," Hoku said. "No one will argue if High Khan Onggur does it in the middle of a contest."

"Hold your tongue, or someone will chop it out for you," Rollin hissed. "What you say is true, and all the more dangerous for being so. Think the thoughts, boy, but don't let them reach your mouth."

Hoku's face flushed with heat, but he only nodded.

Calli lowered her voice when she spoke again. "I heard Dantai say that some of the messenger birds are missing. I wonder . . . if a certain weaver might already be in contact with the High Khan or Scorch."

Rollin sighed. "That's not much better, girl, but points for effort. Don't either of you go into spying." She turned back to her fiddly-bits work. "Truth has a way of showing itself. Suppose we'll see for ourselves soon enough." And then Rollin fell back into her work. She may as well have disappeared off the face of the Above World, for all she paid attention after that.

"Come on," Hoku said. "I've got a screwdriver. Let's see what's inside the commbox."

Calli nodded and carefully maneuvered to the table. As they bent to work, Hoku remembered their time together at Skyfeather's Landing, when he'd just discovered the immense possibilities of Above World tech and Calli had been there to get him started down the right paths. For the first time the entire day, his body relaxed. Aluna was out there somewhere, alive. He knew it. And if she was alive, there was a good chance that Dash and Tayan were, too. He needed to let go of the worry. To focus on the things he could control. He needed to learn as much about tech and artifact-making as he could. He and Calli needed to figure out the bizarre twists and turns of Shining Moon politics. And together, they had to find some way to help Shining Moon beat Red Sky in the Thunder

Trials, so they could kick Scorch and Karl Strand out of the desert.

But for now he let himself be in the moment. He had tech at his fingertips, just itching to be fiddled with, and he had Calli at his side—talking fast, biting her lip, being brilliant, and smelling like feathers and sunshine, no matter what time of day it was. He'd been so uncertain of everything since they got to Shining Moon, so sure Dantai would sweep Calli away with his muscles and braids and "I know what it's like to be a leader" talk.

And maybe he still would. But that didn't change what was important between Hoku and Calli. That didn't hurt their friendship at all. Nothing could.

He finished with the last screw, and Calli helped him lift the face off the commbox. They set it down behind them on the wobbly stack of cracked suntraps.

Calli began pointing at parts immediately. "That's the transmitter, I'm almost positive," she said. "And this is the receiver. Or at least it should be. The transmitter sends our voices to an ancient artifact floating in the sky, which bounces them to other places. The receiver is our ears. It hears whatever someone else sends to the sky artifact. We should check for loose wires first—that would be the easiest problem to fix. And then we should double-check the power source.

If it's spotty, it could be causing a short when you turn it on. . . ."

He smiled and dug into the tech, testing wires and pushing parts more firmly into place. He interrupted Calli with a few ideas of his own but in general was happy to let her voice wash over him like waves at high tide.

CHAPTER 21

IT TOOK HOKU AND CALLI three days to get the commbox working. It turned on and off when they wanted it to, and they were able to talk into its audio input and hear their voices on Calli's radio when they aligned the frequencies. Whether it worked across vast distances would remain a mystery.

Calli shut the machine off with a sigh. "Better save the energy for something more useful."

"That's thinking with your head. Good bird," Rollin said.

"No. Leave it on," Hoku said. "There's almost no chance we'll hear anything, but if it's off, that chance drops to zero. It's worth the energy. I'll go without a fan, or whatever I need to. But please, leave it on." He reached over and turned the knob. The dull hum of fuzzy noise made him breathe easier.

Rollin put down her tools and looked up at him. "That *sounds* like thinking with your head, but it's really thinking with your heart."

Hoku stuck out his chin. "What's wrong with that?"

"Nothing," she said with a shrug. "Just a rare thing to see — thought I ought to point it out."

Three days. The search parties had come back covered in sweat, half dead from dehydration. The iron trail that Tayan left had long since been blown away, but it didn't matter. Aluna had the only metal scanner calibrated for iron. Without it, the searchers had no chance. It was like trying to find a single specific shell on the vast ocean floor.

"Aluna and Dash are okay," Calli said for maybe the twentieth time. "They're both warriors. They're both smart. They'll find a way to survive." She didn't even look at him when she said it. At this point, he figured she was mostly trying to convince herself.

Hoku knew that Aluna was still alive. She'd faced far worse than a desolate landscape and some sun before now. Anyone who grew up with a father like hers could handle adversity. Her family practically fed on it. If he ever made it back to the City of Shifting

Tides, he'd be sure to thank Elder Kapono, Daphine, and every single one of Aluna's annoying brothers.

Calli made a stool out of the dead suntraps and began slowly shifting through frequencies on the commbox. It whined and keened in the process, but Hoku found the noise soothing. They may not be racing across the desert on four hooves, but they were doing something. They were looking.

He pulled out a small sack with the project he'd been working on—an arm shield. Ever since Rollin's first lesson, when Hoku had refused to make a weapon, the idea for this shield had been swirling around in his brain. If he could get it to work, it could change the course of a whole fight.

"Why won't Shining Moon compete in the tech parts of the Thunder Trials?" Hoku asked. "Seems a whole lot safer than competing in the fighting parts."

Rollin chuckled. "How many four-feets have you seen in this tent since you've been coming? Go ahead, count."

"Other than Tayan, I count zero."

"Shining Moon is not the home of shining brains," Rollin said.

"That's not fair," Calli said. "Dantai is very smart. I'm sure he could make something amazing if he wanted to."

Rollin sent Hoku a look that plainly said, "I disagree. That boy is not very smart"—only a lot less polite. Hoku stifled a laugh, but Calli didn't seem to notice.

"Many four-feets are good with tech in other herds. Very good with tech. But not here. Tactics smart isn't the same," Rollin said easily. "It's good for me. If they could fix their own tech, I'd be hunting for another hideout."

Hoku studied the mechanism in his shield. *Hideout?* Who, or what, was Rollin hiding from? Other Upgraders?

"If we make something, can Shining Moon use it as their entry in the tech competition?"

"Not unless we wear the herd colors," Rollin said, "and I don't see any blue and white in here."

He looked around at the artifact-filled tent. "This place hasn't seen the color white in years."

Rollin chuckled.

"I keep suggesting ways we could help and competitions we might be good at," Calli said. "They dismiss me every time. Even Dantai. According to herd law, anyone can join the herd with the khan's consent. I just don't see how we're going to get it."

Hoku pulled out a micro-adjustor and tried to steady his hand. "The Kampii Elders wouldn't listen to us, either, if we were underwater instead of up here.

And I bet we'd have to work really hard to convince your mother, too."

"All the little spots of people, all you splinters, you grew up by yourselves," Rollin said. "Hard to make friends when you're used to being on your own. And when it was other people that drove you underwater or into the desert or into the skies in the first place."

"The Upgraders didn't do that, though," Hoku said. "You didn't flee the Human cities or live in big groups like colonies. Or did you?"

He pressed a button on his shield device, and a jolt of electricity speared his arm. The device tumbled from his hand. He rubbed his arm, then picked the artifact back up again. Carefully he undid the adjustment he'd just made. Trial and error was a lot less fun when the errors came with shocks.

"The Upgraders aren't a people," Rollin said, "although some would treat us as such." She put down her tools, put her good hand at the base of her spine, and stretched. Hoku heard something pop. It was either the bones in her spine realigning or whatever she had in there instead of bones. "Don't know about our ancestors," Rollin said. "Maybe they were from the cities. Maybe they were from the hills or dark places. But somewhere they found tech makers and gizmos and mixers and medics. Somewhere, they decided that survival meant better parts." She laughed and tapped her artifact eye. "Or maybe they just liked what they saw and wanted some for their own."

"You wanted that eye?" Hoku said.

"Like you want food, you gobbly basic," Rollin said. "This eye shows me heat and light and all manner of pretty things you aren't ever going to see. It's a whole new world I've got, an invisible world, a better world. Would have plucked out my own eye if the fixer had asked."

An image filled Hoku's head. An image involving Rollin and eyes and things he didn't want to see.

"I'm going to fetch some food," Rollin said happily. "Talking tech always makes me hungry. Too bad I'll be munching grasses, if the four-feets have their way." She grumbled to herself all the way out of the tent. Hoku could still hear her talking as she lazed down the path to the kitchens.

"I am never going to eat again," Calli said, her face pale.

He grinned at her and put a hand on his own rebellious stomach. But seeing her sit there, hunched over a grimy table, her wings smudged with dirt and oil, made his smile fade.

"We can't stay here," he said. "We have to do something. I don't know. Hire people to look. Go look for them ourselves. Maybe Electra and the other Aviars could come and sweep the desert."

Calli left her seat, wound her way through the piles of junk, and took his hand.

"When an Aviar goes out to scout and gets wounded and can't fly back, they're trained to stay where they are. To make camp, eat what they can, make a signal if possible—but stay. We know their route, and it's the best chance we have of finding them again." She played with his fingertips. "Aluna and Dash know we're here. We can't go after them because we don't know where they're going. And if we leave, they won't know where we are, either. Our chances of finding each other go from small to nothing."

"The Thunder Trials," he said weakly. "We all know where and when those are."

"Yes," she said. "We could easily waste our time looking for them and never find them. If we stay here, you can keep working on your project, I can monitor the commbox and try to get a message through to my people, and we can try to prove to the khan that we deserve to be made members of Shining Moon. I know everyone says that the warrior competitions at the Thunder Trials are the most important, but maybe that's because they don't expect to win the other battles. Not without their falconers."

She talked so fast when she was passionate. Sometimes he almost started fights just to hear one of her speeches.

"You're smart," he said finally.

She smiled. "Tech smart or tactics smart?"

"Both." He wanted to kiss her, but he couldn't. Not without knowing what was really going on between them. Between her and Dantai. And he wasn't brave enough to ask. He looked down at his hands. "If I'm going to win the tech competition, I'm going to have to survive making this shield." He lifted up the device and held it out for her to see. "What do you know about force fields?"

Calli's eyes grew round. "Nothing except the basics," she said. "This is far beyond what I've done."

For the first time ever, Hoku had surprised her with something he'd built. His chest swelled as if a puffer fish were trapped inside.

"Here, let me show you where I'm stuck," he said. "And then maybe you can stop it from killing me."

CHAPTER 22

THE SUN REACHED the middle of the sky before
Aluna remembered to rip another notch in her sash.
Six days. Six days of stumbling across the burning sand
and scrub in the impossible heat.

Her throat ached for water, but they had only a liter
left and it had to last the rest of the day. At night, Dash
worked his desert magic and found them more. He dug
holes, siphoned moisture from plants, and somehow
extracted it from the small animals they killed. If he
hadn't been with them, they would have died days ago.

That Tayan still staggered beside them was a
miracle. Of course, the wound had been near her
Human heart, not her massive horse heart, which did
most of the work. There were times when she seemed

to fall into unconsciousness, yet still her horse legs continued to walk. Even so, they didn't have long. Her fever had come and gone but now blazed hotter than ever before. Dash cleaned the wound each night—using whatever was left of their water—but it hadn't started to heal. Too much walking, too much stress. If they didn't find a settlement soon, she'd die.

Aluna tried not to talk, but there were days when she needed to. It was easy to get lost in her head out here, traveling for hours in miserable discomfort with nothing to think about except past decisions. Mistakes. Plans for the future that she'd never get a chance to realize.

Today she needed words. A connection. To think about something other than the sharks circling in her mind.

"So," she rasped to Dash, "why does Weaver Sokhor want you dead?"

Despite days of marching, Dash seemed only slightly weary. Maybe he preferred marching to being locked up in a tent waiting for a death sentence.

He gave her a wry smile. "Weaver Sokhor did not appreciate his eldest daughter showing interest in an *aldagha.*"

"Interest?"

"He caught us kissing," Dash said.

Aluna chuckled, her voice cracking.

"We had been lucky for weeks, but then one day it was all over." Dash shrugged. "He could not punish me then, as there is no law against what we did. But he sent his daughter to foster with another herd, and I have not seen her since."

"For kissing? That's terrible!" She raised an eyebrow at him. "I'm sure the kissing wasn't terrible, though." For the first time since she'd met him, his sandy skin grew darker on his cheeks. "I'm sorry," she said. "Weaver Sokhor had no right."

"The thing is, I did not blame him," Dash said. "What Equian would want his daughter involved with me? Our relationship was doomed before it began. I just wish we had not lost our friendship as well. We had always been close."

"Friendship is everything," Aluna said gravely. That's why she was out here in the first place.

"I agree," Dash said. "It is . . . difficult to know what will harm a friendship. I have learned to walk carefully."

Suddenly she wondered if they were still talking about the Equian girl. Her heart, exhausted from the heat, found the energy to quicken its pace. Aluna found she had no coherent response to his last statement, only a jumble of thoughts and feelings swirling inside her like a whirlpool. Better to keep her mouth shut than say something stupid.

By evening, Tayan's skin almost burned to the touch.

"She will not make it much longer," Dash said.

Aluna nodded and pressed a damp cloth to the Equian's face. Tayan groaned. She remained barely conscious, speaking only to spout nonsense or cry warnings about invisible foes.

"You need to go," Aluna said. "Take Tal and find help. Any help. Lie if you have to. Tell them your name is Hoku."

"Why me?" he said. "I am better at tending Tayan. You should go. Tal can carry you swiftly."

Aluna shook her head. "Tayan is beyond our help now, and only you will be able to find your way back to us. You know this desert. You understand it in a way I'll never be able to."

"But Tal—"

"She knows you're a better rider, too," Aluna said. Tal snorted her agreement. "You'll make it farther, and you won't get lost. Take the compass." She held out the battered artifact.

He plucked it gently from her hand, then stared at it in his palm.

"I'm not giving up," Aluna said quietly. "I will never give up. This is my best chance for survival, and I know it. You know it, too."

Dash stood up and started to take Tal's packs off

her back. "We will travel faster this way," he said. "You keep the food and water."

"No. If you don't find someone, we're all dead," she said. "Tayan and I will sit here and conserve our energy. You need the supplies more than we do." She didn't mention that Tayan was barely eating or drinking anymore. They both knew the truth.

He gave Tal some of their remaining water, then stored the rest on his belt without argument.

"Go," she said. "Good luck."

He hopped onto Tal's back, seemingly without effort. Like a leaf on the wind. Only then did he look back at her, his dark eyes filled with even darker shadows in the fading sun.

"You are the bravest person I know," he said.

Before she could answer, he whispered something to Tal, and the two of them were off at a gallop, leaving only a trail of dust in their wake.

Aluna helped Tayan down to the ground and tried to make her comfortable. If Dash didn't find help, Tayan would never get up again. Once she was settled and sleeping, Aluna worked on the fire. She didn't need one for heat, but Tayan would.

The fireboxes the Equians normally used produced warmth and light, but they didn't emit smoke. And Aluna wanted smoke—as much as possible. A nice big plume would help Dash find their camp again.

She checked the ground around Tayan's head for scorpions, spiders, and snakes, but didn't find any. *Good.* She'd be safe while Aluna scoured their surroundings for burnable brush and plant life.

It felt good to use her muscles for something other than walking. She bent and tugged at shrubs, yanked them from the soil, and snapped their branches into smaller pieces. A few tasty rabbits scurried out of her way, but they were in luck. She was far too weak and tired to hunt.

By the time she returned to the fire, the shroud of night had fallen. Aluna set up all four of their fireboxes near Tayan and turned them on. There was no sense in rationing fuel if this was their last night.

She allowed herself two swallows of water and gnawed on a stick of cured cactus, the last of her food supplies. The salt burned her mouth and stung the cuts on her lips, but she sucked on it anyway, grateful that her mouth still produced saliva.

One by one, she tested her desert finds with the fireboxes. Branches from the scrubby trees and tumbleweeds burned fastest but produced the most smoke. She headed off into the darkness, armed with her Kampii vision, and collected as much as she could find. If she was lucky, enough for twelve or more hours. But she didn't burn her stash that night. Dash couldn't have made it very far yet, and no matter how big a pillar of smoke she made, he'd never see it in the dark with his Equian eyes.

Before she slept, she examined her legs. There wasn't enough water to wet the new patches of thick skin, and the growing scales looked pale and unsure, as if they had only halfheartedly decided to form. She couldn't even tell what color they would be. The bones in her ankles had started shifting. She could still walk, but her feet now bent back and forth much farther than before. If anyone saw her bare legs, they would know something was wrong.

More things shifted, too, preparing her for the time when her scaled legs would fuse together into a single tail. She'd struggled to hide herself during their trek, worried that Dash would notice. Stupid, really. They were too close to sundeath to be paying attention to such things. The pain had come two or three times a day, but it didn't drive her to the ground anymore. She'd managed to grind her teeth and keep walking.

She looked at the fire, a vast sadness swirling with hunger inside her gut. A part of her had wanted to see the tail before she died.

She slept to conserve what little energy she had left. Tayan cried out once in the night, but Aluna could find no sign of a snake or critter that might have bitten her. In the morning, Aluna scanned the horizon for Dash. Nothing but endless golden flats and scrub, mocked by the cool promise of mountains in the distance. Their peaks loomed closer now, but still not close enough.

"Aluna," a voice whispered.

Tayan had somehow survived the night. Her face had no color, like the pure white of dead coral, except for flecks of red on her cheeks. Aluna hurried to the Equian's side and swapped out her fever-stained pillow for fresher clothes.

"Do not . . . want to die like this," Tayan said, her voice mangled and weak. "Please. I am a warrior. You know."

Aluna pressed a cloth against her forehead, although they'd run out of water to dampen it.

"I do know," she said. "I know that a true warrior never surrenders. Not in battle, not to sickness, not to anything."

Tayan's eyes closed, and she struggled to swallow. "I hate you," she whispered.

Aluna smiled with cracked lips.

Up in the sky, the sun's ever-present face continued to blaze. Aluna returned to the fireboxes and positioned them in a little square. Then she carefully piled her massive collection of branches on top of all four of them at once.

The flames and smoke were magnificent. Even an Equian word-weaver would have felt at home around her bonfire.

Satisfied, she returned to Tayan and managed to get the Equian's head into her lap. Tayan didn't stir. Aluna ran her fingers over the girl's head wrap as if it were hair, just as her sister Daphine used to do to her when she was sick.

And soon, sunsleep took her.

CHAPTER 23

ALUNA FELT HANDS lift her and put her down again. She heard voices but not words. Her eyelids felt stuck to her face with jellyfish goo. And sandy dirt. It invaded everything. Her mouth, her nose, her ears. Dunes of it wafted around inside her lungs. She tried to breathe, and she could feel it everywhere, burning hot and sticking to her like barnacles.

The voices receded, replaced by the rhythm of hoofbeats and a persistent scraping sound. The fingers in her right hand clutched at the ground but found slick plastic instead. Her head bumped against it. She tried to squeeze her eyes closed even more, afraid to see what was happening. She knew she was being dragged across the desert, but she didn't want to know who was doing it or why. She only wanted sleep and darkness. Soon she found both.

She awoke later, although how much later she couldn't say, and in darkness. She opened her eyes slowly, expecting sand, but there was none. Her hands went to her legs immediately, but she found them safely under a thick layer of bedding.

"You are awake," Dash said. Immediately, he was kneeling at her side. "I was not sure . . . I did not know if . . ."

"Tayan?" Aluna croaked.

"Still in danger, but alive," Dash said. "Her Equian heart is strong—it may compensate for the failing Human one."

"Tal?"

"Fine. Eating far too many mushroom jellies for her own good."

Aluna tried to swallow, but her throat was too dry. Dash handed her a clay cup, and she drank. She'd never tasted anything better.

"We are underground," Dash said. "In Coiled Deep, the last of the Serpenti cities."

"Serpenti," she said. "Your allies."

He nodded and pulled out a sash he'd been wearing under his tunic. It had threads of bright red and orange braided together with strands of gold. Had he been wearing that when she'd first attacked him, months ago, in the broken SkyTek dome?

"It's beautiful," she said.

"Nathif gave it to me the night I helped him escape Shining Moon." He rolled it between his fingers. "I never expected him to return the favor."

"I'm glad you did," she said.

He looked up from the sash. His eyes glittered like eelskin. "So am I."

She smiled. Already she could feel strength flowing back into her limbs.

"Are we safe here?" she asked.

Dash nodded. "The Serpenti are peaceful. There are too few of them left to be warlike. They are cautious of visitors, though, as they are still being hunted by the herds."

Aluna studied the room. It was spherical with a flat bottom, like a bubble resting on the palm of a hand. She reached out and touched the wall. Cool, sandy dirt, covered in a clear sealant of some kind. "The whole city is underground?"

"Yes. I must admit, it is far cooler down here than in our settlements in the sun. No place to run with four hooves, but that has never been a concern for me."

"I should visit Tayan and meet our hosts," Aluna said, and sat up. The world spun wildly but soon righted itself.

"You are recovering quickly from sun exposure," Dash said. "Perhaps all that smoke you made shielded you from the worst."

"So it worked? You saw the smoke?"

"Aluna, there are people living in the *stars* who saw that smoke." He offered her an arm to help her stand. "Tal and I would have found you without it, but not as soon. The smoke saved your lives."

She checked under the bedding and saw her familiar trousers covering her legs. Even her shoes and foot wrappings were still in place. She grabbed Dash's arm and stood slowly. Her legs ached and wobbled, but she couldn't tell if the weakness was due to her fatigue or from her growing tail. She nudged one leg forward and was pleased when it obeyed. They hadn't fused together yet. They could still hold her weight.

When she found her balance, she reluctantly let go of Dash's arm. He took a step away but hovered close enough to catch her if she fell.

"I'm ready for my tour," she said finally. "Do I look presentable?" She looked down. Although her face and hands and hair had been washed, her clothing hadn't. She looked as if she'd been swallowed by a whale and spat back up again.

Dash laughed. "Let us hope the Serpenti are not a fastidious people."

They walked slowly out the arched doorway and

into a hallway lined with other bubble-shaped rooms. A Serpenti boy must have heard them. He slithered out of another room, shut the thick plastic door behind him, and came to meet them.

The boy's sand-colored hair almost perfectly matched the color of his skin. His eyes were a light, vibrant green, the color of kelp in the sun. He wore his hair short, cropped close on the sides and back, but longer on top. A clump of it fell into his face and partially concealed his stunning eyes. Aluna liked his features immediately—they were wide and open, marred only by an old scar that cut deeply across one cheek.

The boy's loose-fitting tunic, very similar in style to the Equians', was made of a thicker material and decorated with intricate patterns sewn with colored thread. Below his waist, the boy's tail swept forward for balance, then curved back under him and undulated on the floor in waves. It was so much longer than a Kampii tail, two or three meters at least. Its tiny scales glittered brown and tan and gold.

"Aluna, this is Nathif," Dash said. "He brought you back from so close to sundeath that I think our great sun may feel cheated."

"Brother Dashiyn is too kind," the Serpenti said, grinning. "It is a pleasure to see you awake, Sister Aluna."

Aluna bobbed an easy Kampii bow. "Good to meet you, too. Thanks for saving me."

"Think nothing of it," the boy said. He waved his hand, as if he'd only given Aluna a drink of water. "We are forever pulling mermaids from the desert these days."

"You are?" she said, confused. How could other Kampii even get here?

Then she heard Dash chuckle. "You will have to get used to Nathif and his jokes. They sneak up on you like thieves."

She looked back at Nathif, his expression now one of exaggerated innocence. "Oh, I see how it's going to be," she said.

"You should know right up front that I am not well liked, even by my own people," Nathif continued easily. "There was talk of trading me to the Humans for a camel and five stacks of wood."

"A terrible bargain," Dash said. "I would not pay more than three."

Aluna laughed.

Nathif leaned in toward her and said, "You see? Dashiyn risked his life and his honor to save me, and even he does not like me." He leaned back and sighed, his eyes sparkling. "I wish I could take you to see your friend Tayan, but she is still unconscious and needs rest. I would ask you to wait a little longer."

"We will do as you wish," Dash said.

"I'm surprised you're trying to save her," Aluna said. "After everything between you and the herds."

The boy didn't flinch. "It is true that Brother Dashiyn's tribe killed my mother and gave me this lovely scar, but we Serpenti do not hold grudges. It is our philosophy to remember the past and to honor it, but to give the future more weight in our thoughts and actions. Even if Tayan herself had struck the blow that sent my mother into endless sleep, we would try to save her."

She looked at Dash. "Is this a joke, too?" He shook his head. She turned back to Nathif. "I haven't met many other people who think like that. With the world the way it is, being so forgiving seems . . . dangerous."

"It is," Nathif said. "We consider forgiveness our greatest strength, even as we recognize that it may also be our greatest weakness. But we never want to be the people we were before our war with the Equians. And, truthfully, we don't have much time left. We will survive this generation and the next, but not many more. The Serpenti will end. We have chosen to live out our time in peace, in the hopes of atoning for our past."

"You do not seem as upset about your fate as the Equians would be," Dash said.

Nathif smiled. "To be upset about the inevitable

would be a waste of energy. We have better uses for our time . . . like pottery and singing!"

Aluna laughed again. She couldn't help herself. Something about Nathif reminded her of Hoku.

"Dashiyn, do you see how Aluna appreciates me? Even though we just met?" Nathif said. "You might try something similar."

Dash reached up and clapped Nathif on the shoulder. "I will laugh when you are funny."

"So cruel," Nathif said, hanging his head. In a flash, it popped up again. "But come! I will show you our city. Perhaps we will find the pharos, as I know they wish to meet you." The snake-boy slithered up the corridor. He moved slowly, his long body pushing him forward with its wave motion. Dash tugged Aluna's elbow, and they followed.

The Healer's Hall, as Nathif called it, opened into a vast bubble room twenty times the size of the last one. Aluna could see other ball-shaped rooms in every direction.

"It's like someone stuck a tube into the desert and blew a cluster of huge bubbles deep in the sand," she said. She turned, trying see all of it at once. "The walls glitter."

Nathif laughed. "Once again, you are astute, sister. The ancients did almost what you suggest! Except their bubbles were lined with a sealant that lets air in and keeps the sand and desert creatures out."

"How big is this place?" Dash asked.

"Far too big for the numbers we have now," Nathif said. "As a child, before my sister grew sick, she and I vowed to explore every nodule. We spent months, but I daresay we never made it to half."

A few clusters of Serpenti slithered across the room, barely pausing to look in their direction. Nathif was right; there were far too few for a city this size. Mirage and Shining Moon had been teeming with Equians. In contrast, Coiled Deep was an old, weak city, drifting slowly toward death.

"So you have a leader, a pharo, just as the Equians have a khan?" Aluna asked.

"We have two pharos," Nathif said. "One rules over the material world and the realm of the body. He guides our warriors and healers, our cooks, our farmers and mushroom growers, and other Serpenti who deal mainly with the physical world."

"The other pharo is of the spiritual world," Dash said. "He guides the artists and singers, the holy ones, the thinkers. At least, I believe that is what you told me."

Nathif grinned. "You remember! How pleasing that you actually listen to me at times. Although Pharo

Rashidi passed into endless sleep, and a woman, Pharo Zahra, guides us now."

"It seems like there'd be a lot of crossover," Aluna said, thinking about the Kampii hunters who carved their spears with shark heads and dolphin motifs. And Kampii fighting, with its complex forms, was almost as much an art as it was a warrior skill.

"You are wise, sister," Nathif said. "Our two pharos remind us of the duality of all things. Many of us wear a golden hoop in one ear, to symbolize the circle of life from birth to night. In the other ear, we wear a triangle with its point down, to symbolize the greater internal riches we can discover as our spirits and hearts grow."

And then, in the distance, Aluna heard drums. An energetic rhythm that set the blood dancing in her veins.

"Ah, the cappo'ra warriors have begun their afternoon practice session," Nathif said. "Brother Dashiyn told me you would be willing to kill all the fish in the sea in order to see them."

"I said nothing like that!" Dash grumbled.

Aluna headed toward the drums. "Let's go see if he was right."

CHAPTER 24

ALUNA STUMBLED THROUGH one bubble room after another. Stylized patterns in bright reds, yellows, and oranges decorated the spherical walls. Occasionally a deep blue or green caught her eye, but she spared no time to examine the art. She'd have time for gawking later, after the cappo'ra training session was over.

Dash and Nathif followed more slowly, laughing at her enthusiasm. She let them. She knew how focused she became when there was a new fighting style to be learned. Her brother Anadar had to suffer through her obsession for years, as she begged to be taught the next shark-style form, the final dolphin-style technique, the advanced knife attacks.

The Aviars had taught her so much about Above World fighting, but their techniques had been designed for warriors with wings. The Equians' styles looked interesting but relied on height and a physical power that Aluna could never hope to attain. How had the Serpenti adapted to fight? With their long, sinuous tails, maybe they were the most like Kampii.

The Serpenti fighters moved and twisted in a great circle inside a bubble that seemed devoted to fighting. Weapons hung on the walls — thick spears, slender swords, fascinating circles of silver hung in pairs. She wanted to study them all. But right now, the drumbeat called to her like a mythical siren. She could not resist its voice.

The drummers bobbed and weaved in the circle along with the fighters. Their tall drums bore the same colors and decorative patterns as the walls. Only a dozen warriors stood in the circle — adult men and women, three older Serpenti, and a handful of children. All of them swayed and clapped to the music, as if they were dancing instead of fighting. Their tails came in shades of tan and brown. Desert colors. But now she started to see patterns emerge: diamonds and stripes and spots of black and gold. Each one was different.

Aluna walked up to the circle slowly, not wanting to interfere with whatever ritual was happening. One of the children saw her, a young boy of eight or ten, and waved her over. He slithered to the side to make room.

Inside the ring, two Serpenti weaved as they faced each other, their long snake tails curling behind them like coiled whips. They bobbed to the rhythm, taking their Human torsos lower and lower until their fingers and forearms could brush the ground. Aluna held her breath.

One of the drummers changed her rhythm, and suddenly the sparring match began. Aluna expected the Serpenti to rear up on their snake bodies, to try to wrestle and overpower each other. Instead, the first warrior—a woman in her twenties—planted both her palms on the ground and stood on her hands. Her tail, freed of its job of supporting her weight, swung around in a wide arc, just like one of Aluna's talon weapons!

The woman's opponent, a much older man with rippling arm muscles, leaned backward so far that his short hair touched the ground. His torso seemed as flexible as his snake body. The woman's tail swung right over him. If he hadn't moved, it would have smacked him in the side. The man dropped his hands to the ground, shifted his weight, and swung his tail in a low arc toward the woman's arms, attempting to knock her off her handstand. She saw it coming. She hopped onto her snake body just as his tail reached her hands.

Aluna stood there, trying to understand the concepts—how they shifted and when; how they used the drums; how they relied on the strength in their arms, but even more on the flexibility of their backs and bodies.

Kampii warriors sometimes used their tails to smack fish and stun them, but they never used their tails as a weapon against an equal foe. Tails were too important, too easily ripped and torn by sharks and Deepfell. Serpenti tails were longer and heavier than Kampii tails, but similar in a lot of ways.

A bright light burned like the sun inside her. *Hope.* Even after she grew her tail, she might still be able to fight in the Above World. She might still be useful.

She wanted to yell with joy and cry with relief, but both would have to wait. Right now, she needed to watch the rest of the match, to memorize every move, every strategy. By the end, her body ached to leap into the ring, to dance and fight along with everyone else. But even as she despised courtesy in general, she respected warrior traditions. She didn't belong in this ring. Not yet.

The match ended when the older man managed to wrap his snake body around the woman's torso, pinning her arms to her sides. Aluna wouldn't be able to perform that move with her Kampii tail, but she'd be more mobile. Anadar always said that every fighting technique could be improved by making it your own. By figuring out how to make it work best for you. And that's exactly what she intended to do.

After six more matches, the last few involving the children, the group broke into pairs to practice techniques, and the cappo'ra master slid toward Aluna.

"Sister Aluna, you are welcome in our circle," the man said. "I am Master Sefu." He had skin as dark as her father's and seemed almost as old. He kept his head slick, a style popular with many Kampii hunters, since it reduced drag in the water. Sefu's body was thick with muscle, and he towered over her, yet his eyes were kind.

She gushed at him then. Words spilled out of her mouth in an endless stream. Her history, her love of learning new styles of fighting, her studies with the Aviars. And, before she could stop herself, she told Master Sefu, a man she'd just met, that she was growing a tail. It was a crucial part of her plea, the reason she wanted—*needed*—to learn this style.

When she was done, the Serpenti master smiled at her, nodded, and then spoke to someone behind her. "Healer Nathif, when will you allow your subject to begin training?"

Aluna closed her eyes. She hadn't realized that Nathif was behind her. And if Nathif was there, so was Dash. They'd probably heard everything she'd just said. Aluna turned slowly, afraid to look at his face.

"I would probably earn myself a concussion if I tried to stop her," Nathif said. "But make sure our bloodthirsty sister drinks as much water as possible. A girl cannot live on battle cries alone. And if she looks dizzy, make her refrain from at least one fight. If you need to tie her to a post, do it."

"The post will not be necessary," Master Sefu said. "Sister Aluna, when would you like to start?"

Aluna looked up — not at the master but at Dash. His face bore no expression. None at all. Not the happiness he showed when she awoke, not the seriousness when he said farewell to her in the desert. Just *nothing*. She should have told him about her tail during their trek through the desert. She'd had time. That he had found out like this . . .

"What are you waiting for?" Dash said blankly. His eyes were dark pinpricks, like a shark's. Then he turned and walked away.

She felt a weight crushing her chest, squeezing her lungs and ribs and trying to snap her in two. Her eyes filled, but she managed to stop even a single tear from falling. She'd apologize for not telling him. She'd find some way to make him forgive her. She'd do whatever it took.

But now, in this moment, she needed to sweat. To move. To fight.

She turned to Master Sefu. "Now," she said. "I'd like to start now."

After she'd practiced herself sick with the Serpenti cappo'ra and scrubbed her skin clean in the sand bath beside the practice area, she went looking for Dash. She found him in the Healer's Hall, sitting by the bizarre web of hammocks that held Tayan off the ground.

Aluna touched one of the many bolts anchoring the contraption to the rounded walls. "What is all of this?"

The silence after the question spread like a great chasm between her and Dash. *Please answer,* she thought at him. *Please.*

"Equians must not lie down for long, or their own body weight begins to crush their organs," Dash said. "I was able to tell our hosts and help them construct a healing basket like the ones we use in the herd."

Aluna studied Tayan's sleeping face. Even in the lantern light, there seemed to be more color on her cheeks.

"She's doing better," she said.

"Yes. The infection is gone," Dash said. "Nathif says she will live, although she may never recover her former strength."

Aluna closed her eyes and let her forehead touch

Tayan's flank. She hadn't realized how worried she'd been until just now. "Losing strength is going to really irritate her," she said finally.

Dash chuckled softly. "You have no idea."

"She'll find a way to be just as dangerous," Aluna said. "It might take her some time, but she'll come up with something."

"Just as you will, when you have your tail," Dash said.

She turned to face him, her heart aching as if he'd stabbed it. She wanted him to be angry. She understood anger. She'd spent her whole life dealing with her father's rage, learning how to throw it back at him. Dash's quiet hurt confounded her.

"I'm sorry," she said. "I should have told you."

"You did not trust me," Dash said.

She winced. "Of course I trust you. It wasn't that. I didn't want to burden anyone with it. Worrying is such a waste of energy. And Hoku and Calli, they expect me to be strong. If they knew that I'd be useless soon—"

"Useless?" Dash jumped to his feet, his dark face finally showing signs of color. "When you broke my arm, was I useless?"

"No, never!" she said.

His dark eyes sparked. "Out in the desert, I called you one of the bravest people I knew. But you are also one of the stupidest."

She jerked back, stung.

"You think your strength is in your arms? Your legs? Your body?" He paced back and forth in the small room. "I grew up surrounded by Equians. All taller, all stronger, all faster, all better equipped to live in the desert. Did that make me useless?"

"No," she said, softer. She never thought about his perspective. Tides' teeth, how could she be so self-absorbed?

"You think your friends need you for your muscle, for the way you spin a spear? Would you love Hoku any less if he stopped playing with his tech?"

She thought of Hoku, of his freckled face and goofy grin, about his terrible swimming technique. There was nothing in the wide world that would make her love him less.

Dash stopped before her. He lifted his hands toward her shoulders, but dropped them to his sides without touching her. "Trust us. Honor us," he said quietly. "Believe that we will pay you the respect you already pay us."

He took a step closer. She forced herself to stare into the hot coals of his eyes.

"Regardless of your strengths or weaknesses," he said softly, "you must believe that we love you."

And then her face was in his hands. Tears streamed out of her eyes, and she heard herself sobbing and saying, "I'm sorry, I'm sorry," over and over again. Dash's arms wrapped around her, and she leaned into his shoulder.

"I don't want to be weak," she said. "I'm so scared of being weak."

He held her close. "Everyone is weak sometimes. That is why everyone needs friends."

CHAPTER 25

Dantai met Hoku and Calli at the horse enclo-sure, a fresh bandage on his foreleg. Hoku frowned. Dantai was supposed to be Shining Moon's best chance of beating High Khan Onggur at the Thunder Trials. Going in wounded was going to seriously hurt his chances.

"Your leg!" Calli said. "How did it happen?"

Dantai limped up to the security pad on the enclo-sure's gate. "One of Weaver Sokhor's men," he said quietly. "After time was called on the match."

"What happened to him?" Hoku asked.

"He apologized immediately, so honor did not allow further punishment," Dantai said. He scanned the area before speaking again. "We do not wish to call out the Weaver until we know who his allies are."

Hoku grunted. "I'm guessing High Khan Onggur or Scorch is on that list."

"I fear you are correct," Dantai said. "But for your own sake, do not say so aloud again."

While Dantai punched a number sequence into the security pad, Hoku noticed the black cords that had been woven into the blue and white strands in his braids. Blue and white were Shining Moon's herd colors, but the black . . . the black was for mourning. Apparently the herd had officially given up on Tayan or the other warriors ever coming home. To be missing for so long in the desert meant death. Always.

The gate slid open, and Dantai whistled twice. Two horses immediately trotted over—a frisky midnight-black mare and a slightly mangier stallion the same color as the sand.

"Nightshade and Sunbeam," Dantai said. "You must learn to ride them before the herd departs for the Thunder Trials."

"That's not much time," Hoku said, eyeing the horses. They seemed so much bigger up close. And more dangerous. One misplaced hoof and he'd be enjoying several broken bones. Back home he'd done his fair share of dolphin-drafting, but underwater it was easy to let go of the dolphin's fins when you were done.

There was no hard, unforgiving ground to contend with, and no uncomfortable sitting. It's not like you could even tell the dolphin where to go — you were just a tagalong, holding on for the speed and excitement.

"Careful with your wings," Dantai told Calli. "Our horses do not spook easily, but they are unaccustomed to Aviars." He smiled at her. The sort of smile that made Hoku want to throw up despite not being sick. "They do not yet realize your beauty."

Calli blushed. Hoku expected her to stammer out some sort of thanks, but instead she said sweetly, "If Aviars are so wondrous, why not let me join Shining Moon, so I can compete in the trials? Aviars and Kampii may not be from the desert originally, but we have a lot to offer."

Dantai chuckled as if she'd made a joke. "The khan has remained adamant on this point. Allies are desired — especially the winged kind — but he does not wish to contaminate our bloodline." Hoku and Calli looked at each other. It took Dantai significantly longer to realize what he'd said. "No offense, of course."

Calli shrugged and mouthed at Hoku, "Equians. What can you do?"

"In the spirit of not *contaminating* any existing herds, is there any way to make a new herd?" Hoku asked. He tried to keep the irritation from his voice, but secretly he wanted a little to leak through. "I mean, if your herds die out over time, there has to be a way to add new ones, right?"

Dantai shook his head and swished his tail. "Bloodlines are at the heart of our culture," he said. "Every herd has a bloodline that stretches back hundreds of years to the dawn of Equian creation. Our khans prove themselves in battle and earn the right to wear the bloodline around their neck."

"How many herds are there?" Calli asked.

"Twelve originally," Dantai said, "but there are only eight now. Three—Whispering Gait, Golden Bow, and the hero Chabi's herd, Flame Heart—were destroyed by the Serpenti in the Venom War. Hero Altan's herd, Wind Seeker, was absorbed by Red Sky."

"'Absorbed' seems like a nice way to say it," Hoku said.

Dantai nodded, his face grim for a change. "Now, let us start our lesson."

Dantai was not a patient teacher. Or maybe he wasn't patient with Hoku. Calli kept opening her wings and letting the air pull her off her horse while it trotted. Dantai only laughed and praised her ingenuity. But when Hoku slid off his own horse—admittedly with great frequency—Dantai grumbled instructions in an ever more irritated voice.

"A couple of saddles wouldn't hurt," Hoku grumbled, but not loud enough for Dantai to hear.

Eventually, they mastered mounting, with the help of a stool, and staying on at a walk. Hoku's thighs ached from gripping his horse's body.

"I had hoped we would make better progress, but I must return to my own training," Dantai said. And then, just to be extra irritating, he added, "Calli, can you please help Hoku? You seem to have grasped the basics better than he has."

She grinned, but not from the praise. Hoku knew she'd be teasing him for weeks.

When Dantai was gone, Hoku slumped on his horse. Sunbeam promptly headed for a bush and began chomping the coarse grass growing near its roots. Hoku looked down at his legs as they straddled Sunbeam's back. The gears and gizmos in his brain started whirring.

"Aluna won't be able to ride Tal when she has her tail," he said. "At least not like this." He'd told Calli about Aluna's news as soon as he could. She hadn't even flinched. Maybe having wings makes you less concerned about not having feet. Hoku patted Sunbeam's neck. The horse grunted but kept munching grass. "Stay still," he told the animal. "Let me see something."

He pulled his right leg up and over so that both his legs were hanging down Sunbeam's left flank. His whole body had twisted in the process. The only way he could sit comfortably was facing to the side.

"That's not going to work," Calli said, trotting over. "You can't ride a horse like that. Try twisting your body so you can see over Sunbeam's head."

He followed her suggestion but couldn't turn very much. Not until he'd shifted his knees forward as well. His body looked like a *Z*.

"Can a Kampii tail bend like that?" Calli asked.

"I'm not sure," he said. "But I do know that we lose our kneecaps and become more flexible. Maybe it'll be even easier for her to sit like this."

"It's not very stable," Calli said. "If the horse bolted, you'd fly off the back. You can't hold on with your legs."

"No," he agreed. "We'll have to build a harness for her tail, something that straps around Tal's body."

"Ooh, Tal won't like that, I bet," Calli said.

He pointed to his knees. "Something to hook her tail around up here." Sunbeam shifted to the side, and Hoku's feet thumped against the horse's flank. "And something to keep her tail protected against Tal's side back there."

"With Aluna's tail on the left, we'll want to put

weights on the right. Tal will appreciate the balance," Calli said. "I wish I had some paper! We should diagram this."

Hoku grinned. "Remember those gyroscopic stabilizers that Rollin had me pull out of the broken hovertray? I bet one of those would work as a counterweight, and help Aluna keep her balance, too!"

"Gyroscopic stabilizers," Calli squealed. "Perfect! In fact, I bet I could use those on the bow I'm designing to help the archer aim while she is galloping or flying."

And they were off. Not learning how to ride, but running back to Rollin's tent for supplies and paper and reference books. Rollin's eyes widened when Hoku told her what they were planning—well, her one real eye did, anyway.

"Take all the gyros," she said. "Some folk think the world of animals and the world of tech should never mix. Me, I just don't like things that can bite being anywhere near my legs. But if you can find a way to make the riding safer and easier, might be that I'll head to the Thunder Trials with you, just to see for myself what all the fuss is."

Hoku paused by the tent flap, his satchel stuffed with supplies. "You . . . wouldn't want to *help* us, would you? You see, we need to build a structure for

Aluna to sit on, but Calli and I aren't so good with construction. . . ."

"Please?" added Calli, her face flushed with excitement.

Rollin said nothing but reached into her sack of hand parts and dug around. "I know I got me an attachment for working with hide somewhere. . . ."

Hoku whooped and rushed to help her look.

CHAPTER 26

ALUNA TAPPED THE GROUND, indicating defeat. Her Serpenti opponent—a woman named Subira—released her coils from around Aluna's chest and righted herself. Her bushy red hair bobbed behind her in a bunch.

"Good match, sister," Subira said, breathing hard. "You have learned quickly."

Aluna flopped onto her back and sucked in air. "Thank you, sister. But apparently I need to learn a lot more quickly, if I'm to avoid being crushed into pulp every time we spar."

Subira chuckled. "There are brothers and sisters here who have not yet learned that skill, even after a lifetime of trying. You are in excellent company."

"You honor me," Aluna said.

Subira bowed slightly and slithered off to rejoin the cappo'ra circle, no doubt in search of another victim.

Aluna rolled back onto her shoulders, then flipped up onto her feet. Once standing, she leaned down to adjust the straps around her legs. They'd be fused completely soon. Maybe in weeks, maybe in months. The sooner she got used to life with a tail, the better. Underwater, young Kampii stayed immobilized in sticky beds while their legs fused. She had no such luxury. The best she could do was bind her legs together so she didn't accidentally rip them apart. And the straps provided protection, too, so she could still learn her cappo'ra techniques without the risk of damaging her growing tail.

She was tightening the bottom cinch when she heard the clomp of hoofbeats.

"Did they kick you out of the mushroom stores again, Tal?" she said without looking up. "You're going to forget how to eat cactus."

"Guess again."

Aluna stood up sharply and found Tayan looking down at her. A tiny hint of pink had returned to her pale cheeks. She'd tucked her wavy brown hair behind her ears, but strands of it strayed across her jawline. Tayan's left arm rested in a sling, and might always do so. The healers had told her that if she used it, she might reopen the hole over her Human heart.

"You're well enough to be out of your room?" Aluna asked. "Without an escort?" The Serpenti might live by forgiving their enemies, but the Equians certainly didn't. Someone should be watching Tayan at all times, regardless of her wound.

"Calm yourself," Tayan said. "Even I would not attack the people who saved my life. At least not without a weapon."

Aluna looked sharply at her, and Tayan twisted her mouth into a weak smile.

"A sense of humor," Aluna said. "Did they insert that when you were unconscious?"

"No, I think being close to death did that all by itself," she said. Her eyes strayed to the cappo'ra fighters in their circle. "You don't find the drums maddening?"

Aluna looked back at her fellow warriors, many of whom were becoming her friends. "I like the drums. We didn't have much music in the ocean, except for whale songs and the endless nattering of the dolphins. But our drummers are some of the best. They spend their whole lives dedicated to it."

"I prefer the natural drums all Equians are born with," Tayan said, stomping her foot. Even such a small display of strength seemed too taxing. She wilted as she stood there, her normally strong shoulders curving with exhaustion.

"Are you going to be able to make the journey with us? To the Valley of the Dead? We need to leave soon," Aluna said. "The Serpenti say it will take several days to get there."

Tayan pulled her shoulders back and lifted her chin. "I will make it," she said. "My father may not believe what that traitor Sokhor has done unless I tell him myself."

"Agreed," Aluna said.

She heard more hoofbeats and turned to find Dash riding Tal at a full gallop toward them. Tal skidded to a stop with a snort, and Dash hopped off her back.

"Come," he said, almost too excited to talk. "Tal and I have been exploring. We found a hidden room. If we do not return right now, I might forget the way."

Tal shook her head and huffed.

"Tal won't forget," said Aluna, patting the horse's neck. "What's in the room?"

A smile spread across Dash's face. "Tech!"

A moment later, Aluna sat sideways behind Dash on Tal's back, her bound legs thumping against Tal's flank. She kept one hand on Tal's back and the other gripped firmly around Dash's waist. Tayan insisted on coming along, so they kept their pace slow despite Tayan's repeated claims that she could gallop if necessary.

"Nathif was right," Dash said. "This place is

immense. It could hold a hundred times the Serpenti who live here now."

They walked from one bubble room to the next. Aluna lost track of which direction they'd come from, but Tal seemed confident. Some bubble rooms were small, others vast. The rooms grew dustier and less used the farther they went, until it felt as if they were exploring an underwater citywreck. Except for the water part, they were.

Finally they entered a room covered in row after row of curved viewscreens. A single smooth desk ringed the wall, its ancient keyboards, knobs, and buttons layered in dust.

"It looks a lot like the place we found in the old SkyTek dome," Aluna said. She jumped off Tal's back and hopped over to the closest wall. She reached out and touched the label under one of the viewscreens. A snake symbol, followed by a series of letters. "What does it say?"

Dash dropped to the ground and joined her. "I believe it is a name. GLITTERSCALE. Perhaps one of the other Serpenti cities." He moved over to another group. "Here is TALON'S PEAK—and SKYFEATHER'S LANDING!"

Aluna used her arms to ease her way along the smooth desk and scanned the symbols below each screen. Snakes, horses, birds . . . *a seahorse*!

"What does this one say?" She pointed at the label, her pulse pounding. "Is it a Kampii city?"

Dash squinted at the tiny writing. "It says SEA-HORSE ALPHA. Does that mean anything to you?"

Memories swirled through Aluna's mind. "It means I was right," she said. "Hoku and I tried to break into an old underwater outpost called Seahorse Alpha right before we came to the Above World. The Kampii Elders had sealed it under a jellyfish web. Then Fathom's shark found us, and we had to swim away."

Dash raised an eyebrow.

She turned to him. "Don't you see? If this room in Coiled Deep has a viewscreen that goes to Seahorse Alpha, then maybe Seahorse Alpha has a viewscreen that goes to this room. It's a talking center!"

She looked at him, Tayan, and Tal in turn. None of them seemed as excited as they should be. How could she make them understand?

"We're not meant to be alone," she said, waving to the screens. "The ancients separated us, but they gave us a way to talk. They never wanted us to be alone!"

Finally, Dash's expression changed from confusion to wonder. He turned to the workstations and started wiping dust from the controls. "Look for a way to turn it on," he said. "If only Hoku were here! He and that raccoon could have the whole place beeping and hum-ming in seconds."

Aluna's excitement faded slightly at the sound of Hoku's name. He should be here for this. She could imagine his face at the sight of this place, could picture his hands flying over the controls.

Dash flipped a switch, and the wall of screens flickered on. All of them stayed dark, just an aura of light around their edges to indicate they had power.

Except one. One viewscreen held a flickering scene, faded and jumbled by horizontal lines. Aluna hopped over to it. Dash and Tayan crowded beside her.

"HERD 6," Dash said, reading the label. "Equians!"

Aluna studied the image. The camera seemed to be capturing the scene inside a tent. A tent filled with stacks of unidentifiable things, with other unidentifiable things dangling down from the roof.

"I know this place," Tayan said. "It is the tent of Rollin, in the Shining Moon settlement!"

Aluna opened her mouth to speak, but movement in the image distracted her. Suddenly a fuzzy vision filled the screen. A vision she recognized instantly.

"Hoku!"

Hoku fiddled with something they couldn't see, and then he looked into the screen, a huge smile on his face. "Aluna! And Dash! And Tayan! You're all alive! I knew it!"

His voice warbled and fuzzed out in places, but

Aluna knew it better than she knew her own. Hoku. *Hoku.*

Calli's face appeared, shoving Hoku's to one side. "Skies below! I'm so happy to see you all, I could cry!"

"Quickly," Tayan said. "Fetch my brother or my father. But tell no one else why. I must talk to them immediately."

Calli nodded and started to leave. She turned back, grinning at them. "It's you. It's really you!" Then she disappeared.

Together, they filled Hoku in on their journey to Coiled Deep. He dropped his voice to a whisper and told them what was going on at Shining Moon.

"Weaver Sokhor will stop at nothing to destroy my father," Tayan said heavily. "I do not understand how it has come to this."

"And on top of all that, we're still not allowed to help in the Thunder Trials," Hoku said. "We even asked about forming our own herd, but apparently you need a bloodline for that." He snorted. "I'm good, but I can't fabricate one of those."

"Fabricating a bloodline would be of no use," Dash said. "You are missing the point."

Hoku raised an eyebrow, and even across the tech-garbled distance, Aluna laughed.

"What are you doing?" Nathif's voice came from

behind them. Aluna turned and saw him slithering through the archway, his face tight and dark and anything but friendly. Her talon weapons were in her palms before she even realized it.

"Tal and I found this room," Dash said, his voice calming. "We were only speaking with our friends."

"No," Nathif said. His eyes normally held round pupils, but now they contracted to thin slits swimming in sky blue. "You were not just speaking with your friends. You were telling everyone—including the thousands of Equians who want us dead—exactly where we are."

He slithered toward them with a sudden burst of speed and slammed his fist down on the control panel. Aluna reached for the viewscreen just as Hoku's face blinked and disappeared.

"We may not have much time left, Brother Dashiyn, but now we have even less," Nathif hissed. "You may have killed us all."

CHAPTER 27

Hoku STARED AT THE VIEWSCREEN, hoping Aluna's face would suddenly blip back into view. He'd seen them all turn, had heard the hissing voice behind them and seen a blur of motion when their communication had been shut off. Were they okay?

Think. He closed his eyes.

Aluna hadn't moved to attack. If they'd been in danger, she would have. If they'd been in danger, Aluna's talons would have been spinning and Dash's sword would have flashed. Tayan was scary enough even without a weapon.

Too bad he hadn't gotten a chance to show Aluna his projects. The force shield worked — at least some of the time — and Calli's improved bow was incredible.

The Equians were going to ink themselves when they saw what it could do. In his opinion, she still needed to work on the name. "Better Bow" just didn't inspire the awe the weapon deserved. Of course, his suggestions of "Silent Death" and "Bow-bastic" were hardly brilliant.

They'd been making great progress on the horse-Kampii saddle harness, too. He'd have to make adjustments for Aluna's weight and the specific shape of her tail, but it was almost ready. The horses in the settlement didn't even mind wearing it during his test runs. At least until he fell or was dragged along the sand. Then they probably enjoyed it a little *too* much.

He sat back on his rickety pile of suntraps and took a slow breath. In a moment, Calli would return with Dantai or the khan, and he'd have to explain what had happened. Together, he and Calli would have to convince the khan of Weaver Sokhor's treachery. Two outsiders. What had he called them? *Wetlanders.* Minutes passed, and his heartbeat slowly returned to its normal speed. Tides' teeth, how long did it take to find the khan? His tent wasn't even that far away.

Hoku stood up and headed for the tent flap. Outside Rollin's tent, the sun had dropped almost all the way behind the mountains, bathing the settlement in a cool, shimmering pool of darkness.

"Calli?"

You're being stupid, he chided himself. Calli could

take care of herself. She was probably just having trouble getting the khan by himself. Or maybe Dantai was in the middle of a sparring match. He should go back to the tent and wait for them.

Then again, what if someone had heard the comm-box? Rollin and Dantai had both told him to be careful, and he still couldn't hold his tongue or suppress his excitement at seeing his friends. Weaver Sokhor could have spies anywhere. They could have been right outside the tent. What if . . . ?

He turned and headed down a tight alley between two tents. It was the most direct way to the khan's. The path Calli would have taken.

"Calli? Calli?"

He hated how nervous his voice sounded. He wanted it to sound strong. Calli was fine—he was simply looking for her. Of course, Weaver Sokhor would benefit if Calli didn't make it to the Thunder Trials. Scorch would be angry that her prey was not delivered. Maybe he'd been counting on Aluna's death, and now that she was clearly alive . . .

"Calli!"

He ran. Down the alley, into another. Around a tent. He glanced behind a pile of storage sacks, kicked open some tent flaps, and ran some more.

"Calli!"

His Kampii breathing necklace pulsed at his throat,

working hard to keep up with his increasingly ragged breath. He peered over a stack of rugs waiting for beatings, faced row after row of clean desert clothes hanging from rope lines.

"Hoku . . ."

He stopped, one hand caught pushing aside a drying tunic. Nothing. Nothing but his stupid heart crashing loud as surf. He grabbed the tunic and pulled it to the ground. Clothes surrounded him, thick as a kelp forest. He grabbed and pulled and ripped, making his way through the laundry jungle with all the viciousness of a shark after its prey.

He grabbed another piece of tan clothing and stopped, his hand inches from the fabric.

A red stain. Fresh blood. A jagged tear. The echo of a knife. He poked his finger through the hole, then gripped the fabric and ripped it from the line.

Calli.

Calli.

Crumpled on the sand, like a pile of wings and old clothes.

He dropped to her side, and she opened her eyes. Water leaked from them. Tears.

"Hoku," she whispered.

"Shh," he said. "Shh. Stay quiet. You're going to be okay. I promise. Don't move."

He turned his head and screamed, "Help! Medic! Come quick!"

Shouts answered him, like dolphins keening through the water to one another. He couldn't even understand the words.

"Don't move," he said again, and brushed a strand of Calli's brown hair out of her eyes.

She blinked slowly, then relaxed against him. He should look for the wound, but he was afraid to move her. Afraid he might make things worse. And so he did nothing but whisper to her about Skyfeather's Landing. About her mother and High Senator Electra, and about how amazing it was that Aluna and Dash and Tayan had made it through the desert alive.

He didn't notice the medics arrive until one of them grabbed him by the shoulder and jerked him back, away from her. He watched them roll her over. They found the wound in her side, but he couldn't see anything around their huge horse legs and massive horse bodies.

What he did see didn't seem bad. The wound didn't look nearly as deep as he'd feared. Aluna could have shrugged off that cut in the middle of a fight. But then why wasn't she moving? Why was she struggling for consciousness?

"Poison," one of the medics said.

"Get her to the tent."

Hoku stumbled back. Followed them. Said nothing. *Poison.*

When Rollin arrived, stinking of oil and sweat, her Human hand on his back, a stream of words for his ear, that's what he said to her. Poison. He wondered, briefly, if he would ever think or say anything else.

CHAPTER 28

ALUNA TRIED NOT TO FIDGET as they stood in front of the two Serpenti pharos. She itched to jump on Tal and race back to the communications room. If she could turn the viewscreen back on, maybe Hoku and Calli would still be there. She hadn't even thought to ask how they were doing. Tayan's news about Weaver Sokhor's treachery eclipsed everything else with its urgency.

Nathif stood in front of them, using his snake tail to make himself taller. A nice trick, and effective, too. In the desert—or even underwater—you didn't mess with a creature that looked powerful. And right now, Nathif looked as if he could snap Dash in two.

The two pharos sat on their red-and-gold-enameled thrones and listened to Nathif explain what had happened. Pharo Zahra's face, dark and serene, never changed. Pharo Bomani, ruler of the material world and protector of the Serpenti, seemed less at ease. His massive snake body coiled and uncoiled around the base of his throne, a visible sign of his agitation.

When Nathif finished, Dash spoke before the pharos could respond. "It is no excuse, but I did not know the danger I was putting your people in when I turned the device on," he said. "I will never be sorry enough for what I have done."

Aluna had never seen him look so stricken. Not even when he'd been captured or condemned to death. For him, this situation was far worse than either of those.

"Your regret will not stop your Equian brethren from killing even our youngest child," Pharo Bomani said. "Our entire culture will be snuffed out, as quickly as the last flame of the last candle in the darkest night."

Pharo Zahra chuckled. It was such an unexpected reaction to such dark words that even Aluna gasped.

"The candle was always destined to die," Pharo Zahra said. Her voice sounded like silk. "Whether the flame is snuffed today or tonight, or even allowed to burn down to its last drop of wax, makes no difference to the world. In the end, the darkness wins."

"No," Aluna said. "It does make a difference."

They all turned to look at her, and she wasn't even sure why she'd spoken. Except Zahra's words reminded her of something. Of the way the Kampii Elders had talked, back when their breathing necklaces were failing and the whole colony had been slowly dying. "Wait and do nothing" had been an acceptable plan of action for them—including her father—but not for Aluna. Not for Hoku.

"Every day makes a difference," Aluna said. "Every day you survive is a victory. And every day you're alive and fighting is a day you may find the answer that wins you another month, another year, another lifetime." She stood there, her legs strapped together and slowly turning into a tail, and felt a familiar surge of anger building inside of her. "You're the spiritual leader of your people," she said to Pharo Zahra. "You, of all the Serpenti, should understand how important it is to fight. Hope is the most powerful weapon we have, and you're not even using it."

Hope. That she could save her people from Fathom. That even now, lost in the desert, she could save her people from Scorch, and Karl Strand, and whatever horrors came after them.

Pharo Bomani rose up on his snake coils. The muscles in his arms bulged as he hefted the long ceremonial pike that had been nestled in a holster on the back of his throne. "Finally, an outsider who speaks the truth."

"The truth she speaks will only bring more pain, more suffering," Zahra said. Her placid expression faded into something darker. "If we hear hoofbeats over our heads, we should welcome eternal night, even before we feel the cut of their blades."

Bomani spat on the ground between their thrones. "You would have us drink poison and do the work for our enemies."

"I would have us choose the method of our passing," Zahra said.

"Lying down and welcoming death is not how we should be remembered!" Bomani countered.

"Wait, please," Tayan said. Somehow, Aluna had almost forgotten that the Equian stood in their group. She'd been so silent during the proceeding. "All is not lost. I do not think the herds understand the situation here. They live off memories and feed on dreams of future glory. If they know—"

"That we are barely here, barely alive?" Pharo Bomani said. "You think pity will stay their hands?"

"No," Tayan said quickly, "but I think honor might."

"There is no honor in slaughter," Dash said. "We need only make our people see the truth of the situation."

Pharo Zahra hissed. "The talk of fools. Making the Equians change their ways is akin to asking the sun to withhold its light."

"The whole world is changing," Aluna said. "We can't afford to live alone in our cubbies and niches anymore. None of us can. Not all of the Equians feel the same way. Just as you two disagree, there are some among them who may welcome peace between your people."

"Peace," Zahra said. "There is no peace while the horse clans rule the desert."

"In this we are agreed," Pharo Bomani said. "I have yet to meet the Equian who values peace."

Dash stepped forward. "I saved Nathif, even though I lost everything I cherished in my life to do so. I gave up the desert, and now even my life itself is forfeit."

No one spoke. Even the rasp of Bomani's snake body coiling against itself slowed and fell silent. Aluna held her breath. When she looked at Dash, she saw everything he loved about the desert. She saw honor and self-sacrifice, skill and kindness. She saw an Equian without four hooves but with the biggest heart. What did the Serpenti see?

Finally, Pharo Bomani said, "There is, perhaps, hope for the Equians."

"And if there is hope for our horse brothers and

sisters, there may be hope for us," Pharo Zahra said. Her dark eyes had lost some of their sharpness. "But what can we do? How do we reach out a hand in friendship before it is severed at a distance?"

"My father will listen," Tayan said. "He is khan of Shining Moon, and our reputation is strong. Except . . ."

"Red Sky," Aluna said. "And Scorch. If Red Sky wins the Thunder Trials, Shining Moon and the other herds must pledge their loyalty or be slaughtered."

"But if Shining Moon wins the Trials, we have a chance for peace with the Serpenti," Dash said.

"It's no good," Aluna said. "We can't put all our hopes on a herd that doesn't even want us." She looked at Tayan, still weak and cradling her arm against her torso. "Tayan is the only one of us welcome among Shining Moon, and she can't fight. I refuse to sit back and watch the fate of the entire desert—the entire world—be won or lost through other people's actions."

"I agree," Dash said.

"Then we must make our own herd," Tayan said quietly. "We must recover one of the lost Equian blood-lines, declare our own herd, and march to the Thunder Trials ourselves."

Aluna looked sharply at her. "Do you realize what you're saying?"

"Of course I do," Tayan snapped. "But I do not

need to give up my allegiance to Shining Moon in order to join another herd. Family groups often form across herds, and no one is asked to give up their herd colors. I will always be Shining Moon. But . . . I am willing to be something else, too."

"Khan?" Dash said.

Tayan's brow creased and her tail swished. But her hesitation was brief. She nodded. "Yes. A herd must be led by a full Equian. I am the only one of us—"

"Besides Dash and Tal," Aluna said.

"Besides Dashiyn and Tal," Tayan amended, "with the proper lineage. My presence will make the other herds treat us with more respect."

Aluna wanted to argue, but she couldn't. Tayan would make an excellent khan—she'd been training for the role her whole life. "Will joining a new herd protect Dash from being killed by Shining Moon?" she asked.

Tayan nodded. "Yes. Normally, no herd would take in an *aldagha,* especially one condemned to death by another herd. But our new herd will be different."

"We have no new herd," Dash said. "The Trials are only a few weeks away, and we must first find a blood-line. There may well be none remaining."

Aluna noticed the two pharos whispering to each other on their thrones. Nathif shifted on his coils, a strange grin growing on his face.

"What is it?" Aluna said. "What do you know? We're trying to save you, as well as ourselves!" Even now, the Serpenti fell back into secrecy. Was there truly any hope for the world while silence and distrust held so much power over its people?

Nathif looked to the pharos and raised an eyebrow. Pharo Bomani hissed and sat back on his throne. Pharo Zahra nodded. "Go on. Tell them."

Nathif turned to face them, his snake body quietly slithering to readjust for the change in direction. "Back when there were more than a handful of us, we annihilated three of the Equian herds. Two destroyed their bloodlines before we could capture them, but one did not. We have kept it safe ever since."

"Which one?" Dash asked quietly.

"Oh, one of the lesser bloodlines, I am sure," Nathif said, feigning nonchalance. Even now, the snake-boy couldn't resist toying with them. "Have you heard of Flame Heart? It is the bloodline of your hero Chabi."

CHAPTER 29

HOKU SAT BY CALLI'S SIDE, her limp hand clutched between both of his. The Equian medics had stopped the poison's progress through her bloodstream, but they had no antidote. Either her body would find a way to defeat it or she would slowly die.

He squeezed her hand and ignored the grumbling in his stomach. Sweat dappled Calli's forehead, even in the medics' tech-cooled tent, even at night. Occasionally, she rolled over or moaned. He leaned close when she did, wondering if she might be trying to speak, hoping to hear his name.

Behind him, the tent flap rustled. Hooves clomped on the carpets layered on the ground. Hoku didn't turn to look.

"Weaver Sokhor has fled, along with two dozen of his allies," Dantai said, his breath coming in gasps. "We did not realize so many were loyal to his cause. We suspect he is working with Karl Strand and Scorch directly—High Khan Onggur would never knowingly use poison."

He knew Dantai and the others had been looking for Sokhor for hours, but he just didn't care.

Dantai clomped closer. "She should never have been used like this, friend Hoku," he said, his voice softer and more humble than Hoku had ever heard it before. And still, he didn't care. He felt tears building up in his eyes and gritted his teeth until they disappeared. He would not cry. He would not be weak, even for one moment, while Calli needed him.

Later—he wasn't sure when—Dantai left. Eventually, Hoku saw the sky lighten through the thick cloth walls of the tent. The Equian medics came at regular intervals, bringing water and liquid food for Calli. Someone put a tray of fruit and meat on the carpet beside him. He ignored it.

At some point, he slept, jolting awake whenever his hand started to slip from Calli's. He didn't want her to recover and find him unconscious, unable to perform even the simple task of sitting by her side. And so he recited formulas in his head and tried to solve the remaining problem he was having with the force shield.

The next time the tent flap rustled, he recognized the smell. And the grunting. And the voice.

"Stupid basic, on your butt when there's work to be done," Rollin said.

He started to turn around, then stopped himself and focused on Calli.

Rollin grunted again, and he heard the thud of something heavy hitting the carpet nearby. He couldn't help it. He looked.

"Commbox won't stop squawking," Rollin said, adjusting one of the dials. "Your friends keep calling, wanting to know where you are, wanting to know about the girl, talk-talk-talking as if I don't have work to do. As if I'm your bleeding message service." She stood back up and dusted off her normal hand on her pants. "What else you want from the tent, eh?"

"Nothing," Hoku said, eyeing the commbox. The dials were just out of reach. "I don't want anything."

Rollin stumbled over and kicked him in the arm.

"Ow! What are you doing?" Hoku scooted away from her, but didn't release Calli's hand.

"Waking you up, you ridiculous basic," she said matter-of-factly, as if her words actually made sense. "You think she wants you to dwindle into a stick? You weren't exactly a tree trunk to start. You think she wants you to give up on your makings?"

Hoku looked at Calli, at her eyes jerking back and forth underneath her eyelids.

"Give up if you want," Rollin huffed. "Great way to show her you care. Great way to help your friends. Time-honored method of being ridiculous."

"You don't know what you're talking about," Hoku said. His body felt weak, useless, but a surge of anger lent him strength. "You don't have anyone except your gizmos. You don't know what it's like to almost lose someone you care about!"

Rollin raised an eyebrow, but the twisty smile on her face stayed exactly in place, as if she'd glued it there. "Don't know loss? Don't know love?" She huffed. "Seems the basic knows a lot about me all of a sudden. And like always, he's wrong."

She shuffled toward the tent flap, her hooked hand scratching her hip as she walked. "I'll be bringing your things. The shield and the girl's bow. I'll work on the horse harness myself. Could use a bit of exercise. Besides, maybe the horse will be my friend, since I apparently got no others." She chuckled and left.

The energy drained from Hoku's body, as quickly as it had come. He was tired. That's why he'd said those horrible things. Rollin had kicked him, after all.

He eyed the commbox. Had Aluna and Dash

really used it again? He eased himself toward it, trying to continue holding Calli's hand. He didn't make it very far. Maybe Calli wouldn't mind if he just held on to her with one hand. He slowly unclasped his right hand, stretched his fingers, and scooted toward the commbox. With his arm outstretched, he was still a few centimeters from touching the knobs.

Rollin knew exactly what she'd been doing when she put it there, he thought.

Calli's eyes moved beneath her lids, but less frantically now. Her pulse seemed weak but steady, her breathing even. Gently, he placed her hand on the carpet and released it.

She didn't even notice. He watched her a few seconds longer, then quietly maneuvered to the commbox, grabbing a piece of fruit from the food tray on his way. He bit into its skin and let the juice run down his chin.

When Rollin returned, she didn't say anything about his move. She only grunted and dropped his force shield and bag of tools by his side. When she turned to leave, Hoku said, "The horse harness pulls to the right. I'm not sure I have the gyroscopic stabilizer calibrated correctly. It thinks Aluna weighs twice as much as it should."

"Perfect for me, then," Rollin said with a crooked smile. Then she nodded. "I'll check it."

As she disappeared out the flap, Hoku wondered if he should have said something else. Something a little closer to "thank you."

He disappeared into his work. Once he'd double-checked that the commbox was ready to receive whatever signal Aluna might send, he turned his attention to the force shield. Two more pieces of fruit later, he'd finally figured out why the force part of the force shield was shorting out every time he activated it.

It frustrated him, the fact that they mostly tried to find new uses for old tech. If Rollin hadn't had the tiny little hearts of a force field lying around her tent, his shield would have stayed an idea in his head, instead of a piece of actual tech in his hands.

"Hoku?"

He looked at Calli, but she was still unconscious.

"Hoku!" Aluna said.

He turned to the commbox, and there she was, looking so familiar, so Aluna-like, that he wanted to reach into the viewscreen and hug her.

Her initial smile faded. "Rollin told us about Calli. How is she?"

Hoku frowned. "She's holding on, but I don't know how long she'll keep fighting. She hasn't been conscious since I found her."

Aluna reached out her hand and touched the viewscreen on her end. "I've sent for Nathif. He's a healer, and the Serpenti know a lot about poisons. Do you think he could talk to one of the Equian healers about Calli? He might be able to help."

His heart leaped. "Yes. I'll make them listen, even if I have to dim the video display so they don't know who they're talking to."

"Great! Now listen. Before he gets here, I have to tell you some things." Aluna launched into a description of their conversation with the Serpenti pharos, and by the end of it, he was a member of a bizarre new Equian herd called Flame Heart.

"So our new herd has two Kampii, one normal-looking Equian, two slightly unusual-looking Equians, and an Aviar?" He lifted an eyebrow. "I have to say, we're not all that impressive."

"Yes!" Aluna said, ignoring his sarcasm. "And Nathif, too, if I can convince him."

"Barnacles! Why don't you invite the entire Serpenti population while you're at it?"

Aluna's brown eyes grew wide as clams. "Hoku, that's brilliant!"

"It is? I was joking."

"I have to talk to Tayan about it. If the Serpenti join Flame Heart, the other herds may not be able to attack them as easily." She looked down. He could almost hear the gears in her brain spinning. When she looked up, her eyes sparkled. "It'll be tricky. Our muddle of a herd is already a little light on actual Equians. But Tayan assures me that herd law is a powerful thing, even when they don't like what it says."

The entire Serpenti city, as part of their new herd.

"So . . . anyone is welcome to join?" he asked.

Aluna grinned. "Fins, hooves, tails, wings—we'll take anyone," she said. "Just not Weaver Sokhor or his traitors."

"I'll do what I can," Hoku said, his own gears beginning to spin.

He heard Dash call Aluna's name from somewhere offscreen. "I have to go," she said to Hoku. "I'm going to talk to Tayan. Nathif will be here in two flashes of a tail."

"I'll go get a healer," he said. "But call back soon!"

Aluna touched the screen again. "You know I will." And then she was gone.

Hoku checked on Calli, then climbed to his feet. One of his legs had fallen asleep. He pounded it as he stumbled out of the tent. First he needed a healer to talk to Nathif. And then, after they figured out some way to save Calli, he had a very important question for Rollin.

When they left the Shining Moon settlement, only half the herd went with them. Khan Arasen sent the other half—all the children and non-warriors—north toward the distant mountains. If things didn't go well at the Thunder Trials, he wanted them as far away as possible.

Hoku had argued for sending them to Coiled Deep. What would be safer than an underground city that the herds hadn't been able to find for generations? Even now that the comm signal had been broadcast, he doubted that anyone would look until long after the Trials. But neither the khan nor Dantai would agree, even when Tayan herself got on the commbox and tried to convince them.

At least the Equian healers had been open to speaking with the Serpenti. With Nathif's guidance, they'd managed to bring a little color back to Calli's cheeks. Hoku considered sending Calli north with the fleeing Equians, but the journey to the mountains would be physically rigorous. And besides, Tayan had promised Scorch that Calli would appear at the Thunder Trials. If he sent Calli to the mountains, she'd just fly back and yell at him when she woke up. Calli didn't get angry often, and Hoku wanted to keep it that way. No, it made more sense to take her to Nathif, who might be able to cure her.

He kicked Sunbeam halfheartedly, and the horse cantered up to Rollin's side. She sat astride Nightshade. Hoku wasn't sure which one of them resented the arrangement more.

"When will we get there?" Rollin said. "Saddle needs more cushion. My horse trots bumpy on purpose."

"The horses all hate me" and "the horses are out to get me" were two of Rollin's most well-used complaints. Hoku listened to them gladly. He owed her at least that much for snapping him out of his despair.

When he'd first asked Rollin to join the herd, he had thought she might cry. She lobbed a circuit tray at his head instead. For Rollin, projectiles were a sign of affection. Now she wore her Flame Heart colors proudly. She'd even painted her hand attachments light blue and yellow.

Hoku and Rollin took turns pulling Calli's sandsled. Hoku tried not to think about the Thunder Trials. He was afraid of change. Afraid that Calli might die from the poison in her body, or that Dash or Aluna might get hurt. He was afraid that if they failed, the whole world would fall into the hands of Karl Strand.

Back in the City of Shifting Tides, his dad always used to say, "Hunt fish, gather clams." He didn't mean it literally, although Hoku had thought that for a long time. His dad meant that focusing on practical, everyday things helped you calm down and gave you a sense of purpose. So now, instead of thinking about all the things that could go wrong, Hoku concentrated on his force shield. During the day he puzzled through the remaining issues in his head, and at night, sitting by Calli's side, he tightened tiny screws and adjusted the shield's complex wiring patterns. His dad would have been proud.

CHAPTER 30

WHEN THEY SET OUT from Coiled Deep on their way to the Thunder Trials, Tayan rode at the front of the group, the Flame Heart bloodline amulet around her neck. Aluna followed right behind her carrying the new Flame Heart banner. Nathif had sewn it, based on Tayan's ideas. The top half was blue, but not as dark as the midnight color the Shining Moon wore. More like the sky, or the brilliant blue of ocean water on a clear day. Golden flames licked up from the bottom of the banner, sewn in a shimmering cloth that Aluna wanted to touch every minute.

But her favorite parts were the details. You couldn't see them from a distance, but up close, Nathif's tiny, meticulous designs sewn into the golden flames started to take shape. A falcon for the Aviar. A seahorse for the Kampii. A snake for the Serpenti. A horse for the Equian. And when Aluna had mentioned that Rollin, Hoku's Upgrader mentor, had also joined Flame Heart, Nathif had added round objects with jagged edges called gears.

Aluna patted Tal's neck and apologized again for the bumpy ride. Hoku had shown her the saddle he was making to accommodate her tail, so she was practicing keeping her legs in the right position—knees forward, atop Tal's withers, and calves and ankles together on Tal's left side. A Serpenti skirt clung to her body from her waist down, tapering all the way to her ankles and thankfully covering her unsightly patches of growing scales.

Both male and female Serpenti wore the same style of skirt—they were tight enough that they stayed in place even during slithering and fighting. Nathif had made Aluna's skirts himself—one out of Kampii green with decorations of gold, and the other out of their new Flame Heart colors. He'd even sewn in a thin lining of sponge that Aluna could soak with water. Her legs needed to be kept wet if she wanted the scales to come in healthy. Aluna loved her new skirts more than any other clothing she'd ever worn.

Although all the Serpenti were technically part

of the Flame Heart herd, only Nathif and a dozen Serpenti had chosen to join them at the Thunder Trials. Aluna was thrilled when the cappo'ra master, Sefu, and his prize pupil, Subira, decided to join them. Five other cappo'ra fighters, two healers, and three warriors trained in weapons rounded out the group. Hoku might be bringing the brains, but she was definitely bringing the muscle.

Most nights, Dash practiced with his sword. Aluna sparred with him, hopping onto her hands and swinging her legs around like a Serpenti tail, trying to knock him off his feet. He was fast and quick, and she almost never caught him. But balancing on her legs, even now that they were stuck together, she could still spin her chain whips—her talons, Spirit and Spite—and occasionally catch his sword arm or even his neck. Dash was faster, but she was creative and had picked up techniques from the Kampii, Aviars, and Serpenti. When he tried to guess what move she would do next, he was always wrong.

Back in the City of Shifting Tides, the Kampii Elders had called her wild and unpredictable. They'd always meant it as a critique. But here in the desert, those very same flaws had become her secret weapons.

The Thunder Trials were held in the Valley of the Dead, on a great flat plain of salt called Ghostwater.

Dash said it was an ocean's graveyard, but it comforted Aluna to be close to even the memory of the sea.

As they approached, tents and bonfires spotted the desert in greater and greater numbers. Vendors hawked food and offered to sharpen weapons. Finally they found themselves winding through campsites thick with Equians.

Most Equians would attack Serpenti on sight and not bother to figure out if they were part of a new herd, but Shining Moon had done them a favor. Despite being furious about Tayan's decision to lead Flame Heart, Khan Arasen and Dantai had promised to spread the news of their coming. The Equians watching them now hurled insults and slurs, but no weapons. Aluna changed her grip on the Flame Heart banner so she could hold it ever higher.

"Let them gawk," Tayan said. "The sooner they see that we are here to participate honorably, the better. Already they will be whispering about Chabi and how Flame Heart has been rekindled. And about how strong and noble the Flame Heart khan is."

Aluna laughed. She still wasn't used to Tayan exhibiting a sense of humor, but she liked it.

Tayan led them directly to the heart of the campsite, where a vast arena had been dug into the ground and a huge pavilion constructed above it. Aluna marveled that so large a structure could have been constructed out here, in the middle of nowhere, so far from any settlement.

High Khan Onggur and Scorch stood inside with a dozen other Equians. It looked like a party, with servants offering food and drinks on trays, and a cluster of Equians stomping and playing instruments in one corner. They must have seen Flame Heart coming, but they gave no indication. Ignoring them was apparently part of the game.

Tayan clomped into the pavilion and pulled out her sword. The bloodline amulet glinted around her neck, easy for everyone to see. Her voice boomed, "O Great Khan! Herd Flame Heart has arrived and seeks official welcome to the Trials."

The High Khan turned slowly, as if someone had offered him a snack and he was considering his answer. The smile on Scorch's face glittered, too white and not at all welcoming. They'd had too much time to prepare for this.

"The Flame Heart bloodline was destroyed in the Venom War," Onggur said easily.

"So we all thought," Tayan said, "but we were mistaken. I recovered the bloodline and have resurrected its legacy."

High Khan Onggur glared. "And you will submit to a test of authenticity?"

Tayan nodded. "Of course, High Khan, so long as the bloodline remains in my possession the whole time."

The smile slipped slightly from Scorch's face. She clearly hadn't counted on Tayan being so slick.

"You have brought one of the three prisoners that you promised to our ally Scorch, and I trust that the other two are not far behind," the High Khan said. "But I see no reason for you to defile our sacred games by allowing the enemy of our people to accompany you."

Aluna loosened her grip on the Flame Heart banner. If she needed to, she could toss it to the ground and have her talons out and spinning in a flash. Behind her, she heard the Serpenti coiling their tails into their defensive pose.

"I have defiled nothing," Tayan said. "All who stand with me are members of Flame Heart reborn. As are Hoku of the Kampii, Calliope of the Aviars, and the remaining residents of the Serpenti city, Coiled Deep. Just as our Equian families may forge themselves in any shape so long as there is loyalty and love, so is Flame Heart forged."

The other Equians in the pavilion stomped their hooves. A man wearing the purple and yellow of herd Swift Wind shattered his cup on the ground.

"Insolence!" Scorch said. "My father would never allow such a disgrace." She said it to Tayan, but her eyes strayed to the High Khan.

Tayan touched two fingers to her heart and bowed low. "Fortunately, my allegiance is to High Khan Onggur of Red Sky, not Karl Strand, and to herd law."

Tides' teeth, she is good, Aluna thought. *Someone should have almost killed her a long time ago.*

High Khan Onggur stared at the other Equians until they fell silent, then turned to Tayan. "My heart calls this a disgrace, Khan Tayan, but when I took the mantle of High Khan, I agreed to listen to a higher calling than myself. According to herd law, and assuming your bloodline is true, Flame Heart is renewed. You are hereby accepted into the Thunder Trials, although you are, by no means, welcome."

Aluna and the rest of Flame Heart cheered. Only Tayan remained calm. "We are honored to be here, Great One. Will you guarantee safe passage for my people?"

The High Khan frowned. "You share the same protections as all herds."

"But your earlier promises still stand," Scorch said sharply. "I was promised the three prisoners."

"And you will have them," Onggur said. "They are

yours the moment the last fight ends on the third day. Am I right, Khan Tayan?"

"You are," she said easily. Too easily. An ice crab skittered down Aluna's spine. Tayan would still hand them over to Scorch, after everything they'd been through. Because she'd given her word.

"You will stay, Khan Tayan, so we may examine your bloodline. Your herd may go and set up your camp."

"Of course, High Khan."

Aluna used the banner to lead Flame Heart out of the pavilion and then turned over the leadership duties to Dash. "Find us a good spot?"

"Any spot will do, as long as it is far from Shining Moon," he said. Tal whinnied her agreement.

"You have my vote as well," Nathif said, slithering up to join them. "Serpenti may believe in letting the past go, but even I do not wish to see the people who killed my mother every day."

In the end, they found a small patch of free land around an empty fire pit on the southern edge of the campsite. Closer to escape, if it came to that. They had just pounded the stake for the first tent into the ground when a familiar voice sounded in Aluna's ear.

"Hoku!"

Almost as soon as she said it, he had jumped off his

mangy horse and tackled her with a hug. She toppled over, her splinted legs no match for his enthusiasm. He stood and helped her up.

"Sorry," he said. "You had two legs when you left. I wasn't expecting you to be so . . . easy to tip."

Dash covered his mouth with his hand, clearly trying to hide a snicker. Rollin, who had come with Hoku, didn't even try. Her raspy belly laugh echoed through the whole camp. There were probably people in Mirage who could hear it.

Aluna studied Hoku's face. His skin was a shade darker, sunburned and peeling in places, but essentially he was the same as ever. Only the darkness under his eyes betrayed his exhaustion.

"Here, let me introduce Nathif," she said. "And then you can take us all to see Calli."

CHAPTER 31

WHEN ALUNA SAW CALLI, she bit her tongue to keep from gasping. The girl's face was white, her tiny body even smaller and thinner than Aluna thought possible. She'd been telling herself that Calli was just sick, that it was temporary. Aluna reached over and squeezed Hoku's shoulder. He leaned into her touch. Tal helped them bring her back to the Flame Heart camp to be with her new family.

Nathif placed his satchel on the ground and put a hand on Calli's forehead. "Warm, but not dangerously so." He took Calli's wrist. "Weak life rhythm, but steady." Aluna marveled that the boy who could spew one joke after the next could also be so serious and calm.

"You and the Equians have done well," Nathif said to Hoku. "Few poison victims survive this long."

"What can I do?" Hoku asked. "I'll do anything you say."

"Excellent," Nathif said. "I would like you to leave the tent."

Hoku's mouth dropped open.

"You have to prepare for the Trials, and I need to save a life," Nathif said. He reached into his back and began sifting for supplies. "I work best without interruptions. And with a belly full of sautéed mushrooms. Right now, one of those things will have to be enough."

Aluna tugged Hoku's shirt and pulled him from the tent. She was tempted to close his mouth, too, but he eventually did that on his own. A distraction. That's what he needed. The Serpenti had almost finished setting up their camp, so she'd have to think of something else.

"Hoku, can I see the saddle?" Aluna said. "The sooner I start practicing, the less likely I'll fall on my face during the Trials."

"Yeah. Sure," Hoku said absently. He found Sunbeam and Tal dozing in the shade of the tent and unhooked the saddle from Sunbeam's back. He turned to Tal, but the look on her face was not exactly encouraging. Hoku hesitated.

"Come on, Tal, we talked about this," Aluna said. "You promised to give it a try."

Tal raised her head and flared her nostrils, but Aluna knew she was only posturing. Tal wanted to win the Thunder Trials as much as she did. The perfect revenge for an *aldagha*.

"Here, let me do it." Aluna hopped over to Hoku and took the saddle from his hands. The material felt smooth and soft in her hands, and it had a strange speckled pattern that reminded her of fish scales.

"Snakeskin," Hoku said. "Rollin and Calli and I collected them for weeks. We treated it with special oils to make it tougher."

"It's beautiful. See, Tal? You're going to be stylish in this," Aluna said.

Tal snorted. Aluna interpreted it as, "Not with you on my back, I'm not."

Hoku helped her put the saddle on Tal's back and adjust the straps. Tal grunted and stomped and flicked her tail, but eventually submitted to the procedure. It fit well, especially after Hoku adjusted some seemingly invisible latches and hoops.

"I built in some air bladders, which we can adjust to make the fit more snug," he said. "Climb up, and I'll show you how it works."

Aluna vaulted onto Tal's back and maneuvered her

legs into position. Her arms had grown strong from her cappo'ra training in Coiled Deep. She could walk on them now, if she wanted. Not for very long, but for greater distances every day.

"Hook your knees around that," Hoku said, pointing to a curved piece of snakeskin. "That will keep your tail in place and help you stay attached to Tal if she jumps. Now wrap your ankles to the side, and strap them in here."

Aluna did as she was told, amazed that everything seemed to work. Hoku had to shift the straps forward a little to make them hit her ankles properly, but the fact was, he could. He'd built the saddle so it could be adjusted.

"We may have to alter this slightly when you get your full fins," Hoku said. "I wasn't sure how you'd want them to sit, and we'll need to protect them somehow."

"I'll let you know when that becomes a problem," she said.

"One last step," Hoku said. He walked to Tal's other side. A strange bag hung down from the saddle on that side, the side without her legs. He opened the top, pulled out a spherical device, and began flipping tiny switches along its surface. "Tal, this stabilizer will help balance Aluna's weight on the other side. You'll have to let me know if you want more or less pull on this side, okay?"

Tal whinnied, apparently very pleased that her needs had been taken into account. She twisted her head back and snorted into Hoku's nose. He sputtered.

"She's happy," Aluna said.

"Horse breath," Hoku gasped. "Not my favorite display of affection."

Aluna chuckled. "Is everything set?"

Hoku dropped the stabilizer back into the bag and cinched the top shut. "Yes, go ahead. Please take it slow at first, since we haven't tested—"

"Swim!" Aluna whispered into Tal's ear, and the horse bolted. Hoku jumped back out of the way. Tal would never have hurt them, but he didn't know that. No one knew Tal like she did. Even now, the horse threaded through the crowded camps, nimbly dodging Serpenti and Equians alike.

Aluna felt glued to Tal's back, completely secure. As Tal dodged people and campfires, joy swelled in her heart. When they finally broke free of the congested tents, Tal burst into a gallop. Aluna lowered herself forward, her chest almost directly on top of the crook on her knees.

They were wind over sand. They were sunlight on the surface of the ocean.

Tal cut left and right, testing the saddle. Aluna learned to throw her weight into the turn to help Tal take it faster. Eventually, she pulled out her talon weapons and spun the chains as they ran. She had to adjust her angles and force to account for the wind resistance, but the chain whips whizzed at her side or over her head, ready to be redirected at an enemy.

She and Tal ran and played and drilled for hours. Aluna practiced unhooking the latch on her ankles so she could dismount quickly if she needed to. Tal laughed at her early attempts, especially the ones where she ended up face-first in the sand. But eventually, Aluna could mount and dismount almost as easily as when she rode bareback.

Hoku had given her the best gift ever. Not just the ability to fight from horseback, but a future.

The sun had fallen low in the sky by the time she returned to camp. The Flame Heart banner—now attached to the center pole of a tent—waved clear and proud. She found Dash making their herd's bonfire, and Hoku munching cactus strips while he watched.

She and Tal slid to a stop by the fire. She knew how they looked—dirty, sweaty, and covered in sand and scrapes. Hoku looked at her, a question clearly in his eyes. She grinned at him and rattled off the list of adjustments she and Tal wanted.

"I think I can do most of those," he said, nodding.

His eyes already had that distracted look they got when he was thinking happy tech thoughts.

"Good," she said, still breathing hard. "But before you get into it, I need another favor first."

"What?" Hoku said.

Dash poked at his growing fire and laughed. "The shield, Hoku. She wants you to give her the shield."

Aluna grinned at them both with her grimy, sweat-slicked face. "Show me how to use it," she said to Hoku. "I've got some Thunder Trials to win."

The look on his face drooped. "It's not ready yet. Not unless you want to lop off your arm the first time you use it."

"I'd prefer a non-lopping shield if possible," she said.

"Non-lopping. I can do that!" And he was off, scrambling to his supply packs. When he returned to the fire, he had a small, curved piece of metal in one hand and a bag full of tools in the other. He bellowed for Rollin, and she came out of her tent with a stream of words Aluna had never heard before. But she quickly settled near Hoku and started poking his device and offering suggestions.

Aluna sat next to Dash and watched the fire.

"He is not going to talk to us again the rest of the night, is he?" Dash asked.

She shook her head. "You're stuck with me."

CHAPTER 32

THE NEXT DAY, Tayan held a Flame Heart meeting on a salty-white plain away from the ocean of Equian campsites. Flame Heart numbered almost twenty, a pitiful size for a herd, but it made Hoku's heart swell to see so many people willing to risk everything. They were all his brothers and sisters now.

He sat on Sunbeam, Aluna rode Tal, and Rollin had apparently not managed to kill and eat her horse, Cactus, as she had threatened, because he stood reluctantly beneath her now. Dash now rode a glossy brown mare named Sandwolf, purchased at great price from Shining Moon and only after much negotiating on Tayan's part.

Tayan raised her sword in the air.

"Herd Flame Heart, welcome to the Thunder Trials!" she yelled.

Hoku cheered, along with everyone else.

"Tonight, we will go to the Ceremony of Flames, which begins the tournament. Afterward, you must enter your name in the rolls for one of the three tournament paths — the Path of Sun, the Path of Moon, or the Path of Sand. You may enter only one."

Hoku nodded. The Path of Moon contained the contests for tech, food, art, word-weaving, music, and textiles. Rollin would enter her air-cooling device, and if Calli recovered in time, she could enter her bow. Tayan would enter as a word-weaver, now that she could not fight. A Serpenti agreed to enter the food competition, despite snake bellies being entirely different from Equian stomachs. And Nathif would enter the textiles competition with his Flame Heart banner. Whichever herd had the greatest point total in all the categories combined would win the Silver Disc of the Moon.

Dash and most of the other Serpenti would compete in the Path of Sand, which contained all the trials of skill — spear, sword, bow, strength, agility, and even falconry. Dash was certain to win the falconry contest, if only they could buy or trade for a falcon in time. Shining Moon had refused to sell any of theirs, as it increased their chances of winning if Dash couldn't participate. The Bronze Disc of the Sand would go to the herd with the highest combined total in the Path of Sand competitions.

The final category, the Path of Sun, was both the most important and the most deadly. It contained only one competition: combat. After two days of bouts, the final two competitors would face each other the last night of the Thunder Trials, after all other competitions had been determined. The winner would earn the Gold Disc of the Sun for his or her herd.

The Sun Disc trumped the others. Unless another herd won both the Moon Disc and the Sand Disc, the winner of the Sun Disc was considered the winner of the entire games and would earn the title High Khan and the right to rule the herds for a full year.

Flame Heart would enter six competitors in the Path of Sun: five Serpenti warriors and Aluna. If any of them won, or if Khan Arasen or Dantai from Shining Moon was the victor, then Red Sky would lose power and their alliance would be meaningless. Scorch and Karl Strand would find enemies instead of allies among the Equians.

When Tayan was done speaking, Aluna nudged Hoku. "You should put the shield in the tech competition. I bet you could win."

"No doubt he would win," Rollin said, idly kicking

her horse as it munched on a shrub. "Best tech I've seen in ages, and it doesn't even work yet."

"Then it's decided," Aluna said. "We need that victory. If I don't get the Sun Disc, we'll need both the Moon and the Sand in order to take the desert from Onggur."

Hoku looked at Aluna. She was short, even for a Kampii, but her arms and shoulders bulged with muscle under her brown skin. She wore her hair short—less as an afterthought now, and more like a style. Instead of hiding her growing tail beneath layers of desert cloth, she had wrapped it in a glittering Serpenti skirt.

So far from the ocean, she was more herself than he had ever seen her. Then again, he was more himself, too.

"No," Hoku said.

"What do you mean, 'No'?" Aluna said. "This isn't just your decision. It's about the good of the herd."

"Spoken like a true Flame Heart," Dash said happily.

"This *is* about the good of the herd," Hoku said, squaring his shoulders. If Aluna wanted a fight, he was ready for it. "I didn't build the shield to sit on a judging table. I built it to protect my best friend."

They all stared at him. Even Aluna. He could tell

the anger had washed out of her like a tide. She took his hand and squeezed.

"Spoken like a true Flame Heart," Dash said again. And the discussion was over.

As the sun began to set, the campsites filled with nervous excitement. Over in the Sun Stadium, Equians were building the great flame that would burn throughout the night. Already, a huge plume of smoke twisted and curled into the darkening sky.

Hoku tugged on his shirt and checked the neckline for the third time. Nathif had shown him how to attach the light-blue and yellow Flame Heart colors with tiny stitches. He'd enjoyed doing such simple, focused work while sitting by Calli's side. He wished Calli could join him at the ceremony, but she still hadn't woken. Her face had more color, he was sure of it, but Nathif refused to tell him that she would live. "I do not believe in jinxes," Nathif had said. "But I do have a decent respect for them."

"Hoku," Aluna said. "You ready?" She carried the Flame Heart banner, her eyes dark like deep ocean in the fading light. Dash rode beside her, his chin high, his dark hair streaming behind him. No one wore head wraps to the Ceremony of Flames. They were to "meet and know their Equian kin, bonded by the heat of fire."

"We're together again," he said. "I'm ready for anything."

She smiled, a smile just for him.

Drums echoed in the distance.

"The call," Dash said, sitting taller on his horse. "The drums call to all Equian warriors across the desert, asking them to come and give honor to the sun and moon and sand."

Ahead of them, Tayan raised her sword. "Flame Heart!"

Hoku and the rest of the herd yelled, "Flame Heart!" in response, and they were off.

Tayan kept their pace slow and stately, letting all the lingering herds take a good, long look. Most had never seen a living Serpenti, and none had ever seen a Kampii growing her tail. *If only Calli were here with her glorious wings,* Hoku thought. No one could see them and not want to fly.

They wound their way through the campsites toward the arena. Hoku couldn't speak. After so many months of travel and sweat and tears, his head and heart felt too full, too heavy, too amazed. Six months ago, he'd spent most of his days inside his cramped Kampii room tucked under a coral reef. Now he rode in the Thunder Trials, part of a newly awakened but ancient herd.

The Sun Stadium had been dug out of the salty

Ghostwater ground. In the middle of the vast arena, a huge bonfire blazed. It looked as if the Equians had trapped a piece of the sun itself.

The herds arriving at the arena joined a line that wound down around the rim of the stadium. Once they reached the bottom, they bolted into a gallop. They circled the bonfire three times, once for each day of the Trials, once for the sun, the moon, and the sand. Then, amid the cheers of the other herds, they found their way to an empty space near the bonfire, making sure to leave enough room for the next herd.

Hoku's pulse quickened as Flame Heart edged its way into the stadium, waiting its turn. Some herds had brought hundreds of competitors and thousands of spectators. When Red Sky, the largest herd, entered the stadium, Hoku finally understood why the games were called the Thunder Trials. So many Equians pounding the ground as they ran shook the very sky.

When Flame Heart's turn finally came, Hoku found himself grinning. Tayan yelled and raced forward. He didn't wait. He kicked Sunbeam, and the horse launched itself into the arena, following its leader. Aluna and Tal surged ahead, keeping just behind Tayan. Dash galloped at Tayan's other side. Behind him, Hoku heard Rollin whooping and cheering on her horse, Cactus.

But the Serpenti surprised him most. He'd

expected them to make no noise except the quiet hiss of their snakeskin against the sandy ground. Instead, they spread out behind Tayan and the other horses in a triangle, holding their Human heads and torsos low, just a meter above the ground. Every few seconds, in time with the Equian drums, the Serpenti bobbed their bodies up and slammed them down, driving their fists into the earth.

Boom. Boom. Boom.

Hoku yelled and thrust his fist into the air.

Aluna screamed, "Flame Heart!"

Dash yelled, "For the honor of Chabi!"

Hoku felt the heat of the giant fire on his cheeks, felt Sunbeam's skin break into a sweat beneath him. He wanted to race in that circle forever, yelling with his friends, always on the verge of battle, but never actually entering it.

Too soon, their laps were done, and Tayan led them to their spot in the circle, where they could watch the remaining herds enter the arena.

Hoku's breathing necklace pulsed bright as the sun slipped all the way behind the mountains and the last herd finished its run. When High Khan Onggur finally appeared on the high podium overlooking all the competitors, Hoku knew that he was ready. The drums had called them, and they had answered.

Here we are. Flame Heart. Our hearts aflame.

CHAPTER 33

ONCE ALL THE HERDS were arrayed in the stadium, torches burst to life in the pavilion. High Khan
Onggur, illuminated by the flickering fire, seemed even
larger and more impressive than ever. A ring of Red
Sky warriors stood around him, and Scorch, her red
shirt now embroidered with orange-and-black flames,
smiled easily at his side.

Aluna studied her. She knew exactly how to get
what she wanted from Onggur, and to make it seem like
it was his idea. A whispered bit of advice here, a poke
at something sensitive there. Scorch wasn't the ruler of
the desert by name or title, but she was something far
more powerful. The hidden danger. The shadow controlling everything. Without Scorch, the desert herds

would have united against Karl Strand. Instead, they were about to become his greatest weapon.

Scorch. If Aluna had the chance, she'd have to kill her. If she could. The Scorch they'd encountered in Mirage had seemed indestructible—fast, strong, cruel. Great White with a lot more malice.

Dash moved Sandwolf next to Tal and leaned in. The wind tossed his long hair against Aluna's cheek. "You look angry," he whispered.

"I am," she said. "But it's a good thing. I need it."

He nodded and leaned back.

"Do you think we have any chance of winning the Trials?" she asked him.

Dash looked up at the night sky. The bonfire made the stars hard to see. When he turned back to her, his eyes glowed like embers.

"No," he said. "I want to say yes, but I cannot. We have no chance."

Aluna nodded. "Thank you for being honest."

The corner of his mouth twisted into a smile. "It is the best way I know to show respect."

Aluna watched Onggur speak and Scorch hover in the shadows.

"We're going to fight anyway," she said. "With everything we've got. As if we *do* have a chance."

"Yes," Dash said. "We are."

Aluna returned her attention to High Khan

Onggur just as he held up his hand for silence. The crowd hushed until only the crackle of the bonfire filled the night. "You all know of our alliance with Karl Strand and his esteemed daughter, Sand Master Scorch," Onggur said. Weak cheers echoed up from the stadium. "I am now proud to announce that our bond has grown even stronger."

"Where is he going with this?" Aluna whispered.

Dash frowned. "Nowhere good."

High Khan Onggur unsheathed his sword and held it above his head. "Welcome Scorch, newest member of herd Red Sky!"

Red Sky and their allies cheered.

"You know what this means," Dash said.

Aluna swallowed, her pulse suddenly thick in her throat. "It means Scorch is going to compete in the Thunder Trials. It means Flame Heart has to beat her, too."

When the crowd quieted, the High Khan officially started the games. He yelled, "May we honor the sun!" and slashed his sword through the air. Thunder rolled through the night as more than a thousand Equians stomped the ground and cheered.

Tayan raised her sword and led Flame Heart up the stadium's edge, away from the bonfire. Aluna saw the other herds doing the same.

"The word-weaver competition begins now," Tayan said. "We will each perform one time each night. Stay if you wish, but I recommend you go back and sleep. Tomorrow the Trials begin. You will need your strength."

Aluna touched two fingers to her heart and bowed to her khan. "Wise words from a wise leader."

Tayan bowed in return and granted Aluna a rare smile.

"It's our fault about Scorch," Aluna said. "What we did with Flame Heart, that gave High Khan Onggur the idea of adding Scorch to his herd."

"It gave Scorch the idea," Dash said. "She is the one behind this."

"I agree," Tayan said. "But no doubt he has alienated some of his Equian allies with this decision. Perhaps it will be to our advantage in the end."

"No one can beat her in fair combat," Aluna said. "I think they've just won."

"You have not seen us fight," Tayan countered easily. "Flame Heart's warriors may not claim the Sun Disc, but there is still hope for Shining Moon. Both my father and my brother are highly skilled."

Aluna frowned. She didn't like the fact that Flame Heart's khan had more faith in another herd. But up until a few weeks ago, Tayan had been Shining Moon from the tip of her horsey tail to the top of her Human head. Tayan didn't believe in Flame Heart yet, but Aluna would give her a reason to change her mind.

Tal took her up the slope of the stadium, toward the Flame Heart campsite. Aluna desperately wanted to find open sand and run as far and as fast as she could. She'd done that all the time in the ocean, swimming off on grand explorations minutes before she was due to meet her father or finish a chore. She needed speed. And space. And time away from everything she knew.

Tal huffed and pranced, sensing her mood. Tal wanted to run, too. The two of them were made for each other, a spirit of water and a spirit of sand.

"Not tonight," Aluna said, patting Tal's neck. "If either of us got hurt tomorrow because we were too tired, I'd never forgive myself."

Tal snorted in disgust.

"And besides, we have work to do," Aluna said. "All this time, we've been training to fight Equians. Now we need to figure out how to beat Scorch."

The next morning, Aluna reported to the Path of Sun record keeper and was assigned Ring Three for her day's bouts. Only the warriors with the most victories would continue to the elimination rounds on day two, and only the last two competitors would fight in the evening of day three for the coveted Sun Disc.

Bouts all day! She shook her head and patted Tal. Equians and their stamina. How could anyone compete against a people built from horses? She turned to head up to Ring Three, but Scorch stood in her way. Up close, her resemblance to Karl Strand and Fathom was even more noticeable. If her eyes had the capacity for kindness, she'd look just like a female version of Karl from the photo they'd found. The one taken before his son had died and he'd apparently lost his mind.

"What do you want?" Aluna said.

Scorch laughed. "Why, to wish you well, of course. I hope you survive long enough to fight me."

Aluna smiled. "Oh, I will. I'll survive long enough to beat you."

The humor disappeared from Scorch's face. "Big talk from a fish who couldn't even kill my brother when she had the chance."

Aluna flicked her wrists and felt the smooth silver capsules holding her talons drop into her palms.

"Oh, yes, I've had time to hear all the news now," Scorch said. "Trust me when I say you would never have left Mirage alive if I'd had my way."

"You want to fight right now?" Aluna popped open her talons. She sat on Tal, a good meter higher than Scorch's Human body. But Scorch herself was far from Human. "I'm only here for you. To end you. To drive another harpoon deep into Karl Strand's side. You want to fight right now? Then let's go."

Scorch lifted a hand and pushed a lock of Karl Strand's brown hair out of her eyes. A delaying tactic. Aluna's suggestion had apparently taken her by surprise.

The fake smile reappeared on Scorch's face. "Fight? Now? Why, that's not how we do things in the desert, little fish. It's good to see that none of the Equians' honor has rubbed off on you while you've been here."

"You are the last person in the world who has the right to lecture me about honor," Aluna said quietly.

"You'd prefer my father did it?" Scorch said. "I admit, Father has always had an interesting take on the concept. But, no," she said. "You'll never see Karl Strand or be part of his glorious vision of the future. You won't make it past these trials. I guarantee it."

Aluna should have walked away. She had fights to prepare for, and Scorch was already in her head.

"You remind me of someone," Aluna said, pretending to think. "Oh, that's right! You remind me of your brother Fathom, right before I drove him to his knees."

Scorch's left eye twitched. Her fists clenched.

There, Aluna thought. *Now I'm in your head, too.*

She nudged Tal, and the two of them kept walking. So Scorch knew about Fathom and HydroTek, beyond what they'd told High Khan Onggur back in Mirage.

Even if Flame Heart won the trials, there was no way Scorch would let her or Dash or Hoku or Calli leave the desert alive.

Ring Three turned out to be a large circle of salty earth surrounded by a low wall of sandbags. Competitors prepared on one side of the ring while spectators stood on the other side, eating and drinking and placing bets. Clanking armor and the clop of hoofbeats filled the air. Aluna smelled horse and sweat, metal and oil. A few meters from the ring, Human and Equian vendors sold food to the waiting spectators, adding the scents of sizzling snake and grilled cactus to the air. She even spotted a few Upgraders mixed in with the crowd.

The Equian running Ring Three took her name and gave her a sash to loop across her body, shoulder to hip. It was light blue and gold, with a large golden sun sewn in the middle. She was officially a Flame Heart on the Path of Sun.

She scanned the crowd, looking for Master Sefu or Subira. They must have been assigned to different rings. *Good.* Then all three of them had a chance of making it to the finals. A Serpenti warrior named Okpara had been assigned to this ring, but no one considered his chances good—not even Okpara himself.

"No killing blows," the Ring Three fight master said to Aluna. She wore rainbow colors in her head wrap, a sign that for the tournament, she owed allegiance to all herds and to none. An impartial judge. "You are allowed your horse and whatever weapons you choose. Should you and your horse become separated during the fight, only one of you can continue."

Aluna nodded.

The Equian smiled suddenly. "They'll try to spook your horse," she said. "No one has ever competed with one before. They'll go for her first, to weaken you right away."

Tal snorted and reared her head back. Aluna put a hand on her neck to calm her. She needed them to think that Tal was just a dumb animal, not an animal with full Equian intelligence.

"Thanks," Aluna said. "But why are you helping me?"

The woman shrugged. "I like a good fight. It honors the sun, and it honors us all."

Aluna touched two fingers to her heart. "I aim to give you one."

The woman laughed and shouted, "Next!"

CHAPTER 34

ONCE ALUNA AND TAL were off to the Path of Sun area, Hoku headed to Calli's tent to work on his force shield and keep her company. Or maybe she was keeping him company. He pushed open the flap and almost smacked into Nathif. The snake-boy towered above Hoku and wore a wide grin on his face.

"You're so quiet with your slithering," Hoku grumbled. "Would you consider wearing a bell, or a tiny piece of tech that beeps every few seconds?"

"Keep joking, merman," Nathif said, pushing a clump of blond hair away from his eyes. "After enough tries, you are bound to make a funny one."

Hoku searched for a witty comeback but decided he was too tired. He actually liked the way Nathif teased him. There was no malice to it, and Hoku enjoyed the verbal sparring. At least he did when he was more awake. "I'm saving my brainpower to get this shield working."

"Excellent," Nathif said. "I hope your tech savvy exceeds your wit."

Hoku opened his mouth in the hopes that something brilliant would suddenly appear there, but a weak voice from the back of the tent saved him.

"Hoku's the smartest person I know."

"Calli!"

Nathif's grin grew even bigger as Hoku shoved past him. Calli sat propped up by pillows, her wings arrayed to each side, her eyes bright. He fell to his knees next to her.

"You're awake!"

She giggled.

"Yes, I know that's obvious now that I've said it," he said. He stared at her, at her pink cheeks, her small smile, her hands wrapped around a piece of half-eaten fruit. "I have so much to tell you!"

"I have already told her about Flame Heart and the Serpenti," Nathif said. "I am afraid I was not the most . . . calming image for her to see when she first opened her eyes. I thought she might like to know why a half-snake stranger was changing the dressing on her wound."

"I wasn't scared," Calli said. "Well, not until Nathif started telling jokes."

"You're awake," Hoku said again. It seemed to be the only thought in his head. "I can't believe it."

He heard Nathif chuckle. "I am an exceedingly good healer."

The tent flap opened again. "Good thing, because you make a terrible doorway," Rollin said. "Move aside, you wiggly thing, before I screw on my hook. Taken care of more than a few snakes in my day."

"Hi, Rollin," Calli said. Her voice rasped.

"Good girl, waking up," Rollin said. "Can you walk? Sign-up for the Path of Moon only goes till high sun."

"No," Hoku said. "She needs her rest."

Calli's eyebrow quirked up. "I can speak for myself."

"I . . . of course you can! It's just that you've been so sick. . . ."

"She is weak, but the poison is entirely gone," Nathif said. "The sooner she is up using her muscles again, the better.

"It's okay, Hoku. Really," Calli said. "I promise to drink lots of water and rest whenever I can." She turned to Rollin. "Can you help me up? I think I can make it if I can lean on someone and if someone can carry the bow."

"I will go register at the textiles tent," Nathif said. "Now that my more important work is done."

Hoku stood quickly and grabbed his sleeve. In the filtered sunlight of the tent, the pupils of Nathif's eyes slitted into lines. "Thank you for saving her," Hoku said. "I don't how I can return the favor."

"It was not a favor. Healing the body is what I do," Nathif said. He started to slither out the door, then turned back. "Although I do enjoy a good sandwich every so often."

After he left, Hoku grabbed Calli's bow and Rollin helped her stand. Together, they walked slow as starfish to the "Gizmo Tent," as Rollin called it, and Calli entered her bow.

Rollin had already registered her cooling device in the competition. Hoku wished she'd made an effort to clean it up first. A shiny knob and a sleek surface would have made it look so much more impressive than the bundle of exposed wires and grime she'd submitted. Still, it worked. And it used far less energy to put out a lot more cold than the Equian devices. It just wasn't very exciting. He'd wanted her to enter her mechanical eyeball, but Rollin had just glared at him and screwed something dangerous looking onto her arm socket.

"I'm going to stay here," Calli said after she'd gotten her sash. "Rollin and I can be called up to demonstrate anytime today or tomorrow." She reached over and squeezed his hand. "Don't worry. It feels good to stretch my wings."

"Take care of her, Rollin," Hoku said. "And, Calli, don't let Rollin start throwing things at the other competitors. She has a bad habit."

"Good habit, if you ask me," Rollin grumbled. "Now, go get that shield working. Pretty pieces of metal that lie there and fizz aren't going to do Aluna any good."

He wished them luck and left, an odd pang in his chest. Maybe he should have entered the tech competition after all. Everyone thought his force shield would win, assuming it worked. No one had ever had that much faith in him back in the City of Shifting Tides. To win something like this—entirely on his own— would have been big. *Great White* big.

He changed course and headed toward the Path of Sun rings. He didn't get far before the smell of sizzling scorpions hooked him and reeled him in like a fish on a line. His feet took him to a cluster of vendors strategically located between the fighting fields.

"Tadder's tasty treats, renowned throughout the desert," a Human man called. "Thunder Trials special, a stick of five scorpions for the price of six!" The Equians crowding his tent laughed. "I kid, I kid. I'll give you five for six tokens, I mean. That's how generous I am. After you eat 'em, you'll want to pay me ten. That's how good Tadder's tasty treats are!" The Human, probably Tadder himself, was a burly walrus of a man, with curly brown hair poking out from his head wrap and covering his face from his nose south.

Hoku's nose pulled him toward the tent. He squeezed his way to the front of the line, not trying to cheat, just trying to get a better look at the food sizzling on the grill rock. Sometimes being a scrawny Kampii in an ocean of horse-people was a good thing.

When Tadder saw Hoku, his face brightened. "Ah! A two-legged friend, here to sample my food. Excellent!" He turned to his Equian cook. "Tend the masses for a minute, Jochi." He motioned for Hoku to join him at the side of the counter. "So, what brings a young Kampii to my booth?"

"Well, tasty treats, I guess," Hoku said.

Tadder laughed. He reached over and plucked a skewer from the grill. "A present for the new Flame Heart."

Hoku accepted the gift and bit off a scorpion head. They tasted a lot like shrimp, but better. He moaned in appreciation. "Join us," he blurted out. "Join the herd. You can enter the Path of Moon and compete in the cooking competition. Your food is incredible. You're sure to win. You probably hate Scorch, too, right? Won't be much need for vendors if she ruins the desert."

Tadder scratched his beard, and Hoku tried

to ignore all the grit and gunk that fell out of it. He ripped the scorpion's tail off and sucked the meat from the husk. This was the best idea he'd had in ages. If Tadder joined the herd and won the cooking trial, it would almost be as if Hoku himself had won.

"Thanks for the interesting offer, but no," Tadder said. "I don't like the lady or what she has planned, but joining a herd isn't the answer for me. I'm not Equian, not Aviar, not Serpenti, not Fish-Person or Kampii or whatever. I'm not one of those splinter tribes, those LegendaryTek colonies. I'm *Human*. We're a scattered bunch, more ragtag than not, but we're still proud of what we are, and that's *free*. So join your herd and play your Equian games, but don't expect us Humans to do the same. We haven't adapted ourselves to live in special places. That makes us weaker when we're in those places, but we're not trapped. We can go wherever we want, and we can live there, too. So, yeah. The answer's no."

Hoku found Aluna at Ring Three, standing next to Tal and the Serpenti Okpara. He was going to tell her about Calli, but she seemed so focused on the fight. He didn't want to do anything to jeopardize her focus.

"Fire Tail versus Cloud Hoof," Aluna said. "Fire Tail is allied with Red Sky, and Cloud Hoof is siding with Shining Moon. It's not supposed to matter, but everyone is saying that the bouts this year will be about more than just bragging rights."

Hoku watched the two Equians enter. The Fire Tail woman looked muscular, and her spear seemed nicked and battered. She'd clearly seen some real fights in her day. The Cloud Hoof boy was young, maybe only Aluna's age. The fight master announced the competitors' names and herds. The two Equians bowed to each other. The fight master yelled for the match to begin, and all signs of formality disappeared.

The Fire Tail charged. And screamed. And looked as if she might skewer the Cloud Hoof on the spot. The tip of her spear had been dulled with spongy cactus, but Hoku had no doubt it could do serious damage. The Equian boy dodged, but not fast enough. The spear caught him on the shoulder and twisted him around. He brought his own weapon and swung it in a wide arc toward the Fire Tail.

Aluna hissed. Hoku could hear her murmuring to herself—and to him, because of their hearing devices. "Slow swing. Predictable. Balance wrong. Leaning forward. He's watching her legs, not her chest." She kept at it, narrating the whole fight in a stream of notes. "Good strength, wrong angle. Predictable again. Weak on the left. Favors linear attack."

After a while, he realized that she wasn't talking to herself, but to Tal. The horse's huge black eyes stayed focused on the fight as she listened to every word Aluna uttered.

Then it happened. The boy slipped. The Fire Tail drove her dulled spear into his chest, and he doubled over, his horse legs wobbling and shaking. The Fire Tail pulled back her spear and drove it into him again, and a third time.

"Enough!" yelled the fight master. She cantered into the arena and yanked the Fire Tail away from her prey. "Match goes to Fire Tail. Cloud Hoof, collect your man."

Three Equians trotted in, grabbed the boy, and helped him to the medics' tent.

Aluna turned to Hoku, her brown eyes glinting bright in the sun. "Is everything okay? I thought you were working on the shield."

Hoku kept picturing that Fire Tail thrusting her spear into the boy, as if she were a hunter and he was a tasty bit of fish. If that boy had had Hoku's shield, the fight might have ended differently. It would definitely have ended without him suffering so much damage.

He looked down at Aluna's arm, where the dormant force shield should have been. With a shake of her wrist, she'd be able to summon a glowing aura of force almost big enough to cover her entire body. It only lasted a few seconds at a time, but in a fight, seconds meant everything.

Those seconds could mean Aluna's life.

"Calli," he said, forcing his gaze back up to her eyes. "She's awake!"

"I know." She smiled. "Not all of us are such late sleepers. Nathif is amazing."

Hoku nodded. His brain was already back in the tent, twisting screws and rewiring circuits.

"Be safe," he said. "Be careful." *At least until I can get the shield working.*

She smiled grimly. "I'll settle for being good."

CHAPTER 35

ALUNA KEPT HER THOUGHTS focused and tried to stay ready, not tense. Her brother, Anadar, had made sure that she knew the difference. You wanted to keep your muscles and your mind loose and relaxed, ready to move in any direction, but not anticipating. A tense person carried her shoulders too high, wasted energy keeping her body taut. She'd react more slowly, as clenched muscles were never fast ones. The only time you wanted to tense your muscles, to squeeze them, was in the instant of impact.

Anadar's sparring sessions in the training dome seemed a whole world away, but Aluna could almost hear his voice in her head. He'd trained her well, even though they'd had to hide their sessions from the

Kampii Elders. Girls couldn't be hunters or fighters in the City of Shifting Tides. Up here in the Above World, they had to be.

The fight master whistled.

"Let's do this," Aluna whispered to Tal. Tal tossed her mane and trotted forward with her head held high.

Her opponent for the first match was an arrogant looking Swift Wind man, probably no more than twenty years old. His hooves clomped continually on the salty flat ground. He wore a bored smile and kept looking at the crowd as if to say, "This one will be easy."

Aluna didn't let it faze her. She was used to being underestimated. In fact, she preferred it.

She and the Swift Wind bowed to each other, although he did little more than nod. Aluna adjusted her gaze. She normally kept her eyes on an opponent's waist. All movement started there—if the fighter wanted to have any strength in their blows. You could throw a spear with just your arms, even underwater, but if you didn't twist your waist for power, it'd be useless.

And fights were all about efficient use of energy, about having the strength and speed to capitalize on openings when you saw them.

The fight master yelled for them to begin, and Aluna let her fight-mind take over.

Her opponent swung his spear in wide figure eights

around his body. Aluna hadn't seen many Equians do this, but it was a staple move among the Aviars. If he was expecting to throw her off her guard, he'd be disappointed.

Tal danced to the side, as eager as Aluna to take this man out. Spinning your spear meant that it was out of position half the time. She found her opening and swung her spear low, at the Equian's forelegs.

He tried to block but was too slow. Belatedly, he jumped back. Equians hated to do that; they considered it a retreat.

Her spear connected with his right foreleg, but not hard enough to knock him off balance. Aluna pulled the tip back and struck high with the butt end of her weapon, another move she'd noticed was missing from the Equians' standard tactics.

The solid, smooth end of her spear smacked into the man's collarbone. Hard. He stumbled, the arrogance on his face suddenly gone.

His disorientation gave her time for a slower move. She swept his legs again with the end of her spear that was still close to the ground. She aimed below his knees, not at them. She was trying to topple him, not break his legs and maim him for life.

Her weapon connected solidly, and the Equian went down in a puff of sand and salt. Tal danced forward. Aluna pulled her spear back and drove it down again, stopping the point centimeters from her opponent's neck.

Some warriors thought that power or speed were the ultimate signs of fighting prowess, but Aluna knew it was control. Anyone could lash out with a sword or throw a spear. It was only the true master who could stop her blade before it hit or still her spear a finger's width from her target's heart. She hoped the Equians watching understood.

"Aluna of Flame Heart is victorious!" the fight master yelled.

The encounter had only lasted seconds, but that was true for most fights. And the faster Aluna could dispatch her opponents, the more energy she'd have to last throughout the day.

A few people clapped as she and Tal trotted to the edge of the ring and stepped outside to join the others.

Okpara clamped her on the shoulder and handed her water. "Well fought."

She nodded and took a deep drink, but didn't allow herself to dwell on the victory. There were more fights to watch, more competitors to assess. She and Tal had a long day ahead of them. She reached down and adjusted the straps around her ankles. Her hips ached from sitting in "tail position," as Hoku called it, but she'd get used to it soon enough.

The morning became a blur of spears and sand and the sound of the fight master's voice. By the afternoon, she had a small nick on her shoulder and an undefeated record. Even the Red Sky Equians had fallen quickly beneath her weapons.

This was another problem with isolation, Aluna thought. Except for the few Equians old enough to have fought in and survived the Venom War, the Equians only ever fought one another. They had little practice fighting someone like her, someone who didn't follow the same patterns as they did. Someone whose body worked differently and could twist and react in different ways.

Okpara was faring well for the same reasons. His snake body allowed him to bob and weave in directions that made no sense compared to inflexible Equian bodies. Most of the younger Equians had never even seen a Serpenti, let alone fought one. Tonight they would gather in their tents and discuss the Serpenti cappo'ra fighting style. They would talk about ways to beat it. Today Flame Heart had the advantage of surprise. Tomorrow, when only a few of them were left, they would fight as equals.

As the sun fell toward the horizon, the fights lasted longer, as tired arms and legs slowed competitors' movements. Aluna made more mistakes in these later fights—missed openings, dodged too slow. Tal stayed fast and alert, but Aluna sometimes gave her the wrong cues.

Even so, there were only two warriors in Ring Three that gave her a decent fight—the Flame Tail woman from the first match and a Red Sky man as old as Aluna's father, but smart and fast. Aluna was sure the three of them would advance. She hoped Okpara and the Serpenti in the other rings were faring as well.

Hoku and Calli and Dash were out there, too. Thinking of them made her smile. A few months ago, she would have shoved thoughts of them out of her mind, considered them a distraction. A weakness. Now thinking of them gave her strength.

Aluna's last fight of the day was a slow, grueling battle against a Sun Haven woman with surprising strength. After a few minutes of testing each other, Aluna feinted low. The woman went for it. Aluna changed her attack and swung a hard, fast blow at the Equian's temple. She stopped the blow just before it connected, and the woman let out a relieved sigh.

According to the rules, Aluna could have finished the hit. She'd seen other competitors do worse. Several Equians had been carried from the arena and hadn't returned for the rest of their fights.

But Flame Heart needed to win more than just the trials; they needed to win support. At least one member of Sun Haven now owed Aluna a favor. And if Aluna never mentioned it, even better. The Sun Haven woman would try to help her anyway, driven by her sense of honor. Not all victories were won by the stronger person. Some of the most important were won by the smartest.

The fight master declared Aluna the winner of the match. Aluna bowed to her opponent and headed back to her spot on the rim to watch the last few competitors and stretch.

CHAPTER 36

W HILE THE REST OF FLAME HEART went to the great bonfire to hear the results of the day's competitions, Hoku stayed in his tent, lit all his lanterns, and worked.

He'd gotten the force shield to stop slicing through objects when it was activated, and then . . . it had stopped activating entirely. Despite the fact that it now did nothing, he considered this an improvement. When tech seemed the most broken, it was often the closest to being fixed. At least that was the thought that kept him fiddling and adjusting and squinting his eyes through both the midday and evening meals, and now into the night.

Eventually the flap of his tent flew open and a horde of flushed faces swarmed inside.

"Aluna made it to day two," Calli said. She let go of Rollin's arm and collapsed on some pillows near Hoku's work area.

"She was undefeated," Dash said. Hoku could have sworn he detected pride in the horse-boy's voice.

Aluna, her entire body covered in the dirt and grime of a day of fighting, waved them off. "All the fighters who made it to day two were undefeated. Onggur, Scorch, Khan Arasen, Dantai—all of us. The fight master said that there had never been such a clear set of victors."

"And losers," Nathif said. "Six Equians are still in the medics' tent, and one is so gravely injured that he may see eternal dark before the night is over."

"Scorch fought that one," Aluna said, as if it were obvious. She held a fistful of skewers covered in grilled meat toward Hoku. "Thought you might need some food."

He was about to say no when the smell hit him. His stomach roared like a sea lion and everyone laughed. Defeated, he put down his tools, sat back, and took the meat. "What about the tech competition?" He ripped into the first skewer and almost moaned. The snake was still warm, its flesh covered in a thick, smoky sauce.

Rollin grunted. "Made us stand around all day, then didn't even look at our gizmos. Tomorrow, they say. Lazy four-feets."

"There was only one device that looked good today," Calli said. "You weave it into your mane—if you have one, of course—and it repels insects along your whole body. Whether or not it wins, that herd will have something very useful for trading."

"Not if they all go to war," Aluna said. She hopped to the middle of the tent, leaned against the center pole, and slid down to the carpet. Hoku tried to get a glimpse of her tail, but she kept herself covered—her sleek Serpenti skirt hugged her legs all the way down to her ankles, and her desert boots took over from there. At least she still had two feet. "No sign of Weaver Sokhor, either. Tayan said he didn't show at the word-weaving competition last night."

"He knows that any Shining Moon would attack him instantly," Dash said. "Khan Arasen and Dantai would kill him where he stood, regardless of the consequences."

"Then it's good that he didn't come," Aluna said. "If he's allied with Karl Strand and he got killed, things might get even more messy."

"What about the Path of Sand?" Hoku said to Dash. "How did you and the Serpenti do at the skill tests?"

Calli answered first. "It wasn't fair! They wouldn't let him ride Sandwolf, and they raised all the targets."

"They wanted him to fail," Aluna said.

"It would have been difficult to do any worse," Dash said. "I did not think my own kind would hate me so much. Even more than they hate all of you. Even more than they hate the Serpenti."

"They can make excuses if they lose to us," Aluna said. "They could never forgive themselves if they lost to —"

"An *aldagha*," Dash said.

"I wasn't going to say that," Aluna said. "You know I don't think of you like that. None of us do."

"I know," Dash said with a sigh.

Nathif coiled his tail in a tight circle and sat. At least Hoku assumed that's what he was doing. He looked like the top half of a Human stuck into a pile of snakes. "Do you think the Equians get their arrogance from their horse blood, or does the sun just fry the modesty out of their brains?" Nathif asked. "They are a remarkably condescending race for people who eat cactus on a regular basis."

Calli chuckled. "And who can't even brush their own tails."

Hoku could tell they were trying to cheer up Dash, but it didn't work. Dash stood abruptly. "I think I will walk. I have an idea about where I might purchase a falcon."

"I'll come with you," Aluna said, and started to pull herself up using the tent pole.

"No," Dash said. "You need your rest for tomorrow. Drink water and sleep. I will visit Tal on my way back and see if she needs anything."

Aluna looked like she might argue, but Hoku could see the fatigue in the slump of her shoulders and the dark smudges under her eyes. She eventually nodded and slid back down to the rug.

"I thought Shining Moon refused to sell you a bird," Hoku said. "Did the khan change his mind?"

"No, Shining Moon wants to win and knows that I will hurt their chances," Dash said. The edges of his mouth quirked up. "So I found a herd who wants Shining Moon to lose."

CHAPTER 37

THE RING ASSIGNMENTS were supposed to be random, but somehow Aluna and all her allies were thrown into the same one. High Khan Onggur and Scorch wanted them to defeat one another. Strategically it was smart. Mentally it was devastating.

Aluna's first match of the day was against Dantai.

She checked her saddle. Her knees felt securely wrapped around the hook in the front, and the side strap kept her ankles tight against Tal's flank.

"We're ready for this," Aluna said to Tal. "We can take him."

Tal huffed and nodded. Aluna could feel the horse's muscles bunching. She wanted to fight. Her whole life, she'd been an outsider, living on the fringe of the Shining Moon camp. Aluna had felt the same way about herself, and her role in the City of Shifting Tides. But here, together, they were something strong. Something meaningful. Right now, they both mattered.

Aluna turned her attention to Dantai. His sleek braids had been tucked under his head wrap, but he still looked too familiar, too much like a friend. She'd sparred with friends most of her life, but she'd never fought them for real. If she saw an opening, would she take it? Even the tiniest hesitation could cost her everything.

She thought about Dantai calling Dash an *aldagha*. She remembered what he'd said about Tal, about her being damaged mentally.

"Oh, yes," she said. "We will definitely take him."

The fight master motioned them to the center of the ring. Tal cantered into place, her nostrils wide, her tail swishing.

Aluna bowed to Dantai, and for the first time, Tal bowed as well. Dantai looked surprised. Hopefully, it wouldn't be for the first time.

They stepped back, and the match started.

Dantai charged immediately and thrust his spear at Aluna's chest. She blocked it easily with her own weapon as Tal sidestepped. Tal rushed forward, past Dantai, while he was recovering from his charge. Aluna managed to land a blow across his Human back with the wooden shaft of her spear.

They went back and forth like that for a few minutes. One of them attacked; the other blocked or dodged and counterattacked. Dantai wasn't as foolish as her opponents on the first day had been. He'd seen Aluna fight. He wasn't underestimating her; he was looking for an opening. A weakness. Same as she was doing to him.

Then Aluna thrust her spear, and Dantai dodged. She tried to pull it back before he could grab it, but she was too slow. He wrapped a strong hand around it, just under the spear point, and yanked.

Aluna let it go. He was too strong, and she'd lose the flesh on her palms if she resisted. She watched the spear clatter to the ground meters away.

Tal bolted forward, giving Aluna time to recoup. Aluna twisted her wrists, dropping her talon weapons into place. With a flick of her thumbs, she popped open the silver capsules and swung the thin chain whips out of their sheaths. She spun them in arcs on either side of her body.

Dantai had been ready to charge again, thinking her helpless. Now he stumbled back.

The talons whirred at her side — so fast that they were silver blurs in the air.

"Go," Aluna said.

Tal raced forward. Aluna directed a talon at Dantai's front foreleg, hoping to wrap it and yank him off balance. She got Dantai's spear instead. She pulled, knowing the angle favored her.

Dantai gripped his spear with both hands, refusing to let it go, as she had done. Aluna pulled hard on the line, and his arms jerked forward.

An opening.

She let loose with her other talon. The chain whip struck home, wrapping itself around Dantai's front leg. If he'd been Human, she could have snapped the bone right then. But Equian legs were fortified, stronger than steel. Their ancients had seen to that.

"Back," she said to Tal.

Tal dug her hooves into the crusty white earth and started to walk backward. Aluna used Tal's leverage to increase her own. When she pulled on the chain around Dantai's leg, he went down.

Dimly she heard the crowd around the arena gasp.

But the fight wasn't over yet. Dantai finally dropped his useless spear, and Aluna dropped the talon still wrapped around it. Dantai struggled to stand and pulled his sword from its sheath on his back.

Aluna and Tal never let him get up. Tal charged, throwing the full weight of her body against Dantai's shoulder. He slammed down against the ground. Tal reared as if she would crush his head beneath her hooves. The crowd gasped again. Tal landed centimeters from Dantai's head, on his sword arm instead. He screamed.

This time, Aluna heard the crunch of bones.

Dantai looked up at her, his face locked in a grimace, hate pouring from his eyes.

"Do you yield?" she asked quietly.

Dantai spat at Tal's hooves. "I do."

Aluna and Tal danced away while the fight master cantered in to officially end the bout. Aluna waited until Dantai had been helped out of the ring before retrieving her talons and her spear.

"Well done," she whispered to Tal. "We've made no friends among the Shining Moon, but we did what we had to do."

Tal didn't need any encouragement. Aluna could tell from the way she pranced that this was probably the happiest day of her life.

Her next few opponents fell quickly, incapable of defending against Aluna's talons and unpredictable style. Aluna kept them guessing, attacking a different way each time, using a different rhythm, getting Tal to mix up her speed and approach angles. Unfortunately she had to fight Subira. Subira might best her in the cappo'ra ring, but aided by Tal, Aluna claimed the victory.

She watched the other matches with growing apprehension. Khan Arasen, easily in his late forties or early fifties, dispatched his opponents even faster than she did. His arms and back were strong, his weight always balanced, his breathing never labored. He took out Master Sefu in less than ten minutes. Arasen clearly wanted this win almost as much as she did.

Aluna heard someone approaching and turned to find Tayan standing behind her.

"You're not supposed to be back here," Aluna said.

Tayan smiled wryly and fingered the bloodline amulet around her neck. "They make exceptions for khans."

"Come up and watch with me, then," Aluna said. Tal moved over to make room. "Your father is amazing."

"I am pleased you think so," Tayan said.

Aluna frowned.

"We founded Flame Heart to protect the Serpenti and because we did not want the fate of the desert to rest in the hands of others," Tayan said. "We were worried that Weaver Sokhor had weakened my father and that he would have no chance to defeat High Khan Onggur in the Path of Sun."

"I need to keep my focus," Aluna said. "Whatever you're trying to say, it needs to wait until after the day is over."

Tal fidgeted beneath her, sensing her unease.

"No, I must say it now," Tayan said. She turned her head and looked into Aluna's eyes. "You and I have not been good friends, Aluna. We are both opinionated and horse-headed, and we have rarely wanted the same things. But despite that, we are excellent allies. You saved my life, and without me, there would be no Flame Heart."

"You want a favor? Is that what this is about?" Aluna could feel waves of anger begin to wash over her.

"You may call it a favor, if you wish, or you may call it an order from your khan."

Aluna felt heat rush to her cheeks. Her fists closed around her talons, and she squeezed. "What is this *order*, my khan?"

Tayan seemed unfazed by Aluna's tone. Her own voice remained steady. "My father will win his matches, as you have won yours. The two of you will fight for the honor of the last battle tomorrow." She paused. "You will let my father win."

Aluna's mouth fell open. She felt as if she'd been struck, smacked in the face by someone she'd been foolish enough to trust.

"Is this honor?" she asked quietly.

Tayan nodded. "My father has the only chance of defeating Onggur and saving the desert from Scorch and Karl Strand. You are skilled, Aluna, but not nearly as strong. And the desert needs an Equian to win, not an . . ."

"*Aldagha*," Aluna said.

The word washed away her anger and filled her with something darker. She looked down at her legs. At her saddle. She wasn't Human, she wasn't Equian, and she wasn't even a real Kampii. *Aldagha* fit her better than it fit Dash.

"You are a warrior, Aluna, and I am proud to know you," Tayan said. "But you are not destined to save the desert."

Tal whinnied. Aluna stared at the back of Tal's head, her mind a whirlpool.

"Will you do as I ask?"

Aluna closed her eyes and took a deep breath. When she opened them again, she felt calm waters surround her once again. "I've been in the desert for months, and all I've ever heard you Equians talk about is honor. You say it drives your culture and gives meaning to your lives. But you know what? The person who actually taught me what it *means*—the person who actually showed me by example—isn't even considered a real Equian by your people. You want to really understand honor? Then spend a little time with Dash. No, spend a lot of time with him. Because you, Tayan, don't know the meaning of the word. The answer is no."

Tal whinnied. Aluna spat on the ground near

Tayan's hooves. "I've got to go. I've got to teach a khan and his daughter a lesson."

Tal weaved through the crowd, away from Tayan. Aluna didn't look back. She wrapped the anger around herself like a blanket. But she was more upset with herself than she was with Tayan. She'd allowed Tayan to make her feel bad about herself. For a moment, she'd actually believed what Tayan was saying.

And nobody, not even the khan of Flame Heart, got to do that to her.

When the fight master announced her match with Khan Arasen, Aluna and Tal were ready. The battle lasted past the fall of the sun. A sword danced through the air; talons spun in shimmering arcs; spears blocked and poked and slashed. And finally, in the faint darkness of dusk, Khan Arasen yielded.

The day was hers.

CHAPTER 38

LATER THAT NIGHT, Aluna curled up on her bedding in the dark of Calli's tent. Groups of Equians sang and partied outside around their bonfires, but she had no desire to join in the festivities. Tomorrow she would face High Khan Onggur in one-on-one combat in front of everyone. Tomorrow the desert—and the war—would be lost or won. Her stomach clenched, and the muscles in her shoulders refused to relax. She told her teeth to stop grinding together, but a moment later, they were at it again.

"It must be terrifying, facing all those people in battle." Calli's voice wafted over in the darkness. "I can't remember anything when someone attacks me. Even in sparring. It's like all the training flies out my ears."

Aluna clung to Calli's kindness. She hadn't realized how much she'd missed her. Words started spilling out of Aluna's mouth. She talked about each of her fights. What it felt like when the blows landed. What it felt like to feel the thud of her spear against her opponent's armor. The way Tal's spirited whinnies gave her energy even when she was tired. Calli listened to it all without once interrupting.

"I don't understand why Scorch didn't win in the other ring," Calli said. "She could probably have defeated High Khan Onggur."

"Tayan said that only people loyal to Onggur were in his ring. None of them would risk truly hurting him. Not even Scorch. She came in second, though." Aluna thought about Scorch and her cruel eyes and her face with Karl Strand's smile. "Scorch is smart. She's better off controlling the Equian in charge of the desert instead of trying to control it herself."

Calli grunted. "Is it weird that I miss Fathom? He was horrible and grotesque, but at least he was predictable and kind of dumb."

Aluna smiled in the darkness. "I'd rather face him than Scorch any day." And then, because she needed to tell somebody, she told Calli about Tayan, and what Tayan had asked her to do.

"Outrageous! Despicable!" Calli said when she was done.

"I don't think we should tell the others," Aluna said quickly. "It's over, and I don't want them to think less of Tayan. She's our khan now. We've all done stupid things, me included. I should have told you all about my tail as soon as the battle at HydroTek was over. If you can forgive me, maybe we should forgive Tayan. She's sacrificed a lot for Flame Heart, to give us a chance against Scorch. Maybe she deserves another chance, too."

"Tayan was wrong to ask that of you," Calli said. "My mother would never have done such a thing."

"No, your mother just captured me and forced me to be your friend," Aluna said with a laugh.

"I see your point," Calli said. "I guess honor means something different to everyone."

Aluna reached over and found Calli's hand in the darkness. "I'm glad your mother did it," she said. "I'm glad you're in my life." She knew what Calli wanted to hear, and for once, she felt comfortable saying it. "You're like a sister to me."

Calli squeezed Aluna's hand, her grip still weak. "I couldn't imagine a better one."

Aluna held on to Calli's hand. She felt tears pooling in her eyes. Calli made her feel safe. Safe enough to be scared. "I'm afraid," she said quietly. "Afraid of losing. Afraid of dying. Afraid of letting everyone down, including myself."

"Only the stupid don't feel fear," Calli said quietly. "It's the heroes that keep going anyway."

Aluna stood with her herd in the great arena at high sun on the third day while High Khan Onggur prepared to announce the winners of the Path of Moon and Path of Sand competitions. Aluna watched Tayan move amid the Flame Heart herd, putting a hand on a Serpenti's shoulder, offering a word of encouragement to Calli. They hadn't spoken since their argument yesterday, and Aluna half expected Tayan to publicly humiliate her for daring to disobey her khan.

Tayan's path brought her closer and closer until Tal started stomping her hooves and huffing.

"I know," Aluna whispered. "I want to bite her, too."

Tayan walked calmly toward Aluna, her gaze focused on High Khan Onggur in the distance. When they were side by side, Tayan nodded. "Aluna."

Aluna tried to be civil, but her words came out bitter. "My khan." Tayan's eyelids closed for a moment, but Aluna couldn't tell if the Equian was suppressing her growing rage or was simply bone-tired. Either way, Aluna wasn't done. "Do you have another favor to request?" she asked. "Would you like me to fall on my sword in the fight tonight, or perhaps trip over a rock and sprain my ankle before the match even begins? I'm sure your father would be happy to replace me."

Tayan shuffled her hooves in the sand. Aluna watched color creep into her cheeks. "You . . . fought well yesterday," she said slowly. "You made my father look like a yearling."

"Is that what this is about?" Aluna said. "That I embarrassed you and your father? Because if it is, then—"

"Can you not hold your tongue for one moment? I am trying to apologize!" Tayan's tail snapped back and forth like a whip. She closed her eyes again and whispered something Aluna couldn't hear. When she opened her eyes again, she was back in control. "Aluna of the Kampii and of Flame Heart, what I asked of you was wrong, and I am sorry." She touched fingers to her heart, bowed stiffly, and fled back into the herd without waiting for a reply.

When she was gone, Tal whinnied softly and shifted her weight. Aluna shook her head, stunned. A common Equian phrase popped into her head. "Some days the sun chooses to rise in the west."

Flame Heart cheered for Dash when he won top honors for falconry. Apparently he and his falcon, Odu—a gift from herd Fire Tail—had caught twice the number of rabbits and snakes as the next closest competitor.

Aluna clapped him on the back and shouted his name along with the rest of the herd. His face flushed slightly under his dark skin.

"It was all Odu," he told her. "She is the true hunter. I was only her transport."

"Of course," Aluna said with a grin. "The bird should get all the credit."

A Serpenti named Ramla took the top award in archery, and for a few brief moments, Aluna thought the Bronze Disc of the Sand might be theirs. Then Red Sky took the awards for strength, agility, and sword, and Flame Heart's chances ended. A Swift Wind won for speed, a Cloud Hoof for spear, and the Bronze Disc was awarded to Red Sky. If they had not changed the competitions to favor people with four hooves, it might have ended differently.

Dash and Ramla went to the award platform, joy absent from their faces. Aluna wanted them to be proud of what they'd done. They'd beaten the other Equians despite being hated and feared. Despite being outsiders. When High Khan Onggur placed the glinting bronze sashes over their shoulders, Aluna cheered until her voice cracked.

As the High Khan began to announce the winners of the Path of Moon, he stopped in the middle of his sentence and seemed to waver. For a flash, she thought he might actually topple over completely. Two Red Sky appeared at his side, and soon he was gone, taken away from all the eyes. The Equian in charge of the Path of Moon stepped forward and began speaking as if nothing had happened.

Aluna looked for Scorch on the pavilion but couldn't find her. Not a good sign. It was always better to watch the shark circling than to find its jaws suddenly clamped on your tail.

Tayan did not win the word-weaving competition, although she came in an honorable fifth. At least Weaver Sokhor had never showed up to claim the victory for himself. Nathif came in second in the textile competition with his Flame Heart banner, and the Serpenti Fenyang actually won the cooking trial with his Hearty Desert Stew.

"Mushrooms," Nathif whispered to Aluna. "His secret weapon. Apparently the Equians had never even seen them before."

The tech awards were next. Aluna made her way to where Calli and Rollin were standing. Hoku was still in his tent, still working furiously on his shield. He hadn't slept all night. Aluna held her breath as the results were announced. Rollin came in third with her cooling device—a shock to everyone, including her. She shrugged, grunted, and muttered, "Silly four-feets." The Equian from Cloud Hoof with the insect repellent came in second. Aluna was still watching him rear up on his hind legs and cheer when the winner's name was called.

Cheers erupted all around her, and suddenly everyone was crowded around Calli, trying to pat her back despite the two giant wings constantly getting in the way.

"Calli?" Aluna said. "Tides' teeth, Calli!" She threw herself into the mix and caught a glimpse of the girl's grinning, sun-reddened face.

"Not surprising," Rollin said. "That bow makes good archers out of imbeciles. Got lots of those in the desert."

"I wish Hoku were here," Calli said. "He said it would never win with such a simple name."

"Luckily not everyone is as fixated on naming their tech," Aluna said, and laughed.

Aluna tried to be happy for Calli, but even with her surprise victory, the Silver Disc had gone to Cloud Hoof, who managed to take word-weaving, textiles, and a strange performance art—involving twin swords, stomping around in a specific pattern, and yelling battle cries—called Traditional War Dance.

Calli, Rollin, Nathif, and Fenyang accepted their silver sashes at the podium.

"We did not win the discs, but we earned respect,"

Tayan told the herd. "I guarantee you this: no one here expected us to do so well. We have honored Flame Heart this day."

They hadn't won the Silver and Bronze Discs, and that meant only one thing to Aluna. She'd have to defeat High Khan Onggur herself, one-on-one, or they'd lose everything. She and Calli and Hoku would be given to Scorch, and the herds would either pledge their loyalty to Karl Strand and the war or be cut down where they stood. And if the Equians joined Strand's army? Well, then there was almost no hope for the Kampii or the Aviars or anyone else who dared to fight back.

The crowd started to disperse. In only a few hours, everyone would reconvene to watch the last fight as the sun approached the horizon. Aluna turned to go—she and Tal only had a few hours to stretch and prepare—when Tayan grabbed her shoulder.

"Wait. Look."

Aluna followed Tayan's gaze back to the pavilion. Scorch, flanked by two Red Sky, stepped to the front and spoke quietly with the Path of Moon announcer. He held up his hand, telling everyone not to leave. When he turned to face the crowd, his expression seemed dark.

"I regret to inform you that the Great One, High Khan Onggur, has suddenly taken ill. He will be unable to compete in the final match this afternoon."

The stadium erupted with noise.

"What does this mean?" Aluna asked in the chaos. "Is the fight postponed? Do I fight someone else?"

Tayan looked pale. "I am sorry, Aluna. I am very sorry."

"What? What does it mean?"

"I fear they are about to tell us," Dash said.

The announcer had held up his hand again. "According to herd law, the second-best competitor from the High Khan's ring will take his place."

"Oh, no," Dash said. "This cannot be happening."

Scorch stepped forward and waved to the crowd as if she'd just won an award. The announcer continued: "Scorch, recently made Red Sky, will now fight Aluna of Flame Heart."

This time the noise was deafening.

"I cannot believe she found a way," Dash said. Aluna could barely hear him over the clamoring.

"I can," she said. "I wonder how she did it."

"Poison," Nathif said easily. "You saw how the High Khan wobbled. A man of his stamina does not suddenly become ill without help."

A man in the crowd yelled, "The snakes did this!" A woman answered, "We need to defend our bloodlines!"

"And we need to leave here. Right now," Tayan said. "Do not engage. Keep your eyes down and your tongues silent." She led them quickly and quietly out of the arena. Only when they were safely back at their campsite did she allow them to speak again.

"They will be arguing about this the rest of the day," Tayan said. "The other khans cannot be happy. I'm sure they, too, will suspect poison. But unlike us, they will blame the Serpenti, not Scorch, even though it makes no sense for Flame Heart to have committed such a crime."

"Will they change their minds?" Calli asked. "Aluna shouldn't have to fight that monster."

Tayan shook her head. "Herd law is very clear, and there is no time for a proper debate. The rule will stand, and the fight will happen as the law decrees."

Dash shook his head. "The fate of the desert lies in the hands of two people who were not even born here. We place so much importance on herd law, and this time, it has trapped us. If we Equians learn anything from this, I hope we learn to think for ourselves, instead of relying on the past to think for us."

Tayan's tail swished. "Brother Dashiyn, I promise you this: if I survive whatever happens tonight, I will spend the rest of my life attempting to do that very thing."

After tonight. It was a luxury to think of anything that far away. A luxury Aluna no longer had. Now that she was fighting Scorch instead of Onggur, she was positive that she'd already seen her last dawn.

CHAPTER 39

THE BONFIRE CRACKLED and reached for the sky, even though the sun still hung a few centimeters above the horizon. On their end of the ring, Aluna and Tal cantered and practiced dodging, warming muscles and calming nerves. Behind them, Flame Heart had arranged itself around the edge of the fighting field. Flame Heart minus Nathif and Hoku.

Nathif had slithered off in search of the medics' tent, and Hoku was still struggling with his tech. When Aluna had told him about the poisoning and that she'd now be facing Scorch, he'd let out a strangled cry and bent over his shield with a crazed look in his eye. Unfortunately he was out of time.

Scorch warmed up on the other side of the ring. She wore faded brown leathers studded with a harder plastic material. Unlike her usual outfit of flashy red and black, these clothes looked worn instead of pretty. Scorch stretched in them, easy as an eel, looking all the more dangerous for being dressed so simply.

The entire arena was filled with Equians, vendors selling food, spectators young and old, with the clomp of hooves and the sharp bark of laughter. Aluna could see some Equians talking in quiet groups away from the ruckus; she caught a flash of steel, a quiver of arrows poking over a shoulder. Tayan had been right: no one was happy with this fight. The other herds had been nervous before, but now even Red Sky seemed agitated. Aluna couldn't believe that thousands of Equians had been handcuffed by their own rules. Apparently they couldn't believe it, either.

A motion caught Aluna's eye. Dash waved to her from the edge of the ring. Tal cantered over to him without even waiting for Aluna to ask.

"I do not wish to distract you," Dash said, "but I have something to give you."

"A weapon?" she said eagerly.

Dash deflated slightly. "No, not a weapon. Only a token." He held out a slim feather. One of his falcon Odu's, she guessed. Its stalk had been decorated with blue and green beads, the colors she most associated with her Kampii home.

"It's beautiful," she said.

"My spirit will find yours more easily during the fight this way," he said.

She smiled and studied the feather, suddenly too nervous to look him in the eyes. "Thank you," she mumbled. "Where should I wear it?"

"Lean over," he said. "I will fasten it."

Aluna leaned close to him, ignoring Tal's huffs as the horse adjusted her weight to compensate. Dash took the feather from Aluna's hand and gently pinned it to her right sleeve, near her shoulder. Aluna could smell the sand and soap on Dash's skin. His hair swished around his face like the mane of a well-groomed horse.

"Thank you," she said. "For everything."

He tilted his head. "What do you mean?"

"For being the most honorable person in the desert," she said. "I've learned a lot from you."

"I am merely an *aldagha*," he said, but she could tell he was pleased.

She was about to take Tal back to the ring when she saw Hoku running toward them.

"Wait," he called. "It's done!"

"He did it," Dash said quietly. "I knew he would."

Hoku looked as if a whale had swallowed him for a few days then spat him back up. Everything about him seemed disheveled—his hair, his clothes, even his expression. One of his eyes squinted more than the other, and he ran with a lopsided gait, as if one of his legs had fallen asleep.

He wasted no time on greetings. "Left arm," he demanded. Aluna dutifully held it out while he wrapped the force shield around it and tightened the straps. "Have you been practicing the motion I taught you?"

"Yes," she said. She looked down at the artifact wrapped tightly around her left forearm. In its dormant state, it was simply a hard metal sheath she could use to deflect spear tips and bash against skin. But with a sharp twist and turn of her wrist, a motion she never made in the normal course of battle, a circular shield made of light would supposedly appear.

"Good," Hoku said. "The shield only lasts for a flash, so don't activate it until the blow is about to fall. The device is fully charged, but I'm not sure how many shields that will get you. At least a dozen, maybe twice that. I hope it's enough."

"It's perfect," she said. She wanted to hug him, but she didn't have the mobility. She did the next best thing. "Tal, say thank you, please."

Tal turned her big horsey head to Hoku and huffed air at his face. At least she didn't use her tongue.

"Um, you're welcome," Hoku said.

"Come." Dash grabbed Hoku's arm. "We need to leave the field, and you need to eat. A strong wind might blow you away."

"I'm kind of okay with that," Hoku said with a sigh. But he let Dash pull him away all the same. When he reached the edge of the ring, he turned back and stared at Aluna.

She whispered, knowing that their Kampii tech would carry the words to his ears. "Best friends always."

He nodded grimly and said, "Always."

Aluna patted Tal on the withers. The horse whinnied and cantered them both back into the ring.

"The Path of Sun demands blood," the Fire Tail khan yelled. He'd been chosen as fight master for the final event, no doubt as much for his loyalty to Onggur and the Red Sky as for his showmanship. "This fight will end not when one combatant yields but when one combatant can no longer pick himself—or herself—up off the field. What say you?"

"The sand hears; the sun remembers!" the stadium full of Equians called.

Aluna and Tal stood behind Khan Kutula as he

addressed the crowd. Aluna could feel Scorch waiting to her right, only a few meters away. She didn't look. She didn't want to give that woman any chances to get inside her head before the fight. Even so, she could feel Scorch's presence, sleek and dangerous. An eel hidden in the shadows, waiting to strike.

"Let the sun herself declare our winner!"

The crowd cheered. Tal shifted restlessly. Aluna wanted to comfort her but couldn't. She was too anxious herself. *Be still as a starfish; be calm as Big Blue.* The phrase felt so strange now, when she was so far away from the ocean.

Khan Kutula turned to face Aluna and Scorch.

"Honor demands a clean fight," he said. "To finish as the sun sets will bring luck to all the herds." He looked at Aluna. "To end the fight, stay down. I will give you a few moments to stand, but if you do not, I will call the victor."

Aluna nodded. No one in this entire arena thought she had a chance. She and Tal turned to face Scorch. Aluna forced herself to look at her enemy, expecting to find the same heartless shark eyes that Fathom had possessed. But Scorch's brown eyes were different. More Human. More like Karl Strand's.

"Show your respects," Khan Kutula yelled.

Aluna and Scorch bowed to the crowds. Aluna turned and bowed to Scorch, but her opponent only crossed her arms and laughed. *So that's how she'll play this,* Aluna thought.

"Take your places," Kutula told them. He reached over his back and unsheathed a massive sword of black metal.

Aluna and Tal stepped backward to their starting spots. Aluna kept her eyes on Scorch. Only a tiny part of her watched Kutula slash his sword down and shout, "It has begun!"

Her talons were in her palms, ready to go. She spun them at her sides until they whirred into silvery blurs. Tal reared up on her hind legs, shook her head, and let loose a war cry.

Scorch charged. She held no weapon in her hands, but that only made Aluna more wary.

"Careful," she whispered to Tal. "Give me an angle."

Tal jumped right. Aluna let loose a talon chain, hoping to wrap it around Scorch's arm. She would have aimed for her neck, but back in Mirage, it had been impenetrable. Even so, Scorch had to have a weakness somewhere. Aluna would try every location until she found it.

Her talon whipped around Scorch's arm. Aluna pulled and . . . nothing. Scorch didn't even seem to notice. She continued to speed straight toward them. A glint of silver and Aluna finally saw the blade. It cut through the palm of Scorch's hand and extended almost half a meter. It had been inside the flesh of her arm all along.

Aluna readied her shield. She let her other talon fly and watched it wrap around Scorch's sword.

Something was wrong. Scorch's angle. She'd need to change course to hit Aluna, unless . . .

"Tal, move!" she shouted.

But it was too late. Scorch wasn't charging Aluna at all; she was aiming for her horse.

Time seemed to slow down. Aluna saw Scorch's blade driving toward Tal's chest, straight toward her heart. Aluna yanked on her talon so hard that her shoulder threatened to rip. It didn't do much. Scorch's blade slid slightly left and plunged into Tal's flesh.

CHAPTER 40

TAL SCREAMED. She reared up, and Scorch's blade fell free in a spray of blood. The crowd fell silent, as shocked as Aluna. Equians never attacked each other's horse body. Not near the heart. Not trying for a death-blow. Not ever.

"Away," Aluna said, dropping her talons. There wasn't time to unhook them from Scorch. Tal lurched into an uneven gallop, still crying from the pain. Aluna felt tears well in her eyes and blinked furiously. As Tal ran, Aluna reached down and popped the latches holding her ankles against Tal's side.

"Go," Aluna said to Tal. "You're done. Get out of here!"

Tal whinnied and started to slow. Aluna unhooked her knees and slid off Tal's back. She landed hard on the ground and barely managed to keep her balance. Scorch was already headed for them again, a cruel smile on her face.

"Run!" Aluna yelled again, and smacked Tal's flank. This time, Tal obeyed. Aluna blinked again. Nathif could fix her. Nathif had to fix her. No matter what happened to Aluna, Tal had to live.

The Path of Sun demands blood.

Scorch arrived in a blur of motion. Aluna blocked her blade with the metal band of Hoku's force shield. Even so, the power of the blow knocked her backward. She stumbled and whipped her dagger out of its waist sheath. She swiped it at Scorch's face before she fell.

Scorch jerked her head back, but not fast enough. The sharp tip of Aluna's knife sliced across her cheek, leaving a thin line of blood. A shallow wound. But maybe enough to make her angry.

It did. Another blade slid out of Scorch's other hand. She sliced away the talon weapon dangling from her arm and attacked. Her strikes fell so quickly that Aluna couldn't even see them. She twisted her shield arm, and a huge shimmering circle instantly appeared between her and Scorch. Scorch's blades crashed into the shield and bounced off in a shower of sparks.

That only made Scorch increase the fury of her attacks. Aluna pulled her tail into the protective area of the shield and kept twisting her arm. As soon as the shield disappeared, she activated it again.

"You can't stay down there forever, coward," Scorch hissed.

She was right. The shield wouldn't last forever, and when it failed . . . that was it. And besides, hiding was no way to win.

The next time she activated the shield, she shoved it toward Scorch's face. It hit her like a tidal wave. She staggered back.

Aluna wasted no time. She rolled onto her hands and swung her tail in an arc toward Scorch. It hit her in the knees and she fell hard against the ground. A second later, Scorch hopped back to her feet as if she'd never left them.

"Tricky girl," Scorch said. "It's too bad I'm going to kill you. You'd make an excellent slave in my father's army." Scorch leaped forward, raised her foot high, and brought the heel down at Aluna's skull.

Aluna rolled left and kept rolling. Scorch followed her, landing blow after blow right where Aluna's head had been. Again, Scorch had her on the defensive.

"Have you seen the picture of Karl Strand's real son?" Aluna said. "I have. His name was Tomias."

Scorch faltered. Not long, but it was enough. Aluna rolled into a standing position, her shield arm out, her knife hand ready to strike.

"He has never mentioned a Human son," Scorch said. The malicious grin returned, but Aluna could tell it was forced. "I am his only true child now."

"I'm sure you are," Aluna grunted. "But mention Tomias, and you'll see how much you really mean to him."

Scorch yelled something incoherent and swung both her blades at Aluna's head. She barely got the shield up and activated in time to block the blows. As soon as it disappeared, she made another swipe with her knife. Scorch dodged, and Aluna was forced to hop back and deploy the shield again.

One strike. She was getting only one attack for every ten of Scorch's.

And then she heard drums. A familiar rhythm. The Serpenti cappo'ra warriors were cheering her on the best way they could—by pounding the earth with their tails, as they had done in the training circle in Coiled Deep. She used the rhythm. She ducked under Scorch's next sword strike and kept herself low. She let the beat fill her mind and followed it, hopping onto her hands to strike with her tail, and back again.

She caught Scorch in the knee and saw it buckle slightly. A weak spot. She rolled and twisted, trying to get in another hit at the same place. But Scorch figured out what she was doing and turned, lightning fast, keeping her leg out of range.

Aluna kept dodging Scorch's blades, but she could feel her body tiring. A sharp pain erupted in her chest, and she knew Scorch had landed a kick.

The blow spun her. Her back smacked into the ground hard. Breathing hurt. Moving hurt. Scorch was on her in a flash, slashing and kicking.

"I'll keep your head," Scorch said through gritted teeth. "I'll keep it for your family."

Aluna rolled and spun her legs, trying to get away. She took the worst of Scorch's attacks with the force shield. Its green light flickered on and off. Without it, she'd have died ten times over.

Scorch kicked, and the world exploded in stars and blackness. Aluna clutched her temple with one arm, trying to protect her head. Her mouth tasted like blood. She spat out what she could and begged the world to stop spinning.

"Keep fighting," she heard Scorch say. Not loudly. Not to everyone. Just to her. "Keep fighting, so I can kill you."

CHAPTER 41

Hoku cringed. "Stay down, Aluna. Stay down." He could barely stand to watch. She'd done so well, landed more blows than anyone had expected. But now she was done. Broken. In danger of being seriously hurt. "Tides' teeth," he said louder. "Stay down!"

Aluna didn't stay down. She lifted her blood-spattered face and struggled to her feet in time for Scorch to kick her down again. Scorch slashed her with her swords, but Aluna somehow managed to activate the force shield a flash before the blades hit.

Why hadn't he made the shield into a weapon as well? Why hadn't he ignored his stupid ideals and made her something she could use to fight back?

The shield flickered again and again, as Aluna continued to swing punches and spin her legs to attack.

Even Scorch seemed to grow tired. Aluna landed a hard blow to Scorch's knee, and the leg twisted awkwardly. For the first time, Scorch's face registered surprise.

Then she was all fury and flashing steel again, and Aluna fell in a spray of blood.

The sun slipped closer to the mountains. The Equians wanted the match to end now, to best honor the sun, but Aluna wouldn't give up. Scorch kicked her in the shoulder, and Hoku saw a small object go flying. It looked like a feather.

And still Aluna got up. Again and again. Force shield. Spin. Block. Dodge. He wanted to weep for how tired and hurt she must be. The crowd seemed close to frenzy. They stomped the ground and yelled. He could barely hear Dash and Calli calling out to Aluna at his sides.

Finally, Scorch landed a blow to Aluna's stomach that sent her flying half a dozen meters. She crumpled against the ground with a sob he could hear in his ears.

"Stay down," he whispered, relieved that she was finally close enough to hear him. "She'll kill you if you don't. Please, Aluna."

Dash heard him talking and came closer. The horse-boy's face was taut with worry. "Tell her to stay down," Dash whispered to him. "I will do anything if she only agrees to stay down."

But no. There she was, injured beyond belief, pulling her legs under her, using her hands, twisting herself up. When she finally stood, the whole arena cheered.

Aluna didn't seem to hear them. One arm hung useless at her side. She lifted the other and swung, slow and sloppy. Scorch batted the knife out of her hands with a laugh and kicked Aluna's feet out. She landed on the dusty field with a whimper.

Hoku couldn't breathe. He wanted to turn away, but he made himself watch. He could be that brave, at least. For Aluna. For her family.

"I've grown bored of you, girl," Scorch said. She pulled back both her elbows and prepared to drive her twin swords through Aluna's body.

"Hold!"

All eyes turned to the Equian at the edge of the ring, walking slowly but deliberately across the field. High Khan Onggur. Hoku hadn't even seen him arrive. The crowd fell silent immediately, and even Scorch had the wits to stop her attack and take a step back.

The High Khan's face had a yellow tinge, but his arms still bulged with power. Hoku saw a familiar figure in the shadows behind him. Nathif stood there, bobbing on his tail. So that's where the healer had gone — to save the High Khan.

"This fight is over," Onggur said. "It seems, in the

moment of the sun's passing, that Red Sky is once again victorious." The Red Sky in the stadium cheered and stomped, a thunderous sound. They may have hated watching Scorch fight, but they clearly didn't mind winning.

Scorch straightened her shoulders. One of her legs dangled uselessly from her hip. Her face and arms were crisscrossed with lines of red. None of these injuries kept the smile from her face. "Flame Heart has lost," Scorch said loudly. She raised one of her swords over Aluna, who was once again trying to stand. "The Path of Sun demands blood," Scorch said. "What better way to celebrate Red Sky's victory and my father's call to arms than with the death of a traitor?"

The crowd began to murmur and shift.

Hoku looked to Onggur but couldn't read his expression. The Equian looked tired. Exhausted. The poison had clearly ravaged his body, however bold he tried to appear now. The High Khan seemed too spent to fight with Scorch.

Hoku took a deep breath, then hopped over the sandbags lining the field. He felt the Equians staring at him, saw Scorch's eyes trace him like lasers as he walked quickly and quietly toward Aluna. No one stopped him. He'd half thought they might.

When he got to Aluna, he bent down and helped her up. Her face was a mess, and her body shook. He held her arm to keep her steady. Scorch was so close, she could have skewered them both with one thrust of her blade.

"If you kill her, kill me, too," Hoku said.

Scorch smiled. "That's the plan."

High Khan Onggur remained silent, his brow furrowed, but the Equians in the stadium grew louder. Hoku couldn't make out what anyone was saying. Next to him, he heard Aluna chuckle. Then Dash was there, holding Aluna's other arm.

"You will need to kill me as well," Dash said.

The salty sand around Hoku's feet began to swirl, and he felt a soft breeze against the top of his head. He looked up to see Calli—sweet, wonderful Calli—drifting down to his side. She sagged when she landed, and took his other arm.

Tal hobbled over next, painfully slow, her whole front covered in bandages soaked with blood. A Serpenti tried to hold her back, but she nipped his fingers angrily and kept stumbling forward. Hoku recognized the look in her huge eyes. He'd seen it a million times on Aluna's face.

Nathif and the rest of the Serpenti joined them. They must have looked ridiculous out there. A tiny band of misfits all crowded around one bloody girl.

Scorch laughed. "Perfect! They have all given themselves up as sacrifices, High Khan. The sun will be well pleased with this offering! Let us show the world how Karl Strand deals with traitors."

Hoku heard hooves and was shocked to see another person run out to join them.

Tayan.

She took her place in front of Aluna, not behind her, and Scorch was forced to step back to make room. But instead of addressing Scorch, Tayan turned to the High Khan. "Red Sky has fought well, High Khan. The Sun Disc is yours, and with it, the desert and our lives. I have only one question to ask you first."

High Khan Onggur looked surprised. "Name it."

"I would know how this Human woman can know our ways better than us. She who has never tasted sand. She who does not know honor."

The High Khan stared at Tayan. Hoku had no idea what he was thinking or what he intended to do. One word from him, and they'd all be killed. He looked at Calli on his left and Aluna on his right. If he had to die, maybe this was the best way to go.

Just then, the ground thundered again, and more Equians galloped out to join their growing band. Hoku was shocked to see Khan Arasen and Dantai leading the rest of Shining Moon herd. Even as they arrived, more Equians filtered down from the stands to join them. Arrow Fall. Sand Storm. Cloud Hoof. Sun Haven. Their tiny group suddenly felt mighty.

Khan Arasen trotted forward to stand beside his daughter.

"High Khan Onggur, I believe we have something in common," he said. The crowd gasped. Hoku did as well. "We have both allowed our own sense of honor to be swayed by those less deserving."

Onggur narrowed his eyes.

"I allowed Weaver Sokhor to twist my vision of honor, to convince me that exiling one of my own was in the best interests of the herd." Arasen spoke directly to Dash. "I was wrong." He turned back to Onggur. "These outsiders, now Flame Heart, have shown me a little of the way I used to be. Of how I wish to be again."

He reached out and took his daughter's hand. Hoku saw tears in Tayan's eyes, although her back stayed stiff, her eyes forward.

"I would be glad to ally myself with the man you used to be," Arasen continued. "Before you allowed Scorch to turn you from the path of honor you once championed."

"Ridiculous," Scorch said. "I have done nothing of the sort. High Khan Onggur is a man of great power, and I will help him achieve his rightful place in the world. The Red Sky will rule far more than this bit of dust."

Hoku held his breath. It seemed like every person there was doing the same.

And then High Khan Onggur chuckled. He laughed softly, and then he laughed louder. For one ugly moment, Hoku wondered if the poison had destroyed his mind as well as injured his body. But when the High Khan spoke, he was as clear as calm water.

"That was your last mistake," Onggur said to Scorch. "An Equian does not wish to be known for power. A true Equian wishes to be known for honor."

Every Equian in the arena thundered their hooves against the ground.

High Khan Onggur held up his hand. "That you could fight this brave girl, Aluna of the Kampii, and decide that the sun would be honored by her death . . . that alone should have told me how little you understand us. We do not glory in the deaths of our strongest; we are thankful that their lives better our desert."

Now Hoku and Dash cheered, and all the herds behind them.

"Karl Strand will be angry if you do not kill the girl," Scorch said. She pushed her glasses farther up her nose. "We are allies, and we march to war. This is no time for mercy. That girl and her friends destroyed my brothers, Fathom and Tempest. My father demands revenge."

"Then he must exact it for himself," Onggur said coolly. "This desert does not belong to him, and it never will. Our alliance is ended. I suggest you leave quickly, before my new Serpenti allies determine the true source of the poison they found in my veins."

CHAPTER 42

ALUNA SAT BY THE BONFIRE and let its heat soak into her body. Every part of her felt bruised, sore, mangled. Nathif had told her how many bones were broken, but she lost track after the first handful. She wondered if she would ever feel strong again.

Calli sat next to her, gnawing on one of Tadder's smoky snake skewers. Tal hovered near her head, too wounded to dance but too stubborn to miss the celebration. Thankfully, Tal would live. She might never regain the speed and swagger she once had, but only time would tell. At least now she had that time.

Dash, Hoku, and Nathif danced nearby, their grins matching their awkward attempts to move their bodies to the rhythm. Nathif wore a special black-and-red sash given to him by the High Khan himself, marking him as an ally of Red Sky. It was a strong step toward peace for the Equians and Serpenti.

Calli pointed to the gold sash draped across Aluna's body, from shoulder to hip. "It's a good color on you," she said. "Makes your eyes sparkle."

Aluna ran a tired finger over the slippery fabric. "I didn't know I would get one of these just for fighting."

Calli snorted. "You didn't just fight, Aluna. That's like saying the sun is a little bright."

Aluna leaned back on the pile of pillows Hoku and Dash had built for her. "I wish they had killed Scorch, or at least imprisoned her. Letting her run back to Karl Strand gives him more time to prepare his next move."

Dash plopped down next to Aluna, his face covered in a sheen of sweat. "The High Khan wants Karl Strand to understand the strength of the desert. He wants Strand to know he was beaten."

"He's not going to like that," Aluna said. "He may have lost an army of Equians, but he'll find more people he can control. Or enslave. This isn't over."

Dash shrugged. "All of us live, and the desert is once again a place of honor. It is once again my home." He'd been grinning nonstop since Khan Arasen had welcomed him back to Shining Moon. Like Tayan, he was now part of two herds. "There is much work to be done—we still need more water, more food, a better future. But tonight I see only victory."

She smiled and touched his arm. "You're right. We won in all the ways that are important."

Tayan clomped over, her head wrap newly woven with both Shining Moon and Flame Heart colors. "I would speak to the herd," she said.

Aluna and Tayan hadn't healed the breach between them, but they'd begun the process. For now, it was enough. The others took their places around the fire and waited for their khan to speak.

"We have an old tradition of awarding honor names to those among our herds who distinguish themselves," Tayan said. "And as khan of Flame Heart and khandaughter of Shining Moon, I have decided to grant this rare honor to some of you tonight."

Tayan turned first to Tal. "Your name has always been a dishonor, but one that reflected on us, not on you. From this moment forward, you are no longer Tal; you are Vachir."

"Thunderbolt," Dash whispered. "It suits her temperament."

Tal—*Vachir*—whinnied and tried to prance in place. Her injury kept her from a more elaborate display, but she was clearly pleased. Aluna's heart swelled.

Tayan turned to Hoku. "Hoku shall keep his name,

but among us, shall also be known as Sun-strider, he who walks between worlds."

Hoku's mouth fell open. Aluna reached over and shut it for him. "You do, you know," she said. "You're a Kampii, an Aviar, an Equian, and practically an Upgrader. With your legs and your brain, you'll always be able to go wherever you want."

Hoku nodded, unable to speak.

"And you, Aluna," Tayan said. "You have shown us the path of honor this day, and you saved both our herds and our desert from great dishonor and suffering. You shall also be known as Dawn-bringer, she who leads us to a new day."

Aluna felt tears well in her eyes and was too exhausted to stop them from spilling down her cheeks.

"It's perfect," Hoku said.

"I'll follow you anywhere," Calli added.

Aluna looked at Dash. The bonfire crackled. She could feel the stars overhead, staring down on them from behind a veil of smoke.

"And where will you take us?" he asked softly.

She wiped the tears from her face and chose her words carefully. "It's taken us a long time to find one another, but now we have. Together, we're strong. Strong enough to fight, and strong enough to win." They wanted her to lead, so she would. "We're going to find Karl Strand."

ACKNOWLEDGMENTS

Christopher East and Stephanie Burgis supplied the chapter-by-chapter encouragement I needed to write this book, and as usual, I am in their debt. I also received fabulous critiques from Rae Carson, Deborah Coates, Sarah Prineas, Greg van Eekhout, and the writers at the Blue Heaven workshop. (C. C. Finlay didn't just bring us together; he made us comrades-in-arms.)

Thanks to Joe Monti, who always knows when I need to talk to a friend instead of an agent.

I am grateful to my editor, Sarah Ketchersid, for making this book so much better than it was. Her gentle but brilliant suggestions helped me find my way so many times. The rest of the Candlewick team also has my thanks: Liz Zembruski, Tracy Miracle, Hannah Mahoney, Maggie Deslaurier, Andrea Tompa, Martha Dwyer, and the sales and marketing team. Thanks to Alexander Jansson for another gorgeous cover illustration, and to Kathryn Cunningham and Rachel Smith for turning it into a stunning book.

Thanks to my friends, family, and fellow writers who've supported me on this journey. If I'm doing my job right, you already know how much I treasure you.